T0146482

Praise for Lynn Cahoon and the Tourist Trap Mysteries

"Murder, dirty politics, pirate lore, and a hot police detective: *Guidebook to Murder* has it all! A cozy lover's dream come true."
—Susan McBride, author of The Debutante Dropout Mysteries

"This was a good read and I love the author's style, which was warm and friendly . . . I can't wait to read the next book in this wonderfully appealing series."—Dru's Book Musings

"The menace gradually intensifies; the mystery of who the visiting author is also grips all the town's readers! Lynn Cahoon has created an absorbing, good fun mystery in *Mission to Murder*."
—*Fresh Fiction*

"*Mission to Murder* is a quick, entertaining read with a plausible mystery, and I recommend this series for people who like romantic, cozy mysteries."—*How Mysterious*

"*If the Shoe Kills* was my first visit with Jill and her dog, Emma, to South Cove. However, after . . . just one book I know it won't be my last. I really enjoyed the variety of people that live in South Cove, and the addition of the interns visiting certainly provided a lot of color and intrigue!"—Cozy Mystery Book Reviews

"I am happy to admit that some of my expectations were met while other aspects of the story exceeded my own imagination . . . This mystery novel was light, fun, and kept me thoroughly engaged. I only wish it was longer."—*The Young Folks*

"*If the Shoe Kills* is entertaining, and I would be happy to visit Jill and the residents of South Cove again."—*MysteryPlease.com*

"In *If the Shoe Kills*, author Lynn Cahoon gave me exactly what I wanted. She crafted a well-told small-town murder that kept me guessing who the murderer was until the end. I will definitely have to take a trip back to South Cove and maybe even visit tales of Jill Gardner's past in the previous two Tourist Trap Mystery books. I do love a holiday mystery! And with this book, so will you."
—*ArtBooksCoffee.com*, 4 stars

"I would recommend *If the Shoe Kills* if you are looking for a well-written cozy mystery."—*Mysteries, Etc.*

Books by Lynn Cahoon

The Tourist Trap Mysteries:

Murder on Wheels

Killer Run

Dressed to Kill

If the Shoe Kills

Mission to Murder

Guidebook to Murder

Murder on Wheels

A Tourist Trap Mystery

Lynn Cahoon

LYRICAL UNDERGROUND
Kensington Publishing Corp.
www.kensingtonbooks.com

LYRICAL UNDERGROUND BOOKS are published by

Kensington Publishing Corp.
119 West 40th Street
New York, NY 10018

All Kensington titles, imprints, and distributed lines are available at special quantity discounts for bulk purchases for sales promotion, premiums, fund-raising, educational, or institutional use.

Special book excerpts or customized printings can also be created to fit specific needs. For details, write or phone the office of the Kensington Sales Manager: Kensington Publishing Corp., 119 West 40th Street, New York, NY 10018. Attn. Sales Department. Phone: 1-800-221-2647.

Lyrical Underground and the Lyrical Underground logo are trademarks of Kensington Publishing Corp.

First Electronic Edition: February 2016
eISBN-13: 978-1-60183-419-5
eISBN-10: 1-60183-419-5

First Print Edition: February 2016
ISBN-13: 978-1-60183-420-1
ISBN-10: 1-60183-420-9

Printed in the United States of America

To my sisters, who make me crazy in a good way.

ACKNOWLEDGMENTS

Writing a book is like making a stew. You take pieces from here and there, maybe stored up from late-night dinners where no one finished the corn or the last few green beans from the garden. Then you mix it up, add some broth, and brown up some beef, and you hope the flavors mix together into something not only filling on a cold night, but also tasty.

My mom taught me to hold on to everything, including leftovers. For *Murder on Wheels*, I've mixed several of these tasty ideas that came from a mixture of sources. So, big thanks to my cowboy's best buddy, Dan Moore, for taking us geocaching for the first time. My sister, Roberta, always provides me with interesting tidbits from her cottage on the sea. And, of course, big thanks to the Food Network for their wide variety of shows to distract me, including *Truck Wars*. Or *The Great Truck Race*—it's called something like that. LOL

I'm always thankful for Esi Sogah's careful eye and kind direction in her edits and for loving South Cove as much as I do. Big thanks to Rebecca Cremonese for keeping me from freaking out when I find an error after turning in my last notes, and of course Michelle Forde, Alexandra Nicolajsen, and Lauren Jernigan for getting me and the Tourist Trap series out into the world.

Enjoy the stew.

CHAPTER 1

Fun, just like beauty, is in the eye of the beholder. As I watched Greg and Justin stare at the handheld GPS hung around Justin's neck with a University of California lanyard, two things were perfectly clear. One, Greg King, South Cove's lead detective and my boyfriend, was not having the least bit of fun. And two, Justin Cross, history professor and Amy's boyfriend, was oblivious to everyone else's discomfort. Amy shot me a look as we leaned against an old wooden-post fence. "Do you think we might talk him into lunch at least?"

I glanced at my watch and shrugged. "Are we allowed to leave the hunt without finding anything?"

Justin had talked us into a new activity for our monthly double date. Geocaching. Basically, people go out into the woods, hide an object, and then post the GPS coordinates with a list of clues for others to find the item. Then, apparently, you post on the website that you "found" the spot (without leaving spoilers), take something from the cache, and leave something for the next explorer. It would be fun and all if the people hiding the stuff weren't crazy illusionists.

The hobby was like a big scavenger hunt. Except this game was self-study instead of time-based. Today when we'd shown up at the park outside Bakerstown, there was a group of geocachers milling around the parking area. Most people were the same age as us, thirty-somethings looking for a weekend distraction that didn't take place in a bar. We'd been directed to the registration desk and given our assignments.

Now we were in the middle of the Los Padres National Forest watching our boyfriends argue over our current GPS coordinates. Justin glanced back at us. "It should be here. What was the clue again?"

"Fake rock," Amy called over to him. We were looking at an abandoned water pumping shed. The building had been made of stone, but now it looked more like it had been hit by a bomb. Or a meteor. She pointed up to the still-standing trees. Some of them were small, new growth. Others were old but charred on one side. "The forest fires ravaged through this area about ten years ago, and they let loggers come in to clean up the damaged trees. That's why there's so many dirt trails."

"So, maybe this cache was destroyed in the fire," I said, looking around for any kind of rock.

"The cache wasn't placed here until last year." Greg took my hands and pulled me into a standing position. "Come on, you're not going to find anything by holding up that fence."

I followed him, keeping my eyes on the ground for a plastic rock. After a few minutes, I was into the hunt. I stepped toward a tree and froze. A snake lay curled up next to the trunk. My stomach cramped, and I slowly moved away from the tree, pointing but not saying anything.

Amy came up next to me. "What is wrong with you?" She followed my gaze and laughed. "Jill found a snake."

"It's probably harmless. I don't think there are rattlers in the area." Justin crouched near Amy to examine my find.

I stood at the far end of the group as the three compared notes on what type of snake it could be. All I wanted to know was when we could get out of there. As they talked, I inched closer to the pump house. When I reached the back wall of the building, I saw a pipe coming out of the concrete. Under the water pipe was a rock. Could it be this easy?

I picked up the heavy rock and turned it over. The rock was concrete and had a film canister built into it. I tried to open the lid, but didn't have enough strength. I looked over at the group. Greg was poking the snake with a stick to get it to move along, out of the search area. "Umm, guys? I think I found it."

Justin sprang to his feet and sprinted toward me. He peered down at the bottom of the rock. "You did it. You found the geocache. Good job, Jill."

Yep, that's me. Jill Gardner, bookstore/coffee shop owner, and mad geocacher. I handed the rock to Justin. "You open it. I can't get the lid off."

He took the rock with a gentleness I hadn't seen anyone use before when handling stone. Well, fake stone. He pulled off the lid and dumped the contents into his hand: a scroll of paper, a short golf pencil, and a polished rock. Justin scribbled our names and the date on the paper. Then he handed me the pink tinged rock. "Take one, leave one. Do you have something we can leave for the next guy?"

I dug in my pocket. I had change from the candy bar I'd bought at the gas station when we stopped for snacks. My stomach growled at the memory. Digging deeper, I found a snail shell I'd found on the trail. I handed the miniature shell to Justin. "It's this or a quarter."

He smiled. "This will do just fine. I didn't know you had a fondness for trinkets." He put everything back into the canister, closed the lid, and looked at me. "So, where did you find it? We need to put it back exactly for the next person."

I pointed to the shed and the pipe. "It was right there, on the cement."

Greg put his arm around me. "I looked at that rock more than once, but when the clue said 'fake rock,' I kicked it for weight and moved on. Good thing you thought to pick it up."

I gazed into his blue eyes, pushing his hair away from his face. "So does this mean we can eat now? I'm starving."

By the time we'd hiked back down the mountain to the parking lot, the geocaching club had set up a barbecue grill and was selling hot dogs and cold sodas as a fund-raiser. Greg shrugged. "Want a snack to hold you over until we get into town and find a real restaurant?"

"Are you kidding? Of course." My mouth watered as we walked toward the smell of grilled dogs, mustard, and chopped onions. A dark-haired woman in a WE HIDE THINGS FOR FUN T-shirt motioned us over.

"Dog and drink for five bucks. Can't beat that." She grinned, rubbing the back of her hand over her forehead. "Darn, it's hot today."

I looked at Greg, who like me, wore a light jacket. It might be an unusually warm Saturday in February in sunny California, but it still felt chilly, especially standing here in the shade. "Spring will be here before you know it." I kept the small talk aimed at the weather. "We'll take four dogs and sodas."

"Jimmy will get your hot dogs wrapped up and you can pull your drinks out of the ice chest over there." The woman held out a hand as Greg pulled out his wallet. "The Coastal Geocache Club thanks you for your support."

"Do you do this a lot?" I'd never met anyone who even claimed to like this geocaching stuff. Now, in one day, I'd seen what a draw it could be for people. "I mean, I guess you do, since you're in the club and all." Now I was just stumbling over my words.

"You're looking at the current president! I'm Kacey and I've been a member for five years." The woman looked down at her slim body. "You're thinking how can she be so heavy and be part of a hiking group?"

I stared at the woman. She stood about five-five and might weigh 120 pounds. Her dark hair bounced around her shoulders, and her fair complexion brought out her emerald-green eyes. If I had to guess her occupation, I'd put her in the want-to-be-an-actress category. "Don't even think that, you're tiny. It's just that before today I'd never even heard of this activity, let alone any clubs around it."

"Sorry, I'm a bit sensitive about my weight. I went through a bad breakup, and I think I ate most of Bakerstown's supply of chocolate during that time." She smiled softly. "But I'm back at the gym and back with my husband, so things are good now. Anyway, geocaching. Most people haven't heard of it. We usually get several homeschooler families who use the hobby to teach geography principles. And they get a day out of the house."

"I'm glad to hear that. Good luck with everything." I hadn't even asked for a fifth of the information she'd so quickly provided. Apparently Kacey loved to talk. I took a step closer to Greg, who had walked away, talking to Amy and Justin and ignoring me. I almost sprinted to the cooler.

Greg handed me a cola and looked at Justin and Amy, "What's your poison?"

"Poison's right." Justin smirked. "I'm not much of a soda guy. Just throw me a bottled water. The sodium in the hot dogs is going to be bad enough for my body."

"Give it a break, honey." Amy turned toward me as she took a lemon-lime soda. "Justin's on this healthy food kick. I haven't had a French fry in months."

"Now, that's true love." I grinned at my friend. "I think I'd ditch Greg if he started feeding me health food."

Greg handed me a hot dog. "At least I know where I stand in your priority list now." He nodded toward the condiments table. "You're not going to have onions, are you?"

I grinned. "I love onions."

He shook his head. "I guess necking on the couch is off the agenda for this evening's activities."

Amy shook her head. "TMI, guys." She paused, then pointed to a man who walked toward the concession stand. "Isn't that Dustin Austin?"

I put mustard and ketchup on the dog and frowned toward the approaching figure. It *was* Austin with his Hawaiian shirt, Birkenstocks, and, in deference to the weather, long shorts. The guy's gray dreadlocks bounced as he walked toward us. I hadn't talked to the guy since he had broken my friend Sadie Michaels's heart and dumped her to return to his wife. I hadn't even known the guy was married. "I need to have a little talk with the jerk."

Greg held my arm, which also kept me from throwing my hot dog at Austin as he walked by. When he reached the table, instead of buying his meal, he walked around the table and kissed Kacey on the lips. Apparently she was the mysterious wife, and, of course, she was younger than either Austin or my friend. Sadie had just turned forty; the women's group at the church had invited me for her black party. I wonder if Austin was the one putting the "fat" ideas into her head. I turned away and took a bite of the hot dog, hoping the food would keep me from making a scene.

"You guys already out of here? We have another round starting at one." The man who had registered our group stood between us and the car.

"We've got reservations in town." Justin shrugged. "What can I say, newbies."

The man looked us over and nodded. "We'll just have to make you want to come back." He held out his hand. "I'm Taylor Archer, vice president of the Coastal Geocache Club. Four years running now."

"You must like the hobby a lot." Amy leaned into Justin, taking his hand.

"I love it. You wouldn't believe the stuff I've found just lying around. I have a metal detector, too, but you have to have a permit for it in national forests or state parks. And they've been good about allowing us to hold these monthly get-togethers here, so we don't want to mess with that." Taylor took a breath.

"Besides the fact that you wouldn't want to break any laws," Greg added to Taylor's list of reasons.

He grinned. "Yeah, there's that. But mostly all the stuff we find here is just things people have left behind while they're camping or hiking. It's not like it's a Confederate battleground or a historical site."

I knew from personal experience that historical objects were hiding everywhere, including an old shed that had been turned into an art studio. "You'd be surprised what can turn up where you don't expect it."

"True that." Taylor waved at another group. "I've got to go. Check us out on the web. Kacey over there's our webmistress, and she's crazy-good about keeping our page current."

I looked in the direction he was pointing and confirmed that Austin's latest love was the computer guru Kacey. Now the guy's website skills made sense. Of all the businesses in South Cove, Austin's Bike Shop had been the first on the web and had the best site even now.

The four of us walked back to Justin's car and sat inside as we ate our food. Finally Amy spoke. "Wow, I guess you can't know what anyone is really thinking."

"She doesn't seem Austin's type, that's for sure." Greg took a sip of his cola.

"When I talked to her, she said she'd gained weight when he left her. I can't imagine how little she was before." Kacey seemed to have a thing about her weight, even though I thought she looked amazing.

"There's no way she thinks she's heavy." Greg rolled his eyes. "I don't understand women and their weight obsession."

"She's totally different from Sadie." I peeked around Greg, and watched the couple near the table. "I hate saying this, but she seemed nice. I kind of liked hating the woman for what she did to Sadie."

"We all make our own choices." Greg crumpled the hot dog paper wrappings and held out his hand for mine. "She's not the one you should be mad at. Dustin didn't tell Sadie he was still married. And he's the one who broke it off."

As we drove back into town, I thought about my friend. Sadie had been alone for years after her husband died, and the first man she'd let into her heart since then had torn it apart. I was focusing on the ocean when a thought occurred to me. "Darn, I forgot to ask him what they planned to do with the food truck."

"You think he would have told you?" Amy turned around to look at me.

I shrugged. "Probably not, but who knows? He's the one into New Age honesty and purity. Maybe I could have used his beliefs against him?"

"Tricked him into telling you the truth?" Greg laughed. "Honey, that hasn't worked since they stopped making those Scooby-Doo cartoons."

I leaned up against him. "Well, Austin definitely would be playing the part of Shaggy."

Justin and Amy dropped us at my house when we returned to South Cove. Greg walked me to the porch. "Well, that was fun."

"You're a bad liar." I poked his chest. "I didn't think you were going to make it ten more minutes looking for that fake rock. In fact, I believe I saved you from a boring afternoon."

"Don't tell Amy or Justin, okay?" Greg took my key and unlocked the door. "It's just that I get enough of the search stuff in my day job. When I'm on my own time, I don't want to look for clues or find hidden treasure. I want to drink beer and eat buckets of clams."

"Now, that sounds like a terrific plan. Let's say we do that tomorrow." I had three days off this week—Friday, Sunday, and Monday—and I intended to make the most of my last day to relax. As we walked into the living room, Emma leaned against our legs, whining and yipping. I leaned down and gave her a quick hug. "You want to go out, girl?"

She ran to the back door and barked.

"I guess that's your answer." Greg nodded to the television. "You mind if we watch some of the game? I could go home if you'd rather be alone."

"I can read with you here or gone, so I'm fine." I threw the remote at him. "But I'd rather snuggle on the couch with you while I'm doing it."

Greg chuckled and settled on the couch as I let Emma outside. "Do you happen to have a beer?"

"Beer and chips. And I might just be talked into warming up a frozen pizza if you're good." I opened the fridge and grabbed a couple of bottles, then checked the freezer to make sure we had pizza. I poured a bag of potato chips into a large bowl and headed back to the couch.

Double dating was fun and all, but Greg and I had developed our own routine as a couple. And this was our comfort zone.

If I believed in fate, I'd worry about feeling this settled. Instead, since I wasn't superstitious, I believed we'd have many more nights like this to enjoy each other's company. Change, however, happens when you're not expecting it.

CHAPTER 2

Aunt Jackie put the standing water pitchers away under the counter. "Until the water ban is lifted, we'll only serve water when requested. Do you know how much water we go through in the afternoons? Those kids drink it because it's free."

"Then we should provide it." I looked to Toby and Sasha for support. Neither met my gaze. This was our first monthly staff meeting, and my aunt seemed to be changing everything. "Toby? What do you think?"

Toby didn't even look up from his texting. "If we have to pour water for every kid who asks, we'll be swamped and we won't give great service to the paying customers."

Mayor Baylor had put out a save water decree after the third month of the drought. Businesses were supposed to turn in their plans to City Hall by the end of the week. I didn't mind helping the cause, but this seemed extreme. "Yeah, I'm sure we don't want to add staff hours just to pour water."

Aunt Jackie seemed to consider our objections, then crossed the item off the list. "We'll try it this way for a while. Next topic is new aprons. Who has an idea for a new slogan?"

Toby tucked his phone in his shirt pocket. "Look, I don't want to be rude, but it's my one day off and Elisa's upset I'm not helping with the yard work. Is there anything else we need to talk about before I leave?"

I glanced at my aunt, who narrowed her lips and scanned her list of items. "I guess there's nothing here that I can't update you on at the end of your shift tomorrow." She nodded to me. "Go ahead and give them the envelopes."

I handed out the white business-size envelopes. Sasha took hers like it could bite her. "You're not closing the store are you? I know I haven't been able to work as many hours this semester, but I'll cut back on my schedule for summer and be here more."

"Just open the envelope." I watched as they each pulled out a check. "It's not much, but Aunt Jackie and I wanted to share the amazing holiday season we had. And a lot of it is due to the two of you."

"We just want you to know you're appreciated." Aunt Jackie put her agenda in the manila folder she'd set up for staff meeting notes. Then she went back behind the counter. "I'll see everyone on Wednesday. Josh and I are going into the city for a play tonight."

Toby sank back into his chair as Aunt Jackie left the shop. "Don't I feel like a real heel right about now?"

"You didn't know." Sasha patted his arm, then grinned. "This will take care of Olivia's day care for a few months. I don't know what to say."

"There's nothing to say. But when you see my aunt, please thank her for insisting on the bonus program. She thought the entire thing up. In fact, there's a whole performance-based section for next quarter's bonus. The more traffic we get, the bigger your bonuses will be." I focused on Toby. "Everything okay with you and Elisa? You seem a little tense."

"Nothing I can't handle." His phone buzzed again with a new text message. He rubbed his face with both hands. "I guess I'd better get out of here before she blows another gasket."

Sasha and I sat in silence as we watched Toby leave the shop. "That was interesting," I muttered as I finished the rest of my coffee. "Do you want to take home some cheesecake for dessert? I need to clean out the display case anyway."

She flushed and shook her head. "I'm trying to diet. Of course, being here with all the treats, it hasn't been the easiest food plan in the world to follow."

I frowned. "You don't need to diet. You're perfect." Two days in a row now, women who looked amazing had been complaining about their weight. I pulled my sweatshirt closed. Emma and I hadn't been running in over a week. Maybe the universe was hinting at me and my expanding waistline. I glanced at the single slice of double chocolate cheesecake sitting lonely in the display case. Or maybe not.

"Whatever." Sasha looked toward the door where Toby had exited.

"I'm not trying anything crazy, just eating better and working out every day. I want to set a good example for Olivia."

As we said our good-byes, I wondered about Sasha and her attention toward Toby. Did he realize the young mother had a crush on him? Or did he have one too many women with kids in his life as it was? This thing with Elisa was Toby's longest relationship. At least, since I'd known him. I'd have to pry some gossip out of Greg when he took me to dinner tonight.

Walking home, I slowed as I passed by Austin's Bike Shop. Right in front of the shop, parked on the street, was *my* food truck. Okay, so I had only rented it once for the Mission Walk, but I'd hoped to be able to purchase it for Coffee, Books, and More's first annex. A large pink sign hung on the side proclaiming GOOD FOR YOU DESSERTS— COMING SOON.

Amy hadn't said anything about a new business starting up in South Cove. But here sat the proof. The truck had recently been painted a bright green with flowers bordering the edges. It looked like a hippie mobile from the seventies. As I stepped closer, I could see the tagline for the business written in script under the window. I read the words out loud, "Yes, we are totally gluten-free."

"I'm just in love with the way the truck turned out, aren't you?" A slightly familiar woman's voice spoke to me from behind. I spun around to see Kacey Austin. This time she wore a floral dress with sandals, looking like she'd just auditioned for the role of fairy queen in the next hobbit movie. She moved closer to me, studying my face. I could tell when she recognized me with the smile she gave me. "Hey, I know you. You and your friends were at the park yesterday."

I nodded. "Jill Gardner. I own the bookstore/coffee shop up the street." I looked at her truck. "We sell the not-so-good-for-you-but-delicious desserts."

Kacey giggled. "Don't I know it. Austin took me there last week for an after-dinner treat. I adore your romance section over in the bookstore. I picked up several new releases from my favorite authors."

Okay, now I had a dilemma. I was supposed to hate this woman for ruining Sadie's life and now stealing away my food truck. But she was also a customer who loved my shop. I sighed. Worse, I kind of liked her. "Thanks. I try to stock what my customers want to read. And it doesn't hurt that I love reading the same books."

"Well, you've got a new supporter in me. I have a list of cook-books I was going to go into Bakerstown today to look for, but could you order them for me? That would save me a trip." She dug in the side pocket of her dress and thumbed through some paper scraps. "Here you go."

I glanced through the list. "I can't promise these are all in print, but I'll get them ordered. You should have the majority of them by Friday."

She clapped her hands. "Perfect. I told Austin that today was going to be ultra-special. And it has been. I met a new neighbor and got one chore off my list in less than ten minutes."

Her grin was infectious. "When are you opening?" I pointed to the food truck. Surely her healthy treats weren't going to cut into my business. Who would trade a dry cookie for a slice of cheesecake?

"I'm thinking two weeks. I still have to get permits from the city and the health inspector. There's a lot of paperwork involved in open-ing something like this. I hadn't really considered the delays. I got the truck and painted it, then I thought I'd open the next day." She gig-gled again. "Austin says I'm hopeless when it comes to business planning. He's taken on all the details."

Dustin Austin was the *more* driven of the two? That couldn't be a good thing. The man was so laid-back I think he closed the bike rental place anytime he thought the waves were good down the coast. The way these two were going, I wouldn't have to worry about the competition for customers for months, maybe even years. "Well, good luck." I reached into my tote for one of my council liaison cards. "We have a monthly meeting of all the businesses, maybe you could come to the next one."

She took the card and tucked it into a pocket. "I'll try. I'm not very good with meetings. I tend to get bored easily. I think that's why I keep getting elected as president of the geo club. I keep the meet-ings short and then we go have some fun."

Maybe Kacey had some lessons to teach me, as well. "I'm sure it's more than that. Anyway, I hope you at least try one. We talk a lot about things we can do as a community to bring in more business. We'll be planning a spring sidewalk sale for April. All the stores are invited to participate."

Kacey didn't look convinced. "I'm really always on the sidewalk. Or at least my customers will be."

I couldn't fault her logic. "We do several other activities during the year." I don't know why I was trying to talk her into coming. If Sadie saw her at a Business-to-Business meeting, she'd probably rip Kacey's eyes out.

Or, in actual reality, Sadie would probably break down into tears and go running out the door. She was still really upset about Austin.

"I'll try." Kacey's response sounded weak. I knew she'd never even try to attend, but maybe that was for the better, at least until Sadie's heart healed just a bit.

"Well, that's my cue. I'd better get home. I've got a ton of things to do before I go back to work tomorrow."

"Call me when the books come in. I'll come by and let you sample my newest creation, Summertime Smooth. It's a lemon cheesecake, completely gluten-free." She waved and disappeared into the food truck.

I stared after her. Kacey could have gotten the lemon cheesecake recipe from her grandmother or even the Internet, but I doubted it. It wasn't a coincidence that Austin had asked Sadie for that exact recipe right after he'd broken the I-have-a-wife news. Shaking off my friend's relationship troubles, I started power-walking toward home, hoping for a quick run on the beach with Emma before Greg was due to arrive.

Opening the front door, I got a full-body-slam welcome from Emma. She covered my entire face with one wet slurp and then sat down and whined quietly. I put my tote on the table next to the door and knelt to hug her. "You miss me, girl?" Emma was a full-blooded golden retriever and Greg's gift to me last year. He thought I needed protection since I had just moved into the house I'd inherited when my friend Miss Emily died. Turned out Greg was right, as Miss Emily's distant relatives were none too happy to give up the place.

Now Emma was my running companion and my best non-human friend. I patted her back and stood. "You want to go outside?"

This got me a short bark before she ran to the back door. I let her out and glanced at my home answering machine. Yep, I'm old school. I have a landline and a real answering machine with cassette tapes inside. I've thought about looking for a replacement for when this one bites the dust, but I'm sure the guys at the big box store wouldn't understand what I was talking about. The light was blinking, indicating a message.

Only two people called my landline. Greg, when he couldn't reach me any other way, and Frank Gleason, my contact with the California Historical Commission. I had the original South Cove Mission, or what was left of it, in my backyard. I'd been working on getting it certified for as long as I'd lived in the house. The one thing I could say about the process? They were certainly thorough. I got my new filtered-water pitcher out of the fridge and filled a travel bottle after I pressed the Play button.

"Miss Gardner? This is Sally Walters. I'm Frank's administrative assistant. This is just a courtesy call to let you know that the South Cove Mission Wall certification request is still with the state commission. They are running a little behind due to mandatory staff reduction days so it's taking a little longer than we expected. I'll call you in three months if the project is still pending on their docket." The machine clicked off.

I stared out the window toward the part of the backyard where the wall stood. "I guess you hid back there for years, so a few more months isn't going to hurt anything." Greg wanted to put up a hammock and build an outdoor brick oven where the wall sat, *if* the commission found it wasn't a historic mission. I figured he'd be disappointed when the decision finally came through. I knew it was the mission.

Emma barked at me from the open screen door. If I understood dog language at all, her bark said, *Hurry up and get changed so we can run on the beach. I smell dead fish.*

Or, more likely, *Open the door so I can chew up those couch cushions.*

I decided to believe the former and hurried upstairs to change into my running clothes. Ten minutes later, we were on the beach. The sun had broken through the morning clouds and the waves were light and playful. No one but Emma and I were there, so I unhooked her leash and let her run. I focused on the sound of my feet against the sand and the smell of the salt air.

We rounded a bend and out of the corner of my eye, I saw a couple walking hand in hand toward me. And Emma running full bore to greet them, seawater flying off her body as she flew. "Emma, come here," I called, hoping for once my dog would listen to my plea. She didn't.

When she reached the couple, the woman leaned down to greet her, and Emma sat, enjoying the attention. I sped up my pace to return her to the leash, hoping it wasn't Mayor Baylor and Tina. I'd get a lecture for sure about loose animals on the beach and the city laws. As I approached, I realized it was Austin and Kacey. I clicked Emma's leash onto her collar and stood. "Sorry about that, I thought we were alone."

"Dogs aren't supposed to be off their leashes on the beach," Austin muttered.

Kacey slapped his arm. "Stop being a rule book. Who died and left you king?" She turned toward me. "I know we live in a small town, but how crazy is it to run into you again today. Jane, isn't it?"

"Jill. And this is Emma." I reached down to rub the top of Emma's head, and she scooted over to lean against my leg as we stood there. "I just love this stretch of beachfront. We run a few times a week, especially when the weather's good like today."

"I know." Kacey spun around in a circle. "Isn't it grand today? When Austin mentioned we should take a break and go for a walk, I was all over that idea."

I turned my attention to Dustin Austin. I noticed his wife called him by his last name along with everyone I'd ever met. The guy hated the name Dustin, but when I'd first met him, I had felt weird calling him Austin. That thought was pushed aside by another memory crowding into my brain. The last time I'd seen him, before his wife showed up in town, he'd been in my storeroom, kissing Sadie. I could tell by the look on his face, the memory had occurred to him, too. "So, Austin, it's been a while. I hear you and Kacey are opening a dessert food truck."

He frowned, then turned back to Kacey, grabbing her. "We've got to go."

"Ouch, you're hurting me!" She pulled her arm out of his grasp. "Sometimes he doesn't think. Like the time he kissed me after eating a cookie and I had to be rushed to the hospital."

I stared at her. "How would a cookie send you to the hospital?"

"I've got a mad wheat allergy. I love to bake, but I have to be really careful with the ingredients I use. That's one of the reasons we decided to open the food truck, Austin got tired of eating all my experiments. Besides, people are going crazy on this gluten-free thing, so I thought it was time to let them eat cake, too." Kacey shrugged. "So to speak."

"I'm sorry if I hurt you." Austin put his hand on the small of Kacey's back. I couldn't pinpoint his true age, but I knew he had to be in his late fifties. Kacey, on the other hand, couldn't be more than thirty or thirty-five. "We need to get going. I forgot the health inspector is coming by today."

"No, he isn't, you said he was coming next week." Kacey didn't budge from her spot. She grinned at me. "I put it on my new calendar. You should see all the planner options they have down at that office supply place in Bakerstown. I wanted all of them, but settled on a weekly planner that had a slot where I could put my own pictures on the cover. So it looks just like me."

"That sounds nice." I loved seeing Austin squirm. "I have a lot of friends in the area who are addicted to their planners." *Sadie being one of them.* "Maybe that's a topic for one of our Business-to-Business meetings."

Austin turned stone-white. "The inspector called back this morning and rescheduled. He said that if we don't meet him today, it will be a couple of months before he can get out here." Austin turned Kacey's head away from watching the seagulls frolic on the waves. "We really have to go."

"Fine. I guess we have to go then." Kacey gave Emma a kiss on the top of her head and smiled at me. "I'll see you later. Maybe I'll come in to your shop tomorrow. What time do you work?"

Austin pulled her away and toward the parking lot exit. I called after them, "Five to noon. Come in any time."

I watched as Austin dragged his wife up the stairs to the lot and they disappeared from view. I looked around the now-empty beach and unclicked Emma's leash. "Let's finish our run."

By the time Greg arrived to pick me up for our clams and beer date, I'd finished showering and was dressed. I sat with my legs tucked under me, my formal flip-flops with the oversized flower decoration on the floor next to the couch. Emma slept on top of one of them, making sure I didn't slip out without her noticing.

I'd left the front door open so the sun and air could come through the screen. And also so I wouldn't have to get up to let Greg in. He grinned when he saw me on the couch. "Lady of leisure these days, huh?"

"Get off my back. This is my no-guilt Monday. Although I did run with Emma, it was merely for pleasure reasons, not for the exercise." I stretched and put the book on the coffee table. "We ready to go? Or do you want an iced tea before we leave?"

He glanced at his watch. "Reservations are at seven, so we have a little time. Iced tea would be great."

Emma woke with a start and ran toward Greg as he opened the screen and came into the living room. "Hey, girl. Did you get to go on a run today?"

Emma wiggled her entire body. She loved Greg. Which was good since he spent most of his free time here when he wasn't keeping South Cove safe for its citizens. "I'll be right back."

Greg followed me into the kitchen and kissed my neck as I poured the tea over the ice cubes in two glasses. "Today was crazy. Your friend the mayor has decided that we should do joint training exercises with Bakerstown on surviving a terrorist attack. So now I've been assigned a task force to develop the plan for the exercise."

"More meetings. You must be thrilled." I knew for a fact Greg hated meetings. I handed him the tea. "Porch or kitchen?"

He glanced out the window. "Better make it kitchen. If I get comfortable on that swing of yours, we'll never make our dinner."

"Worse things could happen," I said as I walked over to the table and sat.

Greg joined me. "Yeah, like a terrorist attack on a little tourist town no one has ever heard about."

"That's not true. We do all kinds of advertising in the big California tourist magazines. And we were nominated that one year for best tourist town to walk through with less than six thousand residents," I countered.

"In 2001. Face it, Jill, we're a small fish in a really big pond of places people can go to spend a weekend." He shrugged. "And I kind of like it that way."

I sipped my tea. Maybe we were just going to have to do something about that. I'd talk to Aunt Jackie next week about ways to increase our image in the tourist community. Greg looked beat, and I was sure the mayor was riding his tail about this new project. So I decided to change the subject.

"Guess who I ran into twice today?"

CHAPTER 3

Halfway through my bucket of clams, Greg's phone rang. I didn't even look up, but started eating faster. From experience, it appeared date night was coming to an end. I quickly buttered a slice of their homemade fresh bread and devoured it.

"It could just be a check-in." Greg chuckled, watching my increased speed.

"Not with my luck," I mumbled with my mouth full. "And this bread isn't as good warmed up in the microwave."

He wiped a butter spot off my chin with his napkin, then answered his phone. "Hey, Tim, what's up?"

As he listened, Greg watched me drain my bottle of beer, then handed me his, which was almost still full. I took it and cracked open more clamshells. He sighed. "No, you did the right thing. I'll be there in twenty minutes. I've got to drop Jill back at the house."

He waved over our waitress and nodded to the two clam buckets on the table. "Can you put those in a to-go box and bring me our check?"

The woman took Greg's bucket and reached her hand in to get mine, but I snagged one more clam before they all disappeared. Greg started laughing. "I think she thought you might bite off her hand."

I finished the last clam, then took the bread and wrapped all but one slice into a napkin, putting the bundle in my purse. I buttered the last slice and glared at Greg. "I hate Tim."

He put his hands up. "Not Tim's fault. He tried to call Toby in, but he's all the way in the city with Elisa. I guess we shouldn't try to have date night on the nights he has off."

"If that's even going to be a problem anymore." I polished off the bread and took a sip of Greg's beer. "What has he told you about him and Elisa? Things seemed a little tense today at the staff meeting."

"Even with you handing out bonuses? That's odd." Greg took the bill from the waitress, and handed it back with his credit card. "Typically when you give people money, they're in a good mood."

"I know, right." I thought about Toby's behavior. "Well, actually, it happened before we gave them the envelopes. I think he felt pretty bad about being a jerk then."

"Toby usually isn't a jerk." Now Greg looked thoughtful. "Come to think of it, I haven't heard him talk about Elisa for a while. I just thought he was keeping his private life, you know, private."

"In South Cove? Like that's going to happen." I slipped on my sweater and stood after Greg got his credit card back. He carried a large Styrofoam box with what should be our clams. "Too bad you're not going to get any of those. Or the cheesecake I brought home to serve with coffee."

"You're evil, you know that?" Greg put his arm around me as we walked out of the restaurant. "But I still love you."

The words "I love you" were still new to our relationship. I got a delicious chill every time he said them. Especially after he called me evil. He held the truck door open for me and set the box on my lap. "So, what's going on that Tim needs help?"

Greg kissed me before he answered, making me sad he wasn't coming over after dinner, and not just for the cheesecake. He rubbed my bottom lip with his thumb. "Normally with official South Cove police business, I'd say none of your business, but I'll give you this one. Someone broke into that food truck parked outside of Austin's Bikes and trashed the insides."

"Vandalism?" We'd had problems in South Cove before with businesses being targeted, but typically, there was an underlying reason behind the attack. I grinned at him. "Or terrorism."

He shook his finger at me. "Don't you start." He shut the door and came around to the driver's side. Starting up the engine, he turned toward me. "Your new friend Kacey says someone stole all her recipes."

I didn't even turn my head so Greg couldn't watch me jump to the same connection he'd already made. The only person who would want Kacey's recipes was the woman from whom they were stolen originally. "There's no way it's Sadie," I finally said as we approached the turnoff toward South Cove.

"Honey, even with all the reasons why it could be, I agree with you. Sadie just doesn't have a mean bone in her body." Greg parked the truck and came alongside to open my door. We walked to the porch and I realized I wasn't hungry anymore.

"You'll call me later, right?" I unlocked the door and flipped on the inside light. Greg set the to-go box on my little table and pulled me into a hug.

"Don't worry, it's not Sadie." Greg squeezed me, then stepped back on the porch. "Lock up. I'll talk to you tomorrow."

I locked the door and watched him drive away before I went to the kitchen to put the clams in the fridge. I got a soda and let Emma inside. He hadn't said he would tell me anything, I realized as I wandered upstairs to try to lose myself back inside the pages of the book I'd been reading before our date.

The alarm shrieked me awake the next morning. Tuesdays were always hard, mostly because I typically read until I dropped asleep the night before. Today was no exception. I only had my morning shift now, even though Aunt Jackie had Tuesdays off as Sasha had taken over the evening slot. I stumbled downstairs, let Emma out, and grabbed a cup of coffee. Thank goodness for delay-set brewing pots. I didn't know what I'd do if I had to actually make coffee in this condition. I headed upstairs to shower, sipping the coffee as I walked.

I beat my first commuter customer by twenty minutes and for the next hour, I filled travel mugs with our best brew. Aunt Jackie had finally agreed to a customer rewards card, with one caveat. They had to purchase one of our travel mugs with the CBM–South Cove logo and bring it back in every morning to purchase their coffee. Then I could punch their card. Ten visits, they got a free coffee. And on those days, most of them picked up a treat to take with them to their day job for breakfast.

I had to admit, the program had increased the number of commuter visits a week. They loved the free coffee; I didn't even clip coupons to save money.

Soon, the commuter traffic slowed, and I was able to complete the task list that Aunt Jackie had developed for every shift. Mine just had additional duties, like ordering books and reviewing our P&L statements—which made my eyes cross every time I had to pretend to understand what was happening with the business. As long as Aunt Jackie seemed happy with the numbers, I was happy.

When Toby arrived, I sat slouched on the couch, feet up on the coffee table, and was halfway done with the new YA book Sasha's teen group was reading this month. I heard the bell over the door ring and tried to sit up straighter until I saw it was him.

"Busy morning?" He went behind the counter and threw his jacket through the back door onto my desk. Then he washed his hands and started fresh coffee. He peered over at me as I'd returned to the story without answering. "Good book?"

"Dragons." I closed the book and stretched. I went over to the counter. I'd finish tonight. Typically Greg and I didn't even do dinner together on Tuesdays. He said it was his man cave night. I think he just wanted to watch basketball. "So, what did you hear about the break-in?"

"What break-in?" Toby swung a clean towel over his shoulder. "I was in the city with Elisa for dinner and a movie."

"What did you see?" I was sure he'd heard about the food truck issue, but I'd play his game, for a minute or two.

"Some chick flick. Seriously, if there isn't anything getting blown up or a gunfight, I don't pay much attention. I did get an awesome nap and Elisa didn't even have a clue." Toby sank down onto a stool we kept behind the counter. "She seems to be clueless about a lot of things I do lately."

"Trouble in paradise?" Clearly *something* was going on. I watched as he halfheartedly adjusted a few cups into larger stacks.

He shrugged. "I don't know. We hardly see each other lately, and when we do, she's on her phone texting more than talking to me."

"I thought you were living together?" That had been the last big announcement, but I'd heard it from Greg, who'd heard it from Esmeralda or Tim. The exact source of gossip is hard to pinpoint at times in South Cove.

"We are, except on nights when I work late, I stay at the station. She says it disrupts Isabell's schedule." Toby poured me a cup of coffee and pushed it across the counter slowly. "I think she's seeing someone else."

If anyone would know the signs of juggling two or more "friends," it would be Toby. The boy had been a player of the worst kind before he'd met Elisa. Now, he was a one-woman man, but it seemed like his woman didn't want to play that game anymore. "I'm sure it's just a phase. I mean, relationships have their ups and downs. Have you tried to talk to her about it?"

Toby shook his head. "Nope, I'm pretending like everything is okay. And so is she." He got a water pitcher out from under the counter and filled it on autopilot. When he'd finished, he looked at it like it had just appeared. "Crap, I'm not supposed to provide free water anymore, am I?"

"Only if they ask, according to Aunt Jackie." I took the pitcher over to its regular spot and took cups out of the counter below. "She won't be here today, so don't worry about it. And if she pops in, I set up the water station, not you."

It felt weird worrying about water when we had an ocean filled with the stuff less than a mile away. Too bad some scientist couldn't come up with a way to change salt water into fresh. As I gathered my stuff to leave, Toby's girls started coming in the shop. The man brought in a lot of business for the shop, mostly of the female variety. But as far as I knew, he'd been a total professional since he'd started dating Elisa, even if the women coming in were less than happy about it.

As I passed by the green food truck with yellow crime scene tape all over it, I realized I hadn't found out anything about the break-in. I sat on the curb and dialed my own gossip channel. Amy Newman worked at City Hall as the city planner. Most days, her duties landed smack-dab in the receptionist category. Besides, I hadn't heard from her since the double date on Sunday.

Her line went straight to voice mail. I left a quick message for her to call, then looked at the time. Sadie would be done with her baking and delivery by now; maybe she'd like to have lunch. My stomach growled. Of course, I could just go into Diamond Lille's by myself and eat, but Lille had been a bit cranky lately, especially when she saw me. I dialed Sadie's number.

Sadie's purple PT Cruiser with the Pies on the Fly decal pulled into Lille's parking lot ten minutes later. I'd stayed on my bench, reading the dragon book. She beeped her horn as she passed me, and I stuffed the book back into my tote and crossed the street to meet her. It wasn't that I was afraid of Lille, not exactly. I was afraid of her banning me from the only restaurant in South Cove, if you didn't count my coffee shop and now Kacey's health van.

Sadie gave me a quick hug. "So glad you called. I needed a break. Nick came home from Stanford over the weekend and we ran around the entire time getting him restocked for the dorm. I swear that boy goes through more socks and granola bars than anyone else I know."

"How's he doing? Does he like his classes?" Nick Michaels was one of South Cove's wonder kids. He'd gotten straight As in high school, been the team quarterback for the last two years, and sang in the church choir. I wondered how college was treating him.

Sadie smiled. "He's liking his clubs. He joined debate and has been swamped with the work. Classes have surprised him. He's not the only smart kid in the room."

"I can see that." I held open the door and aimed us toward my normal booth, but I stopped short. It was already taken. On a Tuesday. I peered closer and saw Amy and Kacey waving at us. Sadie started backing up.

"I can't eat with her," Sadie choked out.

I figured Sadie had already seen Kacey around town. There wasn't much that went on in South Cove that everyone didn't know. In fact, the entire dining room seemed to be waiting for our next step. I touched Sadie's shirtsleeve and stopped her from running out of the diner. "Stand tall. We won't eat with them." I pointed her toward a booth where we wouldn't see Amy or Kacey. "Go grab that booth, I'll stop and say hi and then be right over."

Sadie nodded and almost ran toward the booth, weaving through the tables. I stepped over to greet Amy. "Hey, Amy, Kacey." I nodded to Amy. "We had the same idea. I called you earlier about lunch, but you must have already been here."

Kacey nodded. "Amy and I started talking last night after the police left and realized how much we have in common. I used to surf competitively in high school."

Of course you did. What I said was, "I didn't know that. Amy loves talking surfing." I glanced toward the booth where Sadie sat. "I'd better get going. I'm starving."

"I'll call you tonight," Amy said, focusing on her burger.

"See you soon," Kacey called out as I stepped away.

When I sat down at the booth, Sadie's face was bright. "I can't believe that woman."

I opened the menu and handed it to her. "It's not her fault. If you want to be mad at someone, you should be mad at Austin. He's the one who led you on."

Sadie glared at me, then took the menu, slumping into her seat. "I know. It's just I thought things were going so well, especially once we settled that *thing*."

I nodded, already knowing what the *thing* was. Austin had wanted a more physical relationship too quickly. Nick had been still at home, and Sadie wasn't into being a bad example for her kid. Once he'd gone off to school, Sadie had been more open to taking their relationship to the next level. Then Austin had dumped her.

Carrie came by and took our order, and instead of her normal banter, she gave Sadie a quick hug. "I'm so glad to see you today. You need to come in more."

As the waitress walked away, Sadie wiped her eyes with a napkin. "I guess I have been holed up too long over that jerk."

"Exactly." I smiled. "You have friends here, you shouldn't ever question that."

"Or Carrie's just in love with my desserts." Sadie took a sip of her tea. "Did you see that food truck? Seriously, that woman thinks she can sell gluten-free desserts and make a living? People don't want that crap when they're splurging."

I sipped on my iced tea. "I totally agree with you, at least for my own indulgences. However, I might carry one or more of her treats at the store. I'm always being asked for sugar- and gluten-free stuff. I can't think I'll sell much, though."

Sadie gave me a death stare.

"Sorry, it's a business decision." I played with my silverware. "Kacey's not that bad of a person. You might actually like her if you talked to her."

"I will never be friends with either her or that husband of hers." Sadie put her napkin in her lap and leaned back as Carrie brought our food. "Can we change the subject?"

I nodded my thanks to Carrie and attacked the mushroom Swiss burger. "No problem." I took a bite and thought about what had been going on the last few days that didn't have anything to do with Kacey or Austin. Finally, Toby's face came into view. "Toby and Elisa are having issues."

We gossiped through the rest of the meal, and I waited to leave until I saw Amy and Kacey walk out. We didn't need a scene today. I walked Sadie to her car in the parking lot and gave her a quick hug good-bye. "Let's do this again next week."

Sadie didn't answer; her attention was on the food truck across the street. The yellow police crime scene tape had come loose and was flapping in the wind. "I hope they stole everything," she muttered.

"You heard about the break-in?"

She smiled. "I'm on the church's women's group phone tree. We don't just use it for planning purposes. It's a great source of local gossip." She opened her door and slipped into the car. "I know, I'm not acting very Christian-like."

"You'll get there." I waved as she pulled out of the lot and wondered if my prediction was actually true.

Just after seven that evening, I opened my door to Greg holding a large pizza box and a bottle of wine. "Surprise."

I stepped back so he could enter, then closed the door behind him. "What's up? We don't usually have dinner together on Tuesday."

He set the wine bottle on my table, then pulled a DVD out of his coat pocket. "It's impromptu dinner and a movie night." He tossed the movie to me. "Put this in the player while I finish prep on our dinner."

I walked over to the television and looked at the cover. "This is a war movie," I called into the kitchen.

"I didn't say it was impromptu dinner and a chick flick movie night. I felt bad about cutting our date short last night, but I didn't feel that bad." Greg brought the wine and two glasses out to the living room. He uncorked the wine and poured it. "You don't have to let Riesling breathe, right?"

I shrugged, taking my glass. "I have no clue. Maybe we should take another jaunt to Napa Valley this weekend and ask?"

"Sounds like a plan. We haven't been out of town since our Mexico trip." He settled in next to me, grabbed the remote, and started the movie. He looked at me and patted his chest. "Let's relax a bit before we dive in to that pizza."

I glanced toward the kitchen. "Is Emma outside?"

"Of course," Greg said. "If she wasn't, we wouldn't have a pizza by now."

My dog did love her pizza. We let her eat the crusts. I curled up next to him and took a sip of wine before relaxing into his arms. "This is nice."

"Even with the war movie?" Greg kissed the top of my head.

"Yep, even with the subject matter."

His phone rang and I pulled myself upright, pausing the movie credits. I took another sip of my wine. Emma was probably looking at getting more than crusts tonight.

Greg checked the display and then answered. "What's up, Toby?"

He listened for a while, then set his wineglass on the coffee table. "I'll be there shortly."

"Movie night cancelled or delayed?" I still held out hope that we might be cuddled back on the couch sooner than later.

He kissed me. "Cancelled. Some beachcomber found a body."

"A dead body?" I followed him to the door. "Is it a local?"

"Toby didn't say." He stood at the door. "Sorry for leaving two nights in a row. And about this weekend . . ."

I nodded. "Cancelled, too."

I said a quick prayer that the body wasn't someone I knew and went into the kitchen to share my pizza with Emma.

CHAPTER 4

The first customer Wednesday morning broke the news. Darla Taylor, owner of South Cove Winery and promotion queen, waddled into the shop and climbed up at the counter. "Hon, get me a large mocha and a piece of that chocolate marble cheesecake. You know I love Sadie's cheesecakes."

"I'm glad, but aren't you on a diet?" Darla had been dieting and working out with her boyfriend, Matt, for the last year.

"It's my cheat day. I'm taking full advantage of it this week. Matt about killed me on our run yesterday." She dug into the treat as I started her mocha. "So, what does Greg say about Kacey Austin's death?"

My hand slipped off the foaming attachment. "What? Kacey's dead?"

Darla shook her head. "I knew it was a waste of time to come here. You never have the gossip." As lead reporter for the small town paper, Darla typically came to me to weasel out information Greg wouldn't release. Unfortunately, most of the time, Greg hadn't told me what Darla wanted to know.

"All Greg said was that someone was dead on the beach." I resumed my foaming. "Are you sure it was Kacey?"

"Dustin Austin drove to Bakerstown to meet up with Doc Ames late last night to identify the body. He told Mabel at the funeral home that she'd gone for an evening walk and didn't come home."

Strange, since she and Austin had taken a beach walk earlier that day, but maybe that was how she stayed skinny. I knew she was obsessed with losing weight, so it could be true. I finished making Darla's mocha and warmed up my own cup of coffee. Since it was just the two of us, I came around and sat next to Darla. "That's so sad.

I mean, I didn't like what Austin did to Sadie, but Kacey was really nice. At least the times I met her."

"So you don't know if she died of natural causes or not?" Darla pressed. "I tried calling Doc Ames this morning, but he's going all 'open investigation' on me."

I glanced at the clock. "It's only seven. Maybe he doesn't know yet?"

"Maybe, but I'm driving in to talk to Mabel." She nodded to the dessert case. "Box up a couple more of these cheesecake slices. Maybe that will get her to talk more freely."

I put the cheesecake into boxes and rang up Darla's purchase. She used the *Examiner's* credit card. I guess she was on assignment with this one. Darla stood and swung her bag over her shoulder. "It's just a shame. She reunites with her husband, and a few months later, he's a widower. I guess true love doesn't come with a guarantee. I wonder if Sadie knows yet?"

"Do not go see her." Sadie was going to be seriously upset. The woman didn't dislike anyone, so she'd had conflicting feelings about Kacey in the first place. The last thing she needed was Darla poking around into the reasons Austin had dumped Sadie to return to his wife. "I'll stop over as soon as my shift's done."

"You may be too late by then. You know how gossip spreads in South Cove." Darla didn't meet my gaze, instead looking down at the box of cheesecakes. "You know I wouldn't do anything to hurt Sadie, right?"

"Sorry, I didn't think before I said that." It was turning into a crap morning.

Darla nodded and left the shop. I'd hurt her feelings. One more thing on my list to fix. But first, I needed to make sure Sadie was okay.

The rest of my shift seemed to run in slow motion. By the time Toby arrived, I was itching to leave. He watched me pull off my apron and gather my purse as he started his day. "You on a mission?"

"It shows, huh?" I set my purse on the counter and put on my jacket. "I'm heading over to Sadie's to make sure she's all right. I just hope she hasn't already heard the news."

"I would think it would make her happy that her rival was out of the picture." Toby slipped an apron over his head and tied it in the back.

"Don't say that. You know Sadie, she doesn't have a mean bone in her body." Why was everyone convinced Sadie would be happy at the news?

He shrugged. "I don't know. Love makes people crazy sometimes. If I were her, I'd be happy Austin's new relationship didn't work out. Just for the satisfaction."

"Well, you're not her." I stormed out of the shop, letting the door shut a little too hard behind me. I felt furious that Toby thought Sadie would be enjoying someone's death, but then as I walked to Sadie's house, I began to think about the situation. If Toby, who I knew had a good heart, thought this, what were others saying?

Sadie Michaels's house sat on Beal Street, a block away from the Methodist church. It was an old Victorian with that gingerbread trim all over. For being a single mom for so many years, the house looked well-tended, even if the paint was a bit faded. I knocked on the front door, but no one answered, so I went around to the garage she'd refurbished as her bakery and opened the door. "Sadie? Are you here?"

The smell of brownies hit me as soon as the door opened and my stomach growled. I hadn't taken the time for breakfast, and now the sensory overload of baking chocolate almost did me in. Sadie was at a counter, pouring more ingredients into her oversized stand mixer. She waved me over. "Hold on a minute. I'll get this started, then I'll take a break."

She hadn't heard. I could tell by the way she hummed as the flour and cocoa drifted down into the brownie mix. As usual, my friend was dealing with her own issues the old-fashioned way, by baking.

Sadie pulled her gloves off, poured two cups of coffee from the pot on the cabinet, and met me at a small table in the corner. She pushed a file filled with paperwork to the side and closed her laptop. "What's got you out on a Wednesday? Brownies will be ready any minute. You can taste-test my new recipe. Double chocolate with dark chocolate chips. They may just be too much chocolate."

"That's impossible." I sipped my coffee slowly, not wanting to ruin my friend's good mood. *Chicken.* I took a deep breath.

"It's a great day. I guess Austin changed his mind about using my recipes for his new food truck." Sadie pulled a loose-leaf notebook out from under her counter. "Look what I found on my front step today."

I used a napkin to open the red cover. *Sadie's Marble Cheesecake* was written on the first page, with ingredients scratched out and new ones added to make the final product gluten-free.

"You need to show this to Greg."

Sadie laughed. "I don't think Greg's going to arrest Austin for conning a silly woman out of her best recipes. Besides, I'm done with that man. I had a long talk with Pastor Bill after Sunday service, and he helped me forgive Austin for his treachery." She took the notebook back and slipped it under the counter again. "This is just God's way of telling me the man is out of my life. Whatever punishment He has in store for Austin won't be pretty."

"Don't say that." I patted the chair next to me. "Come over here, I need to tell you something. Then we need to call Greg."

I quietly explained what I actually knew about Kacey's death, which was almost less than nothing, then dialed Greg's number when I finished. Sadie looked pale, so I poured her more coffee as the phone rang.

"Hey, I'm in a meeting. Can I call you later?" Greg's voice filled my ear.

"I think you need to come talk to Sadie. She found something on her doorstep this morning." I pushed a brownie toward my friend, but she just stared at the temptation.

The pause at the end of the line worried me. "I was planning on stopping by later anyway."

That didn't sound good. *Don't jump to conclusions, Jill.* I knew she was watching me, so I put on my best service smile and nodded. "Sooner would be better. I'll wait here for you."

"Please tell me it's nothing incriminating." Greg sighed and I could hear him rustling papers on his desk.

"You just need to see this." I hung up, not wanting to explain more about the mysterious notebook that at the very least made Sadie look guilty for trashing the food truck. Not that I thought she'd do a thing like that, but maybe someone else had. Nick had been home last weekend. Would he have taken steps to protect his mom?

"Greg will be right here." I tried to sound soothing, but Sadie didn't respond. She stood and began to finish the batch of brownies she'd started when I'd arrived. I took a bite of the chocolate heaven and sipped on my coffee. There was a new dead body in town, and of course, I was already knee-deep in the investigation. Something that Greg hated, but this time, it wasn't really my fault. All I'd done was visit a friend.

Keep telling yourself that.

* * *

By the time Greg arrived, Sadie was putting the last batch of brownies in the oven and a large pan sat on the counter, waiting to cool. And she still hadn't said anything.

I excused myself, telling Sadie I'd be at home later if she wanted to talk, but I wasn't sure she even noticed me leaving. Greg took me aside.

"You okay?" He brushed a brownie crumb off my lip. "You're not too sugared up to drive, are you?"

I wiped my hand over my mouth. "I'm not driving. I'm walking." I looked back at my friend, who now slumped in the chair I'd vacated. "Be gentle with her. I think her heart is still tender from the breakup."

"I'm not insensitive," Greg responded. "I'll stop by the house later."

I knew better than to ask if he'd catch me up, but I knew at least he'd tell me what happened with his discussion with Sadie. There was just no way she was involved with any part of Kacey's murder or the break-in at the food truck. I paused one more time. "Do you think she needs a lawyer?"

This time, Greg was the one to pause, which worried me. "You may want to see if one of your old coworkers is available." He held up his hand as I moved to go back into the garage-turned-bakery. "I'm not going to arrest her, at least not today. Today, I just need to know what she found and what she knows."

As I walked home, I thought about the law firm where I'd spent ten years and wondered who owed me a favor and could take on Sadie's case if she was arrested. I dialed the number from memory and left a message for Matt Clauson, the lawyer who had handled Aunt Jackie's legal issues to call me back.

Walking by Esmeralda's, I admired her green lawn. Due to the drought, we'd been put on a watering ban for our landscaping. February and my lawn was still a dull brown; waiting, hopefully, to come out of its dormant season. My neighbor's lawn looked like it was out of a landscape painting. I'd have to confront the woman about her watering, even with the ban. It was my civic duty. Besides, her failure to comply was making me look like I didn't care about my little house. I thought about walking back into town to catch her at her job as the police dispatcher, but I didn't want to run into Greg. At least not yet. His comments about Sadie needing a lawyer were bothering me. He couldn't believe she would break into the food truck, not Sadie. *And what about the murder?*

I unlocked my house and ran upstairs to change into my running clothes. I didn't want to even consider the possibility, and running would help me clear my mind of these crazy thoughts. With Emma leashed, we headed down to the beach.

Halfway through the run, thoughts of Kacey and Austin walking the beach rolling through my mind, I realized my plan hadn't been the best. In fact, there was still yellow crime scene tape where they'd found Kacey's body. I stopped at the large rock that typically served as my turning-around spot and stared at the section of sand marked off with four sticks with the yellow barrier wrapped around the area. All I could see was sand and a few seashells that would disappear as soon as either the tide came in again or the beachcombers found the more perfect ones. Nothing was left of the vibrant woman whom I had begun to like, even though she was the reason Sadie's heart was broken.

Well, not quite true. *Austin* was the reason for Sadie's heartbreak. He was the one who'd led her on while planning on reconciling with Kacey. Greg needed to question that pile of crap, not my hurting friend.

Emma growled, low in her throat. I reached down to settle her and scanned the area behind me. A man was walking toward us. He saw me watching and waved.

"Hey, hold on," he called as his walk became a jog. Emma growled louder.

I motioned her to sit and put my hand on her collar, just in case. I'd hate to have her bite an unsuspecting tourist, but if the guy had bad intentions, I had Emma and a tube of pepper spray in a pocket of my running shorts. I slipped my other hand into the pocket, just in case.

"Hey, remember me?" the man called again and as he got closer, I realized he was one of the geocachers we'd met on Sunday. Tim, Ted, Taylor—Taylor, that was it.

"Mr. Vice President, right?" I was sure that had been his title. "Are you setting up a new hidey-hole?"

His lips pressed together for a slight second. If I hadn't been looking right at him, I would have missed it. "Now, you know I can't release information about possible geocache sites." He stepped closer and nodded to Emma. "Beautiful retriever. Is she papered? I have a friend who has a stud a few towns over."

"Emma's not old enough to breed." I rubbed one of her ears, and she scooted closer to my leg, all the while keeping an eye on Taylor. "I'm not sure if I want her to have babies at all."

"You're missing out. Raising dogs is a gold mine. My buddy lives off the money he makes. Of course, he's got several bitches." Taylor reached toward Emma. "She'd be a fine breeder."

Emma growled deep in her throat, and Taylor jerked his hand back.

"Sorry, I've never seen her react this way to anyone." I put my hand on Emma's head, trying to comfort her while I kept a tight hold on her leash. She didn't like Taylor, not one bit.

He stepped back two big steps and held up his hands in surrender. "I get it. She's protective and that's a good thing. You never know what can happen to a woman all alone on a stretch of beach like this."

A chill went down my spine as I thought about Kacey and her solitary walk. I pointed to the crime scene tape. "You're right about that. One of our newest town residents was killed right there."

He studied the area where I'd pointed. "No. Seriously? That's awful." He glanced at his watch and whistled. "I didn't realize it was this late. I'm supposed to be picking my date up in thirty minutes and I'm an hour away from her house. I hope she doesn't mind waiting."

I watched Taylor sprint toward the beach parking lot and then looked at the crime scene one more time. Kacey hadn't deserved this. Turning and picking up my stride to finish my run, a thought stopped me in my tracks. I glanced at the lot, but the sound of an engine confirmed Taylor's exit. He'd known Kacey. She was the reason he was never elected president of that club. And now she was gone. I wondered if the coincidence had occurred to Greg. At least there was one person besides Sadie who wasn't upset that Kacey was out of the picture.

I ran the rest of the way, chewing on that thought. Taylor at least had a reason for wanting Kacey gone. But was that strong enough to want her dead? I could just hear Greg now if I tried to tell him.

"Stay out of the investigation, Jill." I lowered my voice and Emma turned her head, questioning my baritone. It was *not* the best impression in the world.

When I got home, I went to my office and got a new notebook. I opened it to the first page and wrote two words: "*Kacey Austin.*" My murder investigation book had begun, and I sat at my desk, filling in the pieces I knew and listing off the questions I had. The questions page was bigger.

Greg isn't going to like this. I closed the notebook and put it in the top shelf of the desk. Turning to close the door, I stopped and looked at my reflection in a mirror I'd hung on the office wall. "He doesn't have to know."

I heard my good side chuckling as I left the office.

CHAPTER 5

When Greg was on a case, I typically didn't see him for days at a time. When I heard a knock on my door, I closed the travel log I'd been reading and checked the time on the banister clock. Almost nine. Peeking out the window, I saw Greg's truck in the drive so I opened the door. He leaned against the door frame, all Cary Grant and Matt Dillon rolled into one. I couldn't help myself. I sighed.

He chuckled and opened the screen, letting himself in, and then pulled me into a hug. "Glad to know I still have some effect over you." I felt his breath in my hair and he squeezed just a little tighter. "This was just what I needed after today."

I looked up into his eyes and saw the worry he carried. "You want to talk? I'll try not to pester you with questions."

He put his arm around my waist and walked me into the kitchen, kicking shut the front door behind us. "Let's sit for a minute. Do you have something cold to drink? Non-alcoholic?"

I snagged two sodas from the fridge and set them on the table. I plated three of the brownies I'd brought home from my visit to Sadie's that morning and put the plate in front of Greg, who inhaled, then mimicked my sigh. "Sure, the food gets that response." I sat and opened my soda, taking a sip before I spoke again. "You don't really suspect Sadie of anything, do you?"

"Sadie? No. But maybe someone was trying to help. Someone who just happened to be home this last weekend?" Greg didn't meet my eyes as he spoke.

I stared at him, understanding his implication. I'd even thought the same thing for a few seconds. "That's impossible. Nick's a good kid."

"Unless it protected his mother. Then the kid would do anything." Greg set the brownie down and ran a hand through his sandy blond hair. Dark circles were starting under his eyes, and I knew he still had to go back to the station for a while.

I shook my head. "No way. Nick wouldn't hurt a fly. Not even to help his mother." I took a sip of my soda. "I guess if she was being mugged or something in front of him, then maybe. But breaking in to the food truck? And don't even suggest he could have killed Kacey."

"I'm not suggesting anything. I just find it interesting that the weekend the truck gets broken into, Nick's home from college. Not to mention that Sadie's recipes were returned to her in the dead of the night. You remember how he helped that girl break into The Castle, maybe he was thinking this could help his mom?" Greg rolled his head in a large circle, then opened his eyes and smiled at me. "Even if I agree with you, I've got to question him. It's my job."

Realization hit me as I broke off a piece of brownie and popped it into my mouth. As I chewed, the heavenly chocolate flavor didn't brighten my mood. I pointed my index finger at him. "You want me to tell Sadie."

"Tomorrow morning after I'm on my way to Stanford. I don't want her going all tiger mom on me and keep me from talking to Nick." Greg rubbed his face. "I know she'll want to know he's all right after I talk to him. I'd call her, but she doesn't trust me much right now."

"If I play messenger, she might not trust me ever again." I knew Greg had to talk to Nick, and, additionally, I knew I should be the one to tell Sadie. She deserved to know as soon as possible rather than getting a call from her kid or worse, the school, reporting Nick's arrest.

My cell rang, the display showing Bill Sullivan, owner/operator of South Cove Bed-and-Breakfast, city council member, and chairman of the Business-to-Business group. I frowned. It wasn't like him to call this late just to chat. I put on a smile I didn't feel from the interruption and clicked on the phone. "What's going on, Bill? Is Mary all right?" Mary was his wife and my aunt's BFF. The pair were the Thelma and Louise of the South Cove set.

"Mary's great, thanks for asking." Bill's voice wavered on the cell. "The council has ordered an emergency meeting. The mayor has a project he's rolling out for South Cove."

"When?" Next week would be hard to pull together. Maybe I'd be lucky, and they wouldn't want to meet for two weeks.

"Great, I'm glad you're on board. The meeting will be tomorrow at ten. Can we still hold it at your shop? I don't expect you to close for the period, so we'll just have to watch for the random customers." Apparently he'd taken my single-word question as agreement, if not full-fledged approval. All I'd wanted was to find out a day and time to see if it was possible to pull together.

When I hung up, I realized Bill had set in motion the emergency protocol the council had put in place if the town was attacked by a wave of invading aliens, or even just the occasionally drunk driver. The phone chain had been started, and I'd have at least ten business owners in my shop tomorrow expecting coffee and a dessert. I stared at Greg. "I'm hosting a Business-to-Business meeting tomorrow, per special directive. Do you know anything about this?"

"No, I swear. Look, I'm running on fumes." He stood and drained the soda out of his can and put it into the recycling bin. "You think about what I asked you. I'm heading back to the station and sleeping for a couple of hours. Then I'll drive up to Stanford so I'm there first thing in the morning."

"I'll tell her." I stood from the table and put my hand in his as we walked toward the front door. "I can't let her find out from someone else."

Greg kissed me at the door, and as he left, I watched him walk toward his truck. Typically, the role of lead detective for South Cove fit Greg like a glove. Tonight it looked like he was dragging a ball and chain.

I called Sasha and asked her to work my shift tomorrow so I could focus on the meeting. Whatever the mayor and council had planned, I had a feeling it wouldn't be an easy sell. I e-mailed a quick order of three dozen brownies to Sadie, knowing she was already probably asleep. And if she wasn't, I really didn't want to call her and risk blurting out Greg's mission to go question her son.

I closed up the house and trudged up to my bedroom, where I lay in the dark, not sleeping and thinking about how things had gotten all jumbled around. Sadie and Nick were solid people. No way would they do anything that even approached the line to illegal. And yet, the recipes were back in her possession.

The morning commuter rush over, Sasha helped me move tables to get ready. I'd called Aunt Jackie that morning to let her know about the impromptu meeting, but as usual, the news had already reached her.

"I'll be down at nine thirty. Did you call in Sasha or Toby?" I could hear my aunt lowering the volume on her television; she loved her morning talk shows.

"Sasha's already here." I wanted to say, *Duh, I already thought of that*, but I didn't think my aunt would appreciate my sass this morning.

"Be sure to make a fresh pot of coffee and fill the carafes before people start arriving." She hung up the phone before I could respond.

I put the receiver down. "I wish I would have thought of that."

Sasha wiped down the last carafe filled with fresh coffee. "Thought of what?"

"Jackie wants to make sure we have coffee available." I waved my hand at the tables set up for the meeting with coffee, cups, and a couple of plates of Sadie's brownies. She'd called that morning to tell me she would bring extras to the meeting when she came.

"She likes to make sure the t's are crossed and the i's are dotted. That's for sure. She reminds me of my grandmother. That woman runs a tight ship." I thought that was one comparison Sasha should keep to herself. Even though my aunt had ignored her last birthday, the woman was pushing her seventies—and didn't like to be reminded of it. Sasha glanced around the shop. She leaned under the counter and pulled out a novel. "You think I'll have some time to finish reading this? My after-school group meets this afternoon, and I'd like to be done before they come in."

Sasha had taken over our teen and young adult book clubs as part of her duties. She'd also redesigned our website and put in an online ordering system for both coffee drinks and books. Sales were increasing daily as customers found out about the service. I was going to have to increase her salary soon just to make sure we kept her around.

"I'm sure you'll have plenty of time during the meeting. If you don't fall asleep from boredom." I considered my upcoming conversation with Sadie. "Why don't you just stay on the clock through Toby's shift, that way you can be ready."

"You sure? I hate to have you pay me for just reading." Sasha ducked her head. "I could run home after Toby gets here and then drive back."

Her reaction surprised me a bit. There were lots of times when the job was really all about reading, when the walk-ins dwindled down to nothing. "No need to waste gas or your time. Besides, if he gets busy, you'll be here to help."

She shrugged. Before I could ask her if there was a problem, Bill and Mary arrived, followed by Sadie and Josh. The Business-to-Business regulars were starting to show up. I made a mental note to talk to Sasha later and went to greet the new arrivals.

Ten minutes later, the table was filled with committee members and Bill was calling the meeting to order. "Thanks, everyone, for coming on such short notice." Bill shot a look at Mayor Baylor, who was sitting next to him and ignoring his pointed look. "The council felt that we needed to act on the mayor's special committee request as soon as possible, so I guess I'll turn the floor over to Marvin and he can fill you in on the new project."

Bill sat down and Mayor Baylor stood. This time it was Bill's turn to ignore the glare from our mayor, probably due to the use of his first name rather than his title. "Thank you, *Bill*, for arranging this get-together." Mayor Baylor smiled down on the rest of us.

Uh-oh, we're in trouble now. I felt tingles all over the top of my head. The last time Mayor Baylor had shown up at a meeting with a special request, he'd put his wife, Tina, in charge of our holiday planning. Which was a disaster before she dropped the ball and Mary picked it up at the last minute.

"You all know California is in the middle of a drought. Even with the large body of water just a few miles from this very spot, freshwater is in short supply. So South Cove is going to do its part in helping our lovely state make it through this natural disaster." Mayor Baylor glanced around the table. "I know our local businesses are more than willing to assist in this worthwhile cause."

Josh Thomas, owner of Antiques by Thomas, and Aunt Jackie's boyfriend, even though I don't think she'd ever used the term, interrupted the mayor's monologue. "My business doesn't use a lot of water"—Josh shot a look at me—"not like a coffee shop. So why am I here?"

I sat forward, ready to tell him that he didn't need to be here, now or ever, but my aunt put her hand on my arm. I pressed my lips together to hold back the comment and leaned back in my chair.

Mayor Baylor answered the question. "The council has given approval for a special committee dedicated to holding businesses and residents accountable for their excess water usage. We were hoping, Mr. Thomas, that individuals like you would step up and be a part of the solution rather than just griping about the problem. Can I put your name down as a volunteer?"

Josh's face burned red, but he nodded.

My aunt raised her hand. "I'll join the committee, as well." She patted my arm in some sort of *there, there* gesture. I was less than reassured since my aunt had wanted us to stop serving water to our customers.

A third member joined the committee. Harrold Snider, the owner of The Train Station, put up his hand. "I guess I should be carrying my weight as the newest member of this group. I'll be part of the committee, too."

Thank God for rationality, I thought as Mayor Baylor beamed at the model train store owner.

"So glad to see you participating." He glanced around the table, and when no one else said anything, he nodded. "I'll assign Amy as the city's representative to the committee, and she'll drop off the reading material the state sent us on water conservation. Can I expect a starting report in two weeks?"

Harrold, Josh, and Aunt Jackie all nodded. "Looks like we've got some work ahead of us," Harrold said. "Why don't you all come over to The Train Station after the meeting and we'll set up some times to get together? Maybe Amy can join us?"

"Perfect," Aunt Jackie said. Her voice was a little too bright, causing me to look over at her. She blushed and poured herself more coffee.

Harrold looked at Josh, who shrugged. "I guess that will be okay." Josh never went against what Jackie said. At least not in public.

"As long as she's not away from the phones too long, you may ask Miss Newman to attend your meeting today." The mayor looked at his phone. "I'll be in the office until two."

He then turned the floor back over to Bill, who looked at me. "I believe that completes our business for the meeting? Jill, we can count this as our February meeting, correct?"

I thought of all the agenda items in my file and realized that most of them were from one person, Josh. I tried to keep my grin from taking over my entire face when I answered. "Of course, I'll move the other items off until March."

"But—" Josh protested.

Bill slammed down the gavel. "Then the Business-to-Business

meeting is adjourned. Make sure you send your agenda items to Jill a week prior to the March meeting."

Chairs pushed back from the table and people filled their to-go cups with the last of the free coffee. Brownies disappeared into napkins, and in less than five minutes, the shop was empty except for six people. Sasha, who sat reading behind the counter. Me. Sadie. And the new committee.

"We could just talk here," Josh mumbled, looking at Aunt Jackie.

She shook her head. "I believe a short walk over to The Train Station would do us good. Maybe we should order lunch from Lille's and extend our meeting so we can start planning?"

"I need to open the shop." Josh looked at Jackie like she was talking treason.

Aunt Jackie pulled her Burberry trench coat on over her peacock blue pantsuit and picked up her purse. She turned to look back at Sasha, who tucked the book away under the counter. "I'll be back in time for my shift."

Sasha nodded her head quickly, looking like a deer caught in the headlights.

"We'll be fine. Take all the time you need," I said, trying to divert my aunt's attention away from Sasha.

The three walked out of the shop and the rest of us started moving tables back into their regular places. "Josh didn't look too happy," Sadie observed as she wiped down a table I'd just moved.

"He doesn't like sharing Aunt Jackie with anyone." I put chairs around the table and moved to the next one. "And he's totally paranoid she's going to find someone better than him."

"Are they dating?" Sadie watched out the window as the trio made their way to Harrold's shop. "I didn't think Jackie was interested in that type of relationship with him."

"She's not sure about what she wants. Josh, well, he's still trying." I lifted another table and carried it to a place right in front of the window. I watched my aunt walk away, sandwiched between the oversized Josh and the tall Harrold. For a minute, seeing Harrold from the back next to my aunt, I remembered my uncle Ted. He was just about Harrold's height. The memory made me smile. They'd had a perfect marriage. One I hoped to mirror someday.

Sadie grabbed her purse. "Looks like the shop's back together. I guess I'd better head home. I've got Lille's order to finish."

"Hold on, I'll walk with you." I went to the back room and got my own purse. I paused when I walked by Sasha. "If you need help before Toby shows, just give me a call."

Sadie waited by the door. "I'm the opposite direction of your house. I don't really need an escort."

I pushed the door open. "I need to talk to you about something."

She followed me as we crossed Main Street, no cars coming from either side. "What's going on? You're making me nervous."

I slowed down, not sure how exactly to approach the subject. "Greg wanted me to tell you something."

"Please don't tell me he really believes I could have done something to Kacey. I feel bad for the girl, despite my past relationship with Austin." Sadie put her hand on my arm, slowing my progress. "You don't believe I could do something like that, right?"

"Of course, I mean, I don't think Greg thinks you're a murderer either, but he had to—" My words were interrupted by Sadie's phone chime.

She took her phone out of her purse and held up a hand. "Hold on, it's Nick."

My heart sank. I was too late. "Sadie, listen to me," but she'd already answered the call and put her hand up to stop my words.

"Hey, honey, how's school going?" She leaned against the side of The Glass Slipper. The glass shop was closed for the day. Typically the owner, Marie Jones, only opened the shop on weekends and the nights when she held classes. Wednesdays, the place was deserted.

I watched Sadie's face as she listened to Nick, who was probably telling her what I had been about to say. That Greg had come to question him about his activities that weekend and where he'd been when the food truck was vandalized.

"So, you're okay? He didn't take you into custody or anything, did he?"

I heard Nick's laugh from where I stood.

Sadie shook her head. "Fine, but next time, tell Mr. King that you're not talking to him about anything without an adult being present."

She clicked off the phone. "I take it you knew?"

"That's what I was trying to tell you. Greg went up this morning to make sure Nick wasn't involved in the food truck incident." I sagged into a bench on the sidewalk. I decided not to point out the fact since Nick was over eighteen, he really was an adult himself. "Is he okay?"

She nodded. "He thinks it's funny. The good news is, he has an airtight alibi for Monday night as he was with his debate team, including his professor, getting ready for their first event this weekend. And yes, your boyfriend talked to Mr. Allen and verified his story. Which probably makes Nick look like a criminal or something."

"I'm sure Greg was discreet." I took in Sadie's erect posture and clipped words. She was furious.

"I don't want to talk about this anymore. And I don't need an escort home. You've delivered the message, a little late, but I know now." Sadie turned toward home.

"Sadie, come have lunch with me, we'll talk," I called after her. Food could fix anything, including hurt feelings. At least that was my mantra.

"No, thank you."

I watched Sadie walk away and hoped that she'd be able to forgive. Even though I hadn't done anything, apparently since I hadn't told her immediately, I was as bad as Greg in her mind.

The good news was, Nick was in the clear. The bad news was, I might have lost a friend in the process.

I turned and walked home, hoping the sun would break through the clouds and lift the gray from the day if not from my mood.

CHAPTER 6

Thursday's shift was quiet, but I wasn't able to lose myself in the novel I'd been reading. I picked up several of the new release advance copies our sales rep had dropped off, but nothing kept my attention. I kept thinking about Sadie and the scene from yesterday.

I took out the laptop and spent the next few hours reviewing the accounting. Usually Aunt Jackie had to badger me into approving the last week's figures, but today, the numbers stopped my racing mind and gave me something to think about other than Sadie.

"I can't believe you've already approved the book order." Aunt Jackie stood over me as I sat on the couch. I'd moved from accounting to book buying and had probably spent my budget for the entire quarter already. "What's gotten into you?"

"I'm worried about Sadie." I blurted the statement out before I could think about my aunt's reaction.

Instead of the lecture about staying out of Greg's investigations that I'd expected, my aunt sat on the couch next to me. "She'll be fine. It's unfortunate that Kacey had to die so unexpectedly, but you and I both know Greg won't be able to charge Sadie with the murder because she didn't do it." She patted my hand. "You really need to have more faith in the justice system."

"People are falsely accused and convicted all the time." I decided not to share the fact that Sadie's recipes had mysteriously appeared on her doorstep with my aunt. No need to add fuel to the gossip fodder already running through town. "I do trust Greg. I just feel bad that Sadie has to go through this."

"I understand." My aunt sat in silence next to me. Finally, she turned toward me. "I need you to cover my shift on Friday. I asked Sasha and Toby but they both already have plans."

"And you know I don't have plans since Greg will be unavailable due to the investigation." I shrugged. "Sure, I haven't worked an evening shift for a while. I'm probably getting rusty."

"Perfect." She stood and headed toward the back of the shop.

"Hey," I called after her. "What's going on? Is Josh taking you to the city for dinner?"

Aunt Jackie froze midstride and turned back, studying my face. Then she checked out the empty store to make sure no one was in earshot. She came closer, then whispered, "You can't tell anyone."

"I can't tell anyone what?" Now I was intrigued. "Don't tell me you and Mary are breaking and entering again? What is it this time? A shady art dealer?"

She pressed her lips together. "No." She framed the word with her mouth. "I'm not doing *anything* illegal."

"Okay, now you have to tell me. What's up?" I closed the laptop and focused on my aunt.

She took a big dramatic sigh. "If you must know, Harrold and I are going to the city for dinner and drinks to talk about the water conservation committee."

"Without Josh or Amy?" I got it now. My aunt was going on a date.

She turned beet red. "Fine, it's a date. But don't go getting all 'what about Josh' with me. I never said our relationship was exclusive."

"I wasn't even thinking about questioning you on that subject." Okay, so maybe I had been, but I liked Harrold. He and Aunt Jackie would make a nice pair. I did feel sorry for Josh though. In a weird way.

"Just cover my shift and keep your mouth shut on my business." My aunt looked at me, waiting for a response. When I didn't say anything, she blurted, "What?"

"You didn't say please." I heard the bell over the door ring and saw Toby walk in for his shift.

"Please," Aunt Jackie whispered.

I stood and put the laptop under my arm. "Your wish is my command."

"Uh-oh." Toby smiled as he walked toward us. "Your aunt must have conned you into covering her shift."

"Yep." I smiled back at him. "And since I'm working tomorrow, I need to get home and take a run into Bakerstown to the Pet Palace. Emma's almost out of dog food."

My aunt mouthed the words *"thank you"* before disappearing behind the office door toward her apartment upstairs.

Toby watched her go. "I felt bad saying no, but Elisa set up this dinner thing and she's been pretty adamant that I need to be there. I even had to have Tim cover my police shift. I hate leaving Greg so shorthanded during an active investigation."

"Sometimes people have to come first. I'm sure Elisa must have something very important planned." I left the front of the shop and put the laptop on the office desk. Grabbing my purse, I decided to stop by City Hall and see if Amy wanted to get an early lunch. Okay, really I wanted to see what had happened between my aunt and Harrold at the water conservation meeting. So sue me.

Toby was making fresh coffee when I returned to the front of the shop. He drummed his fingers on the counter, waiting for the pot to brew. I studied him as he tossed an empty cup from hand to hand, his attention elsewhere. "What's up with you? Don't tell me you're still worried about taking tomorrow night off? Greg will understand."

He shook his head. "That's not what I'm worried about." His attention moved to the group of women who were getting out of a large van and walking toward the door. "I wonder what Elisa wants to talk about that's so important."

Our conversation ended as the women entered the shop and rushed to the counter to order. Toby's girls, as I called them, were students at the local cosmetology school down the highway toward Bakerstown. There were a lot of coffee shops or restaurants closer where they could take their study breaks, but only one that had the sexy police deputy–slash–barista working the counter. I put a hand on his arm. "Call me or Jackie if you get swamped."

Amy was balancing a pencil on her upper lip when I opened the door. She dropped the pencil and reached for the phone that hadn't rung. When she saw it was me, she hung up the receiver. "Crap, you scared me."

"You alone here?" I glanced around the empty waiting room and through Mayor Baylor's open office door.

"He's been gone all morning but he keeps calling to give me one more thing to handle." Amy yawned and stretched her arms. "I guess I should be happy for the distractions. Besides the water conservation committee, the office has been dead all month."

Bingo, there was my opening. "Can I buy you lunch? I'd love to hear about the meeting."

Amy pulled her purse out of her desk along with a BACK IN AN HOUR sign. She turned off her computer and went over to shut and lock the mayor's office door. "You don't have to buy. I'd give my firstborn to get out of here today."

"You don't have any kids," I reminded her as we walked out into the courtyard.

Amy turned toward me, flashing her outdoor smile. "Haven't you ever heard of a figure of speech?" She leaned her head back and stretched out her arms. "I love sunny winter days."

The weather had been beautiful, except the longer we went without rain, the more serious the area's drought problem got. "So, tell me about the meeting. Did they come up with any good ideas?"

Amy narrowed her eyes as we approached the diner. Lille's Thursday's lunch specials were written on a chalkboard set up on the sidewalk. Meat loaf plate and a spring chicken salad. Even the soup of the day sounded amazing—chicken tortilla. She held the door open for me. "Why are you so interested in water conservation? I thought you were going to slip under the table when Marvin was looking for volunteers."

I slid into our favorite booth, and as I unwrapped the silverware from the paper napkin, I kept my head down. "Believe me, I have no interest in serving on the committee."

"Then, why would you . . ." Amy stared at me. "I knew something was going on. I could feel it. Jackie and Harrold?"

Carrie tapped menus on the table. "You two know what you want? Or do you need these?"

I pushed one of the menus toward Amy. As I opened the other one, I focused on Carrie, giving her my best innocent smile. "We'll need a few minutes."

"Seriously, you have to spill, I can't believe the two of them would . . ." Amy took a breath and I kicked her under the table. "Ouch." Amy leaned down and rubbed her leg.

"Keep your secrets. It's not like I won't find out soon anyway. This is a small town, remember?" Carrie waved at a couple coming in the door. "Just let me know when you're ready to order. I can't stand all this drama."

I watched her walk away, then turned to Amy, who was staring at me like I had seven heads. "You can't say anything. Aunt Jackie will think I told you."

"But you didn't, I guessed." Amy flipped her pixie cut behind her ears. "Wow, I never would have seen that coming."

"You and me both, sister." I tried to focus on the menu. My aunt and her love life had surprised me from the moment she'd decided to move into town to *help* me with the store. I turned to the page describing the salads and told myself to be happy with my choices. The pep talk wasn't working.

Amy gasped, pulling the menu away from my eyes with one finger. Even though Amy surfed more weekends than not, her nails still were pretty and polished, something I hadn't done in years. "Does Josh know?"

I shook my head. "I don't think so. She swore me to secrecy about their date tomorrow night. I'm covering her shift." I guess my version of keeping a secret meant I didn't take an ad out in the local paper or post the information on my Facebook page. Although I had thought about announcing I would be working in case any of my regulars wanted to stop by and keep me from being totally bored. Friday evenings often got a lot of date traffic, both from the local teenagers and from the day tourists who just wanted to get away on a date night. But not during dead season. Not for the first time, I thought about adding music to the mix by hiring a local band hoping to make it big by playing just the right gig where they'd be discovered. I pointed my finger at my friend. "Don't tell anyone."

Amy leaned forward in the booth. "Do you want to know what happened?"

I leaned over just as I heard Carrie clear her throat.

"Are you ladies ready to order?" Carrie sounded tired. "Or should I come back at a better time. Like Christmas?"

"Sorry." I listed off my salad order and watched as Amy struggled to make her food decision before Carrie turned toward her. I think she just panicked when Carrie looked at her.

"I'll have the meat loaf platter." Amy held out her menu. "So how are you feeling?"

Carrie leaned against the table. "You can say it, I look worn out. My doctor thinks I might have a gluten allergy. I totally laughed at him, but I was planning to try to clean up my diet before Austin's wife died. You never know when your ticket's going to be drawn, so it's better to live life to the fullest."

I'd never met anyone with a gluten allergy before and now, in a week, I'd talked to two people. "What are the symptoms? Tiredness? Is that all?"

"Migraines, mood swings, digestive issues, the symptoms run the gamut. Even if I am allergic, I'm not as severe as some people. My doctor said he has patients who can go into anaphylactic shock if they eat something with wheat, barley, or rye." Carrie eyed the menu. "Aren't you sorry you asked?"

When she left the table, Amy leaned closer. "Are you feeling all right?"

"I'm fine. I was just interested. Did you know that Kacey had a severe wheat allergy? She told me about it when we were talking about the food truck." I sipped my water and wondered exactly how Kacey had died. Greg had been less than forthcoming about the cause of death, but that could have been because of Sadie and her possible involvement. Or *im*possible involvement, to be exact.

"The day we went to lunch we talked about her health. She was really limited as to what she could order on the menu. I don't think she kept her condition a secret from anyone." Amy studied me. "You don't think that's how she died, do you? What does Greg say?"

"Nothing. Which makes me think there is something fishy about her death. If it was an accident, he would have already closed the case and wouldn't have questioned Nick." My eyes widened as I clamped my mouth shut. I hadn't meant to tell anyone, even Amy, about that part.

"You're kidding me? Greg thought pure-as-snow Nick could have murdered someone?" Amy shook her head in disbelief. "I think your boyfriend is grasping at straws."

We paused as another server dropped off our iced teas. I lowered my voice. "You can't say I told you this, but Sadie got a notebook left on her doorstep with all the recipes Austin had conned out of her when they were dating. And Kacey had notes on the pages on how to turn them gluten-free." I shrugged and took the paper sleeve off my straw. "At least I assume it was Kacey's handwriting. Austin is a Class A jerk. I bet Kacey didn't even know where the recipes came from."

"I don't think he actually hurt Sadie intentionally." Amy crossed her arms. "You're making it sound like the only reason he was dating her was to get ahold of her recipes. That's cold, man."

I put my hands up in mock surrender. "All I know is, the notebook was on Sadie's doorstep. Someone had left it there in the middle of the night. So Greg had to make sure that Nick didn't break into the food truck to steal back his mom's recipes. That's all."

Our food arrived and we ate in silence for a few minutes, each one lost in her own thoughts. Or at least I was. Amy had rented the second-floor apartment from Austin for years. She probably knew him better than anyone else in South Cove. The man was a mystery. He never talked about his past or people he knew. I'd never even suspected he and Kacey had been married and separated.

Amy's phone chirped and she looked at the text message. She read it aloud. "The geo club is having a memorial out on the beach on Saturday at noon. Do you want to attend?"

I thought about my Saturday plans and decided laundry could wait another day. "I'll be there. Are you going?"

Amy nodded. "I'd like to get to know who Kacey was a little bit better through someone's eyes besides Austin." She took a bite of her mashed potatoes and grinned. "We aren't really investigating, right? Greg can't find fault in us just going to pay our respects."

I didn't know how Greg or Sadie would take our attendance, so I shoved a large bite of my salad into my mouth to avoid having to answer. By the time I could talk, Amy had moved on to another subject.

"So, Harrold and Jackie, huh?" Her eyes brightened. "I could totally see the attraction. Jackie needs a man who wants to wine and dine her."

"She kind of has that with Josh." I couldn't believe I was sticking up for the guy, but a part of me felt sorry for him. My aunt needed to figure out what she wanted and quickly so no one got hurt. Of course, I suspected that no matter what, someone would be holding the short straw, and if I had to bet, my money would be on the portly antique dealer. Josh and Jackie had little in common except the fact that Josh adored my aunt.

"You need to keep me in the loop. This is as good as the soap operas I was addicted to in college." Amy pushed away the almost empty plate. "I guess I'd better head back to the office. My lunch hour was up five minutes ago."

She pulled out cash for her part of the bill, but I waved it away. "I'll buy today. I was the one who asked you to come to lunch. See you soon."

I watched as Amy walked through the crowded diner. I wasn't the only one watching her. The men in the diner were also watching my friend. Amy was oblivious to her effect on men; she always had been. But they noticed her.

Carrie tapped on the table with the folder that held our bill. "You get stuck with the check?"

Turning my attention back to the table, I shook my head. "Nope, I asked for it. Besides, Amy had to get back to work. I'd like a piece of that blueberry crumble and another iced tea. I've got a book I want to finish before I go home and take Emma to the Pet Palace."

"Sure thing." Carrie disappeared, and I opened my tote and took out the latest release in a fantasy series I'd been devouring for the last week or two. I had three chapters left, and since I'd given up my full day off tomorrow and now with plans on Saturday, I wanted to finish the book today.

When Carrie brought the dessert, I paused my reading to take a few bites, then went back to the story. When I reached the end, my crumble and my iced tea were also done. I packed up my stuff, left money for the check, and headed home to a list of chores including a shopping trip to Bakerstown.

Greg should be happy. Not one item on my list had anything to do with solving Kacey's murder.

CHAPTER 7

I'd made three of my four stops in town. Town, being Bakerstown, the county seat and the closest place to actually buy groceries and dog food, and it had a Linens and Loots, the last stop on my list. Well, the last stop before I pulled the car into Wheeler's, my favorite hamburger place.

Jen McKarn, the store manager, looked up when I entered the shop. "Uh-oh. Did Emma eat the sofa cushions again? I'm not sure I can sell you more without feeling like I'm contributing to her addiction."

I crossed the gleaming floor and stood next to the counter where Jen had been working on a spreadsheet. "Nope, today I'm here for sheets for the new guest room. I finally found a handmade quilt for the room, and I need something besides the old sheets I've been using."

"Do you have a picture of the quilt? Maybe we can match a color or two so you have coordinating options." Jen closed the file and tucked it under her arm. "Besides, helping you shop will keep me from messing with this staffing schedule. I swear, the bigger we get, the more problems I have with keeping employees."

I'd been lucky in the staffing department. My aunt had been my first employee, and she'd hired Toby. Sasha came from an internship we'd participated in for the Work Today program last winter. The program could have been a complete disaster, since the director had been killed less than a week into our project. But the good news was, he had been a complete jerk anyway and we'd gained an excellent employee. I realized Jen was staring at me, a clear sign I'd missed a question as my mind had gone on a walkabout. "Sorry, what?"

"I asked if you had a picture. I know you can't help me with staffing. You're perfect in that area." She actually made air quotes when she said "*perfect*."

"Hold on, I've got it on my phone. Besides, my shop's tiny compared to Linens and Loots. I didn't even think I needed Aunt Jackie's help." I thumbed through photos until I found the one of the quilt. I handed her my phone. "Here it is. I'm thinking baby blue and maybe a rose?"

Jen studied the photo. "Very nice. The quilt looks like Sarah's work. Did you get this from the senior center's consignment shop over off of Grand?"

I stepped back, stunned. "How did you know that? I looked for months for that quilt. Then one of my regulars at the shop mentioned the store and they had several I wanted to buy."

"Each quilter has their own style. Even if they use the same pattern, the materials are different, or the stitching. You should have asked me last time you were in the store for pillows. I would have recommended the shop." Jen handed me back the phone and came around the counter. "Let's go look at what we've got in stock. I might need to special-order a color."

As we walked toward the back, past the scented candles and cookware, I wondered if my new guest room would ever be done. New sheets, fluffy pillows and shams, and maybe a walnut nightstand with a pewter lamp. Oh, and a dresser. I pulled out my notebook and wrote down the still-to-purchase items. Once that was completed, we were at the linen shelves and Jen had found two sets of sheets in the exact colors I'd asked for.

"Perfect, you're a miracle worker." I looked at my list and scratched off *find sheets*.

A middle-aged woman hurried up to us, frantically trying to get her arms through the company apron all the employees wore. "Ms. McKarn, I'm so sorry I'm late. I was helping the group set up the memorial, and then my car wouldn't start and I had to wait for a tow, and then the rental place was super-slow."

Jen held up a hand. "I'm just glad you made it, Ginny. I had just started trying to find someone to cover your closing shift."

I felt the pause in Jen's voice and realized the word she didn't say was "*again*." I pressed my lips together so that she wouldn't see the smile and turned to examine a patterned sheet that wouldn't match anything I'd ever own.

"Oh, I'm so glad you didn't. I really need the hours. I was going to talk to you about increasing my shifts this week anyway." Ginny Dean pulled out a piece of paper from her apron. "I can work any day but this Saturday. Next week, I'm clear on Monday morning until ten, Tuesday afternoon between one and four, and any time on Wednesday or Thursday. Unless the funeral is scheduled those days. And of course, I can't work the weekends."

This time the sigh was audible. Jen put her hand on Ginny's shoulder. "Just put a note in my mail slot and I'll see what I can do. You know, we really need people to work full six-hour shifts."

"I know, and I can on a few of these days." Ginny peered at her crumpled schedule.

Jen glanced at me and rolled her eyes. "Let's just see what I can work out, okay?" She pointed to the back room entrance. "We got a delivery today of the new Home Chef cookware. Can you restock that section?"

Ginny's head nodded like one of those bobblehead dolls they give out at baseball games. Greg had a collection on a shelf in his office—they always creeped me out.

We watched her scurry away, and this time, Jen leaned against a display bin of pillowcases. "The woman has a big heart, but she's the worst at keeping a schedule. I'm always having to fill in part of her shift because of car trouble or this crazy group she belongs to."

"Which makes me very glad I've got a small shop and there are only four of us." I glanced at my watch. "The bad news is, there are only four of us, so like tomorrow I have to take Aunt Jackie's shift. If no one else is available, it's up to me to work."

"The joy of management and ownership." Jen laughed and reached for another set of sheets. "Of course, I'm just a manager. I don't get to make the big decisions, not like you."

"Seriously, sometimes I wish I didn't have everything on my shoulders." I grinned, picking up the blue and pink sheets. "Of course, I have Aunt Jackie to tell me what to do, so I guess I am in the same boat."

"Hold on, let me see that photo again. I'm worried the rose is too pink for the quilt." She held out her hand.

"I'm sure it will be perfect. No need to be so detailed." Jen didn't drop her hand, so I handed her my phone. *Please be a match, please.*

I watched as she set the phone down on the sheets, turned it one way, then the other, and then shrugged. Jen handed me my phone back.

"I would go with a shade deeper in the blue, but if you're really happy with what we found, who am I to push?"

My shoulders dropped in relief. I imagined setting up the room tomorrow before going to work Aunt Jackie's shift. I might even take a quick picture and post it on my Facebook page. My joy decreased a bit with Jen's next words.

"Remember, you need to wash the sheets before you use them. They'll be all stiff if you don't." Jen looked at the list. "You want to look at pillows and shams today? We have a pretty set of cream cro-cheted pillowcases that would be perfect."

I nodded and followed her to the next station.

By the time I'd stuffed my too-hot-to-handle credit card into my wallet and the bags of fluffy warm linens into the car, I felt worn to the bone. I'd not only purchased new fluffy pillows for the guest room, but had added on new ones for my room, along with a Memory Foam mattress pad for my older mattress that Jen had sworn by.

I'd planned on a quick in and out, but instead had spent over twenty minutes in the store. My cold items from the grocery were stuck in a cooler in the back of the Jeep with ice packs for the drive home. I hadn't purchased ice cream, so I quickly calculated my suc-cess at stopping at Wheeler's before I left town. My growling stom-ach made the final decision, so I just hoped I had packed enough ice to keep my half gallon of milk and the sea bass I'd bought chilled. On tonight's dinner menu? A mushroom and Swiss burger on their homemade buns with an order of steak fries and a large vanilla milk shake. With the amount of calories, fat grams, and sugar, I could sur-vive being locked in a cave for a week before I'd start losing weight.

Arriving home, my stomach filled and my hunger sated, I still had half of my milk shake left. After unloading and unpacking the gro-ceries, I threw the sheets into the wash and took the shake and a new book out onto the porch with Emma. We watched the light dim as the sun sank over the ocean.

*   *   *

The next morning, I awoke with the sun, dressed in running clothes, and sipped a cup of coffee before I took Emma for a run. She sat at the back door, a small whine coming out of the back of her throat every three minutes. Finally, I set my cup in the sink and picked up her leash.

The morning was glorious. The sun bright but not hot. The beach sand clean from the last high tide but with just enough uncovered treasures that Emma was intrigued. Since we were alone, I let her off the leash and she ran to the shoreline, walking in the waves that lapped the edge of the world. When I reached the place where Kacey's body had been found, I stopped. Now around the entire section, still barricaded with yellow tape, was a ring of flower arrangements and candles. And on each of the glass candle holders was a picture of Kacey, smiling at the camera.

This must be the place where the geo club was holding their memorial tomorrow. Ginny really could have been here setting up this shrine to Kacey. I hadn't even put the two things together until now, sure Ginny was making up excuses for her lateness. Of course, it still could have been an excuse—just because the shrine existed didn't mean Ginny had set it up herself, or even helped.

Emma plopped down into a sitting position at my side, her wet nose finding my hand. I absently rubbed her head as I thought of the woman who had died. "She'd been loved," I said to her, even though Emma was the only person—well, dog—around. Some ideas were just too big to keep in your head.

Emma pushed her nose into my hand again. Which either meant, *Whoa, dude, too deep*, or *Aren't we supposed to be running?* I decided it was the latter and we carefully moved away from Kacey's memorial and headed farther up the beach.

This time the sound of the waves and the feel of my feet hitting the sand didn't block out the unanswered question circling in my mind. *Who killed Kacey?*

The rest of the day was filled with chores right up to the time I left for the shop to cover Aunt Jackie's shift. Sasha was manning the counter when I arrived. She waved and poured me a large hazelnut black, just the way I liked my coffee. "Hey, you didn't have to come in early. I don't have to leave until five to pick up Olivia."

"I thought Toby was working the midday shift?" I sat at the counter and slid the book Sasha had been reading closer. The YA dystopian series had been selling like hotcakes after the movie released last month. "Is this what the book club is reading next month?"

Sasha handled our tween book club as well as the older teen group. Since I'd hired her on, book sales in the YA category had doubled, and even Aunt Jackie had realized it was an uncharted market for us. "We're having a movie night. They can read anything that's been turned into a movie in the last five years."

"That should be interesting. How are you going to talk about the books?" I read the back cover and thought I'd put this one on my own reading list for next week.

"We'll divide up in groups. From the books they purchased through us, I'm pretty sure we'll have four groups with a few outliers. There are some rebels in the bunch." She smiled at the thought of her book club members.

I pushed the book toward her. "Whatever you're doing, it's working. I got a call from the high school principal thanking us for the increase in students reading during study hall. I guess she's even seeing them parked on the hallway floor during lunch with their books."

Sasha blushed. "The kids just needed a reason to read. Now that we get to talk about the books they want to read, instead of the ones they have to read for English class, they're all about it."

I thought about my own high school years. "You know, I don't think we've ever done a service project with the school library. Why don't you visit the librarian next week and see if we can do some type of event for them? Maybe there's an author they'd like us to bring in for a talk?"

Sasha's eyes widened. "We could do that?"

"We have a promotion budget for a reason. Besides, the book club is making us some money now that you're running it." I nodded as I considered the idea more. "We'll have to get Aunt Jackie on board, but after tonight, she owes me at least one favor."

"This is going to be so rad. I just hope the librarian and the high school go for it." Sasha did a happy dance behind the counter. "I love working here. Just saying."

"We love having you." I sipped my coffee and glanced around the shop. Typical Friday night customers, a few kids with their tablets and earphones at a table and a couple of women who appeared to be here as a first stop on a Mommies Night Out. The rest of the evening would consist of random walk-ins and a few who'd had dinner at

Lille's but wanted coffee and a dessert before they called it a night. I figured I'd have a lot of reading time. "You never said what happened to Toby working with you today."

"Oh, he was here." Sasha started restocking cups near the coffee machine. "He needed to leave early. Elisa and him had a date night planned."

She didn't meet my eyes when she told me the answer, but something in her tone made me look up from my coffee. "Are you all right?"

This time I saw her shoulders rise and her eyes widen, putting on a good show for me, I assumed. "Of course, I'm perfect. Just thinking about the things I need to get done tonight with Olivia. Dinner, bed, bath, and story. It's a ritual."

"Sounds like a busy Friday night." I had a lot of respect for Sasha and her ability to juggle being a good parent along with going to school and working.

"Add in studying for an accounting test next week, and you've got my entire weekend." She looked at the clock. "Better get moving. I've got a lot to get done before I'm back here tomorrow."

I stepped around the counter and blocked her way. "You'd tell me if something was wrong, right?"

She froze and I could see the debate going on in her head. Now I was really worried. "Sasha?"

The bell over the door rang, and a tourist couple walked into the shop. The woman paused at the local history and travel display table I had set up near the front. The man power-walked to the counter. He waved his hand to get my attention. "We need two large coffees to go, please."

Sasha nodded to the counter. "Go. I'm fine."

When I didn't move, she let her lips curve into a warm smile. "Look, it's man trouble. Nothing that I can't handle. I'm just being a little sensitive right now."

"Hello?" The man tapped his wallet on the counter. "Can I get some help here?"

"Two coffees. I heard you." I turned back toward Sasha. "You're not in danger, right?"

The girl laughed. Not just a chuckle. She let out a belly laugh and went to pour the two coffees. When she put lids on the cups, she set them in front of the customer. "Four-fifty." She nodded to the woman still looking through the books. "Unless the lady is buying something?"

"She can shop tomorrow. We're on our way to The Castle for the night tour and we're late." The man threw a five and two ones on the counter in front of Sasha and tucked his wallet back in the front pocket of his pants. "Keep the change."

I watched him hand over the coffee and take his wife by the elbow, leading her out. *A man with a plan.* I saw movement from the corner of my eye. Sasha was trying to sneak by me and out the back door. I put my hand on her arm, slowing her movements. "Hold on, I'm worried now."

Sasha sighed and stopped. "Look, I'm okay. I just got my emotions in a nicker about someone I have no reason to be thinking about. I appreciate the concern, but can we just drop it?"

"If you're sure you're safe." I didn't want her to go flying off into some relationship that would be bad for her. So kill me if I'm a big mother hen.

Sasha held her hand up in a mini Scout salute. "I swear, I'm all right."

"Then what are you still doing here." I let her arm go and made swooshing movements with my arms. "Fly, little bird, go explore the world."

"You're a nut." Sasha rushed toward me and gave me a tight hug. "Thanks for caring."

By eight, the shop was dead. I stood by the window, gazing out on empty Main Street. Even though it was a warm Friday evening, it was late February, and the tourist season hadn't really taken off yet. The streetlights were slowly brightening as the dusk fell on the town. I saw a couple walking down the sidewalk arm in arm, and as they approached, I realized it was Amy and Justin. They waved at me through the glass, then entered the shop. "Hey, guys, what's got you still in town on a Friday night? I figured you'd be chasing a wave somewhere?"

"We decided to stay tonight since the memorial's tomorrow." Amy explained as she gave me a quick hug.

"Here for coffee or something decadent from Sadie's stash?" I scurried toward the counter.

Justin followed me. "Neither."

"Speak for yourself." Amy slapped his shoulder. "I'll have a frozen latte. I'll probably be up for hours, but I don't care."

"You want me to make it decaf?" I paused over the espresso machine, waiting for her answer.

Amy's brow wrinkled. "Heck, no. What's the fun in that? Give me the real stuff."

I started brewing her drink and looked at Justin. "You sure you don't want anything?"

"I do want something, just not coffee." He slipped a sheet of paper toward me. "Can you order these books for me?"

I glanced at the list. "Probably. I mean, as long as they aren't out of print." I read the titles. "Are these all about geocaching?"

"Yep. And I bet you could sell a lot of these if you stocked them in the store." Justin climbed onto a stool. "Taylor said it took him a year to find all of those on the list. You could be the preferred bookseller for the club. I bet they'd frequent your store a lot. Taylor says he's always on the lookout for a new book or magazine article."

I tucked the list into my desk calendar I kept on the counter. A small sheet of paper fell out and I peeked at it. It was Kacey's cookbook request list. I'd never gotten the chance to fill it. I went to throw it away, but something nudged me and instead I put it with Justin's list. "I don't really have room for a lot of nonfiction books. The young adult and mystery section keeps growing to feed the book club groups."

Justin looked around the bookstore section like he'd never even considered my lack of space before. "I guess you're right. But you could order the books for people, like you're doing for me, right?"

"I'll order books for anyone. I love the business." I finished up Amy's iced coffee and put a lid over the top. "Sounds like you've been talking to Taylor a lot."

Justin handed me a ten for the coffee and I rang it up, giving him back his change with the receipt. As I did, he continued to gush about the former VP of the geo club. I wondered if a president dies in office, did the club run like the country and the VP stepped in?

"He's so experienced and smart about this. He even showed me what machine I should buy. Saved me a bundle since I was looking at the top-of-the-line GPS device."

Amy unwrapped her straw and poked it into the cup. "Man crush. And a pretty serious one, as far as I can tell."

Justin pulled her closer and gave her a quick kiss. "You're the only one I have a crush on, man or woman."

"Good to know." Amy brushed his hair out of his eyes, then she turned to me. "We're doing a *Star Trek* marathon tonight. Want to come over? We have pizza and popcorn."

"Tempting, but I think I'm cuddling on the couch with Emma and clearing some shows off of my DVR. I'm approaching its max limit, so I need to clean out some things before the machine does it for me."

With Justin and Amy gone, I started the closing chores, knowing I'd be the one opening in the morning, I didn't worry about stocking the dessert case or sweeping the back room. I figured I'd have lots of time tomorrow after the locals left with their morning coffee fix. I'd just set up the starter pot for the morning and was turning off lights when the bell rang over the door. Crap, I hadn't locked the door. "We're closed," I called out, not turning around.

That's when I heard the front door lock engage.

CHAPTER 8

I froze, my hand shaking as I dropped the dishrag I'd been using to wipe up spilled water. Maybe I hadn't heard the lock. I thought about the pepper spray Aunt Jackie insisted on keeping on a shelf under the cash register. I turned my head and calculated how many steps it would take to reach it. Maybe we should keep several canisters spread out in different places in the shop. Typically, my elderly aunt worked this shift. If I couldn't reach it, how would she?

I took a deep breath and ran the few steps to the cash register. I kept my head down, swept up the pepper spray, took off the safety, and swung my arm up in a defensive move. Only then did I recognize the man standing in front of me.

Josh Thomas.

"Hey." He dodged and threw his arms up to cover his face. "What the heck are you doing? Are you insane?"

I kept my arm outstretched. "What am *I* doing? Why did you lock the shop door?" My voice sounded a little loud and stressed. Okay, so I sounded like a screech owl. The man had scared the crap out of me. "What are you doing here?"

"I always come by after dinner and help Jackie close up." He pointed at the pepper spray. "Put that thing away, Miss Gardner. If I planned on doing you harm, I wouldn't have left the lights burning so anyone passing by could see my misdoings."

I thought about his logic and dropped my arm. Adrenaline surged through my body, and I sank against the counter, hoping it would hold me upright. "Okay. So maybe I overreacted."

"I blame the obscene amount of coffee you drink on a daily basis. I'm sure you have caffeine poisoning." He looked around the coffee shop. "Why are you working tonight?"

My heart rate had slowed and I took several deep breaths before I spoke. "There's no such thing as caffeine poisoning." I picked up the rag I'd been using and threw it into the laundry bin we kept just inside the back office door. The promise I'd made my aunt was weighing heavy on my mind. I couldn't tell anyone where she was, especially not Josh. "Can I get you a drink or maybe a slice of cheesecake?"

"I just had my dinner, and I'm not thirsty. So, where is your aunt?" Josh peered at me through the layers of fat around his dark brown eyes. "She's okay, right? She's not in the hospital or ill, is she?"

A little white lie formed and was out before I could stop it. "Aunt Jackie wasn't feeling well so she decided to turn in early. She's probably already asleep. I'm sure a good night's sleep will fix her up."

He considered my words, and for some reason, I felt like he could feel the falseness in the statement. Or maybe it was my inability to look him in the eye. No matter, he finally nodded and headed to the front door. "You should follow me and lock up when I leave. It's not safe for a woman to work alone this late at night."

I did follow him and lock the door after he left. However, I didn't tell him that five minutes after nine wasn't late for most adults. I stood, watching his retreating figure disappear into the dark. Aunt Jackie owed me big after this. She could have warned me about Josh's nightly ritual. The man would do anything for my aunt. And if she chose Harrold over Josh, the loss of her would break his heart.

I turned off the last of the lights and checked the locks one more time. Then I walked toward the light coming from the back room, hoping for the first time that my aunt wouldn't break up with the portly antique dealer.

The next morning came too quickly, and as I dressed for my shift, I remembered the exhaustion I'd felt when I'd run the shop all by myself. All I did was work the first few years after I'd opened Coffee, Books, and More. Work, read, and a weekly lunch date with Amy, that had been my life. And even though it had been hard, grueling work, it was ten times better than the hours I'd spent as a corporate family law attorney.

I let Emma out and filled my travel mug with coffee. I had twenty minutes before I opened the shop. Time enough to throw a load of jeans into the washer and make sure Emma had food and water on the porch. I'd kept her in the house last night during my shift because of the coyotes Greg had seen while he reviewed security tapes of Main Street. Apparently at least one pack of wild dogs was making itself at home late at night in South Cove. A fact that explained my often overturned trash cans behind the shop.

I stifled a yawn as I gave Emma a hug and locked up the house. Maybe I'd wake up on the walk into town. The fog was still heavy and it made the road look as if I was out in the middle of a field covered with snow, instead of on a city street. The street lamps glowed in the fog like the old-fashioned gaslights they'd been constructed to resemble.

When I reached town, the sidewalks were still eerily void of people. I hadn't even heard a bird chirp or the sound of a passing car down on the highway. In the middle of tourist season, these streets would be filled from sunrise to way past sundown. People liked to wander through South Cove. They'd leave their room at the bed-and-breakfast where they were staying, pick up an iced coffee from my shop, or an ice cream cone from Diamond Lille's. Then they would walk down past my house and enjoy some time on the beach. I understood the attraction.

Today looked like it was going to be slow in the shop. I should have time to order Justin's books and maybe make a flyer to send to the geo club. I'd been thinking about his promotion idea, and it just might pull in a few visitors, like the train books I stocked for Harrold.

Thinking of Harrold made me think of my aunt and her date. I hurried the final feet toward the shop and quickly unlocked the front door, turning the sign to OPEN. I started the first pot of coffee, then dialed my aunt's number using the shop phone. Leaving it on speaker, I started working on brewing the hazelnut coffee.

"Hello?" Aunt Jackie sounded sleepy, and for a second, I wondered if she was alone.

I stepped closer to the phone and began stacking more sleeves of cups near the register. "How'd your date go last night?"

I heard rustling and I knew I'd woken her. "It wasn't a date," she snapped. "Why are you calling so early? Is there a fire? Do I need to evacuate the apartment due to a swarm of tarantulas?"

"Ewww. No. Nothing's wrong, I was just checking in." I decided not to push her further. She sounded a little grumpy.

"Then I'll talk to you at a more suitable time." And she hung up. Miss Emily, my friend who'd left me the house, had always ended her conversations the same way. If she was done talking, the phone got hung up. No *good-bye* or *have a nice day*, just dead air.

The morning went slow. Dense fog was a walk-in-traffic killer. The locals stayed home, choosing to brew their own and stay in their jammies on days like this. Hopefully the fog would burn off by midday and we'd get a few customers. So after I finished last night's list of chores and this morning's, I still hadn't had a customer. I made myself a mocha with extra whipped cream, grabbed a Western off the shelf that I'd been meaning to read anyway, and got lost in the wild, wild Old West. The author was funny, but the description kept me deep into the story. I almost didn't hear the bell over the door go off.

I pulled myself back to reality and looked up at the clock. Ten twenty and my first Saturday customers had arrived. Aunt Jackie and I really needed to talk about "winter hours." I stuck in a bookmark to keep my place and walked back to the counter, my book and cup in hand.

"What a charming little store," the redheaded woman gushed to her friend. "I'm so glad you made me come early for the event."

The women were dressed in jeans and black T-shirts. I guess that was their memorial attire. And, to their credit, it wasn't a funeral, so the dress code could run a little more casual. I stepped up to the counter. "What can I get for you?"

"Two large black coffees." The woman leaned toward the dessert case. "You got anything gluten-free in there? I'm really craving a treat."

I glanced at the Black Forest, New York, and Wild Berry cheesecake in the display. I knew cookies were off the agenda, but maybe cheesecake qualified. "I'm not sure. I have a nice fruit cup that you might like."

"That's the first thing everyone offers, a fruit cup. You know there are ways to make desserts gluten-free. Like a flourless chocolate cake." The other woman looked out the window. "This is why we were so excited for Kacey's new business to open up. She totally understood dietary restrictions. I've lost so much weight by just watching my diet closer."

"Me too. Kacey was a treasure trove of information about the subject." The redhead nodded. "Once I heard her tell a story about how one day she had to be rushed to the hospital because she ate an apple that she sliced with a knife that husband of hers had used to make himself a sandwich. She took way too many risks living with that jerk."

"He probably did something stupid this time and his thoughtlessness killed her." The other woman sniffed. "You know he never took her health into consideration."

"I told her to stay away from him, but no. She was so happy when he started sniffing around her again," the other woman added.

I assumed they'd forgotten I was even here, as I finished pouring the coffee and put lids and sleeves on the cups. "So, about that fruit cup?"

The redhead looked at me. "Whatever. That will work if you don't have anything else."

"I'll ask my supplier if she can provide a better alternative. She makes a lot of desserts for not only me, but for the diner down the street." I grabbed two of the fruit cups and keyed in their purchases. The other woman handed me a card and I ran the charge. Glancing at the name, I handed her the receipt and a pen. "Thanks, Gloria, I guess I'll see you at the memorial later today."

"Oh, you're going?" Gloria signed her name, then pushed the paper back toward me. "I didn't realize Kacey knew many people here in South Cove."

"I didn't know her well, but I thought I'd pay my respects. My friend's boyfriend is going crazy over the geocaching thing and keeps taking us out on new adventures. I met her at one a few weeks ago." I leaned on the counter, not willing to end the only conversation I'd had with anyone but my grumpy aunt that morning. And the one-sided conversation I had with Emma every morning.

"I guess we'll see you then." The women collected their coffees and fruit cups and headed over to a table near the window. I'd been dismissed.

I watched the fog start to swirl and disappear out the window for a while, then I returned to my spot on the couch. "Let me know if you want a refill," I called out before putting my feet up and returning to the fictional world.

By the time Toby had arrived to relieve me, I'd almost finished the novel. I joined him at the counter, stuffing the book in my tote. "Hey, how are things with you and Elisa?"

"Fine." Toby didn't look at me as he restocked the counter. There wasn't much to do since Kacey's friends had been my only customers all shift. "You must have had a great reading day."

Okay, then. I guess Toby didn't want to talk about his concerns about Elisa. Not wanting to push, I pointed to the still foggy street. "The weather killed us this morning. Kacey's memorial is at one today, and I'm not sure the sun will be shining by then." When he didn't comment, I continued.

"Maybe the weather is appropriate, though. The two customers I had seemed very close to Kacey, and the gloom seems to match their emotions for the day." I waited until Toby had finished the few chores and had paused for a minute, watching out the window. "Are you okay?"

He transferred his gaze from the window to me. "Fine." He looked at the clock. "If you're going to the memorial, you'd better get going. Did you drive this morning or walk in this crap?"

"Walked. I couldn't see town until I hit The Train Station and then I went from lamppost to lamppost. Kind of reminded me of *The Lion, the Witch and the Wardrobe* when Lucy finds the way into Narnia. It made the walk kind of magical."

"I would have thought about Stephen King's short story 'The Mist' and wondered if there were monsters in the mix." He smiled.

"That's why you're the police officer and I'm the bookseller. We think differently." I glanced at the display case. "Have you had people ask about special diet items, like gluten-free desserts? I get the feeling that there were a lot of people interested in Kacey's new food truck. Do you think we'd sell enough to make it worth Sadie's time to make something special?"

"Definitely. The girls from the cosmetology school are always on some diet. I've heard a lot of them talk about the fact they might have a wheat allergy and that's why they can't lose weight. Of course, I think it's more an issue of eating dessert every morning with their coffee, rather than a real medical thing." Toby looked past me at the door. "And here they come. You should be paying for an advertisement in the college's newsletter. You get a lot of their business."

"Yeah, but word of mouth is always a better sales tool. Especially when they're all talking about Barista Babe." I threw my tote over my shoulder. "I'll see you on Tuesday. Have a nice weekend."

"Sure."

His tone made me turn back around. The boy was keeping something from me, and from the responses I'd gotten when I asked about Elisa, I knew it had to be something there. Of course, I'd already dug into Sasha's personal life yesterday and got shut down. Then the conversation with Aunt Jackie had basically been a mind-your-own-business answer. Maybe I should give Toby a little leeway. I'd reevaluate on Tuesday and make him tell me if there was something wrong. I called out a good-bye and held the door open for the first wave of Toby's girls.

Walking home, I still didn't see a lot of traffic on the road or inside the businesses. Diamond Lille's had a weekday lunch crowd instead of the standing room only she typically got during the tourist season. I wondered if she was cutting back on serving water to her customers like we were.

My aunt had come back from her water conservation meeting convinced the no water station rule was on target. I'd given in even though I knew it caused more work for Toby and Sasha when they worked the afternoon shift and most of our teens didn't order food or drinks, but instead filled up on the free water. As long as they weren't causing trouble in the shop and occasionally bought a book or a soda, I didn't mind the shop being the teen afterschool hangout. It made us look busy, which drove in walk-in traffic. Lille had a one drink per person minimum if they were going to use a table for a study group or just get together. I hated that they would have to wait in line now, just for water, but I guess it was for the common good.

At least I hadn't gone all-out with landscaping last year. I peered at Esmeralda's lush green lawn and wondered how long it would be before it turned as brown as my dormant grass appeared. Maggie, her black cat, meowed at me from the other side of the picket fence as I passed. I reached through the small opening between slats and petted her soft black fur. Maggie and I had a history. She liked to cross the road and sleep on my lap when I sat on the porch. And I liked listening to her purr. Emma even liked the cat. I guess I was bilingual in the animal world. I spoke both cat and dog.

I finished up Maggie's minute, rubbing the tiny white spot on her neck. "Now, you stay home. The road's too busy on weekends for you to be crossing on your own."

Maggie meowed again, then walked back to the porch and jumped onto the rattan chair where Esmeralda sat at nights watching the traffic. Or maybe watching my house. I couldn't be totally sure. Today it appeared she was inside doing a reading for a customer, as there was a powder-blue BMW in her driveway. I guess even the rich and famous needed direction from the great beyond.

When I opened my front door, the landline was ringing. I ran to catch it, only to hear the *click* on the other end as the caller disconnected. I put my purse on the table and opened the back door to let in Emma. I walked back to the front to close and lock that door, when my cell went off in my purse. I quickly locked the door and ran back into the kitchen.

"Yes," I panted into the phone.

There was a pause on the other side of the phone, and I thought maybe I'd missed this call as well. Finally, I heard my aunt's voice. "Where are you?"

I sank into a kitchen chair and kicked off my shoes. "At home, why?"

"Then why do you sound out of breath like you've been running on the beach?" She didn't wait for an answer. "Tell me what you told Josh last night."

"I didn't tell him anything. He scared the crap out of me. Does he always lock the door behind him when he comes in?" I walked over to the fridge and got the iced tea. I poured a glass and drank about half while I waited for her answer.

"Don't change the subject. I want to know what you told him about where I was." If I'd thought Aunt Jackie had been grumpy earlier, this was all-out war. Emma left her spot at the door and went to lie on her outside bed, not wanting to get in the middle of a fight.

I had to think for a minute. What excuse had I used? "I think I said you were tired and had gone to bed early."

"No wonder." She paused, then jumped back into the conversation. "Why didn't you say I'd gone to town or met an old friend?"

"Sorry, next time you ask me to keep a secret, give me something to say." I returned to the table and leafed through an old magazine. "Besides, you're lucky I didn't blab everything I knew. The guy scared the crap out of me. You could have warned me."

She sighed. "You're probably right. I should have left an alibi. I just didn't want Josh to feel bad if he found out. Now I have an expensive flower delivery on my table and a get well soon card from the man. I feel like a total heel."

"Did you have fun with Harrold?" I thought a change of subject was appropriate. Aunt Jackie could beat herself up about the lie on her own time. I wanted gossip.

"Harrold is a very interesting man. Did you know he traveled through Europe during summers while he was in college? You can't believe the places he's been. He makes me look like a homebody." Her voice raised a few notches, excited about the topic.

"I didn't know that. You two must have a lot in common." I didn't push. I liked Josh; I just didn't see him as relationship material for my aunt. Harrold, on the other hand, he seemed more like Uncle Ted.

"I thought I was all past this dating angst. I'm too old to be worried about anyone's feelings but my own." I could hear her thrumming her fingers on the tabletop.

"Are you telling me you said yes to a second date?" I held my breath and crossed my fingers.

"Do you think I'm stupid? Of course I said yes. I just need to tell Josh I'm seeing someone else. I'm sure he'll understand."

I glanced at the clock. I needed to get changed and head down to the beach for the memorial. "Hey, I've got to go. Come by tomorrow if you want to talk. With Greg working the case, I'm sure I'll be alone most of the day."

"I've already got plans for the day, but we'll catch up." She hung up the phone.

I clicked off my own phone and looked at Emma. "Your Aunt Jackie is smitten."

Emma woofed at me.

I took that as a "good for her" and ran upstairs to get showered and changed into a pair of nice pants and a dressy shirt. I wore flats that I hoped would keep the sand out of my shoes, but I wouldn't have bet the farm on the fact.

As I went out the front door, I texted Amy to see where she was. The return message told me that she and Justin were already at the parking lot but would wait by the stairs for me to arrive. I hurried toward the highway and the beach. I could see the cars on the highway lining up to turn into the small parking lot and then coming out the other side to drive to the next lot a few miles down. Both had access to the beach where Kacey's memorial would be held.

And both were access to the place where she was murdered. I paused, looking down the road, and wondered whether her killer had waited there for her to arrive.

Of course, I still didn't know how Kacey had died, so my mental gymnastics over the problem were only speculation.

But I still couldn't take my eyes off the other parking lot, shimmering in the distance.

CHAPTER 9

When I finally arrived, Justin and Amy were right where they'd said they'd be, heads bent looking at something on his phone. I wondered who else had texted them and thought maybe I'd be seeing Greg at the memorial. It made sense in a television detective sort of way. The killer always showed his cards when the memorials occurred. He was probably here, watching and gloating about his perfect kill.

When I stopped in front of them, Justin looked up like he didn't even remember my name. "Oh hi, Jill." He held out his phone. "Check out this geo-app Taylor just hooked me up with. You don't even need a handheld GPS to play the game now. The app is available on any smartphone platform."

"Nice to know." I looked at Amy. "Is he for real?"

"He's just excited about his new hobby," Amy whispered in my ear. "Be glad you don't hang out with him. I'm going a little bit crazy, and if I hear what a wizard Taylor is one more time . . ." She hugged me. "Well, let's just say Greg will have one more murder to solve."

"Our secret." I hugged her back, then stepped around her to look at the crowd. "Wow, I didn't realize there were so many club members. I had a couple of women stop in this morning for a bite, but this is amazing."

"Kacey seemed to be well-liked," Amy agreed, standing close to me by the wooden railing.

"Well-loved, I believe is the term." Greg appeared on the other side of me. "Glad you decided to come to this. I thought it might be weeks before I saw you again."

"Kacey was a nice person. Austin, on the other hand, can rot for what he did to Sadie." I scanned the crowd. "Speaking of, I don't see him down there, do you?"

Greg shook his head. "Of course, I was pretty hard on him at the station this morning. Maybe he decided he didn't want to answer any more questions about Kacey's death."

"You questioned him? Like a suspect?" I turned toward Greg, wanting to hear more.

Greg put his arm around me and led me down the stairs. "More like a grieving widower. The guy just lost his wife. If I need to, I'll play hardball next week. Give him some time to pull it together. He looks like he was the one who died."

I leaned into Greg's body as we walked across the sand to where a small platform and microphone had been set up. "You have a good heart, you know that, right?"

"Baby, I just know what a mess I'd be if I lost you." Greg kissed the side of my head, and I melted into him.

"You know just what to say." I nodded to a few people from South Cove who'd also been invited by someone. Bill and Mary Sullivan were there, along with Aunt Jackie and Mary. Next to my aunt was Harrold. And next to Harrold, was Josh. "Uh-oh. That doesn't look good."

Greg and I watched as Josh tried to maneuver his way between Harrold and Jackie. Finally he gave up and with the grace of an elephant, lumbered over to the last row of chairs and lowered himself onto an aisle seat. He glared in the direction of Jackie and Harrold, and when he caught me watching him, he glared at me.

"How is this my fault?" I muttered. Greg looked over at me and I shook my head. "Don't ask." We headed to the chairs and sat on the other side of the aisle, in the same row as Josh. At least this way, he couldn't throw dagger eyes at me during the entire ceremony.

"Kacey had a lot of friends." Greg scanned the crowd. "I don't know a lot of people here. A few I saw the day Justin took us geo-surfing, and of course, the people from South Cove."

"Geocaching, not surfing." I put my hand on his leg and he put his arm around me. "She seemed really involved in this club. I think Justin has caught the bug, too. He's all about the game and his new toys."

"Great. Does this mean we'll have to do another double date tracking down a buried penny? Or maybe we'll get a shiny rock. If he's that into trinkets, I could go to the dime store in Bakerstown and buy him a bag full."

"Bakerstown doesn't have a dime store. In fact, there's none in the entire United States." I watched people gather around the front of the area. It appeared that we'd be starting in a few minutes.

"Not true. Wall Drug Store in South Dakota is a classic dime store. You can find anything in that place." Greg grinned. "And in Nashville, there are a couple of shops off the main drag with anything and everything, including some voodoo charms and trinkets. You just need to look for the out-of-the-way shops."

"Like in South Cove." I leaned my head into his chest. "We're all about the original and unique."

"I'd love to see a Goonies shop open. It could carry magic tricks, gag gifts, and stuff any twelve-year-old boy or adult male would love." He kissed the top of my head. "Maybe I've found my calling for when I retire."

"That would be a pretty narrow customer base." I drew a heart on his jeans with my fingernail.

"Are you kidding? Men are fifty percent of the population. They may act grown-up in the business world, but inside every guy is a kid waiting to burst out." Greg nodded to the front. "So there's Taylor, but who's the redheaded woman standing next to him?"

"Not sure, but she and that blonde were in my shop today. The blonde's Gloria something." I tried to remember the rest of the name on the credit card but I couldn't. The overwhelming smell of the tons of lilies all around the chairs and aisle had my head pounding.

"Gloria March," Greg filled in. "I talked to her a few days ago about the club's finances. I thought she looked familiar."

I pointed to another woman running down the aisle. "And that's Ginny. She works with Jen at Linens and Loots. She really loves the club, too."

"I guess some people enjoy their hobbies more than their jobs." He looked at me. "Like you and investigating."

"I'm not investigating anything," I protested.

Greg turned my head toward his so he could see my face.

"Really, I'm not," I pleaded with him, conscious of the people starting to sit around us. I suspected we only had one or two minutes left before Taylor would start the memorial.

"Then how do you know the names of some of the suspects?" Greg raised his eyebrows to emphasize the point.

"It's a small town. I can't help it that when I go shopping I meet new people. Or when people come into the shop, I check the name on the credit card before I hand back the plastic so I can use their name in closing."

"You do that? I'm always taken aback when someone I don't know calls me by my name. I'd rather just go by 'sir' or 'kid' or even 'dude'." Greg pointed to the front. "Looks like the service is about to begin."

Taylor tapped on the microphone. "Folks, will you please take your seats? There's plenty of room up here in the front. We won't bite, I promise."

The old joke got a few chuckles, but as I watched, all the seats were filled and the rest of the people stood in a semicircle around the chairs. When Taylor was certain everyone had settled, he pointed to the guy on the portable keyboard, and he started to play "Memories." I heard people sniff around me. Me, I never loved the song, but it wasn't my memorial, so I suffered through.

After the music had stopped, Taylor returned to the podium. "That was Kacey's favorite song. I can't tell you how many times we'd run the food booth at our events and she'd be humming that tune. For hours. It drove me crazy at times. Now I just wished I could hear her humming."

He paused, looking at the notes in front of him. "Kacey Elizabeth Pope Austin was born in Nampa, Idaho, on . . ."

As I listened to Taylor read the obituary that had been published in the *Examiner* this week, I thought about how full of life the woman had been. Even the day I'd first met her at the food booth for the club, she had exuded energy. If Dustin Austin had a good side, it had been the women in his life. Both Sadie and Kacey were good people. Austin, not so much. As if my thoughts of him had made him materialize, the grieving widower walked slowly up the aisle to a seat at the front.

"Way to make an entrance," I muttered to Amy, who now sat on my left side. She slapped my arm. I guess she was still in the poor Austin camp.

After a few more speakers talked about how much Kacey would be missed, the memorial seemed about to end with another song. But then Taylor stood, taking the microphone from the singer. "One more thing. There's a collection jar on your way out. The group is setting up a Kacey Austin Memorial fund to help with club costs. Your donations in her name would be much appreciated by the board." He handed the microphone back to the woman who'd been ready to sing and she stared at him, obviously uncomfortable with his blatant fundraising plea in the middle of what should have been about Kacey and not him or the club. This time it was Amy's turn to be outraged.

"That was totally tacky." Amy didn't whisper and her voice carried over several rows of chairs, causing people to turn to see who had spoken. Justin took her hand and shushed her.

We were the first row released by the ushers, who all wore T-shirts announcing them as part of the Coastal Geocache Club. As we walked past the collection jar, I was surprised to see a line of people using the table to write checks and donate. We just kept walking. When we reached the parking lot, Justin turned on Amy.

"Look, I know you don't like Taylor, but wasn't that a little out of line? You embarrassed all of us." He looked over to me and Greg for support.

I shrugged. "I was thinking the same thing. I guess I just have a better filter."

Greg burst out laughing. He wiped his eyes with the back of his hand and shook his head. "You have *no* filter. Amy just beat you to blurting out the obvious this time." He looked at Justin. "Seriously, dude, you have to admit, the call for money was a bit crass."

Justin squirmed uncomfortably. He was clearly outnumbered, but he didn't want to go back on his original support of Taylor. Finally, he rolled his shoulders. "I guess you're right. But Amy shouldn't have said it out loud."

Greg slapped him on the back, and the boys started walking back to town. "Get used to it. We're dating strong, independent women who have a voice and like to use it." He paused, then added, "A lot."

I called after the retreating men, "I heard that." I put my arm in Amy's and we walked after them in silence for a bit.

Amy broke the silence first. "I'm a little worried about Justin. He's so gung ho about this geo stuff and Taylor. Anything that man says, Justin does—or at least repeats."

I was a little concerned, too, but I didn't want Amy to worry. "You know men. They jump in feet first, then check the level of the water. Justin's smart. He'll figure this out sooner than later. You just have to be patient."

"You're probably right." Amy paused on the sidewalk, looking at Esmeralda's house. "Did you get the letter about the watering ban?"

I nodded. "It was in my mail this morning." I knew she was calculating how many gallons of water it took to keep my neighbor's house green. "Esmeralda probably hasn't even opened her mail yet. She's been doing readings."

"If she was that good of a fortune-teller, she would have known this was coming." Amy pursed her lips. "I'll let this slide for now, but let me know if you see her watering this week."

"No," I said.

Amy turned around and stared at me along with Justin and Greg. "What did you say?"

I didn't back down. "I said no. I decided I won't be a snitch on my neighbors." With that, I turned and went directly to my front door. When I reached the porch, I waved at the trio and called out, "Have a nice day." Then I disappeared into my house.

I kept myself busy cleaning the house and the backyard, trying not to think about the hurt look on Amy's face when I told her no.

I got a text from Amy about two hours later canceling our standing Sunday morning breakfast. Yep, she was steamed. I sighed and set down my phone. Water conservation was important, and I was acting like a jerk. I would take her cookies on Tuesday after my shift to say I was sorry. Bored with cleaning, I called Darla, hoping to reach her before the Saturday night rush on the winery.

"South Cove Winery, can I help you?" Darla answered on the first ring.

Maybe I could talk her into going for a walk with me, or maybe even dinner. The winery had to have slow days, especially in February. Coffee, Books, and More was feeling the winter blahs. "Hey, Darla, it's Jill. You got time for a quick bite?"

"You're kidding, right? The winery has been slammed since three. I guess we're getting the group from Kacey's memorial. We're seating people outside with the heaters running full-blast. Glad it's a warm day." Darla paused and I heard her telling a waiter to tie his shoe before he went flying. "Maybe we can do breakfast tomorrow? I'd love to pick your brain about this Kacey thing. What's Greg say?"

"Not much," I admitted. "But yeah, let's do breakfast. How about nine at Lille's?"

I heard a tray crash in the background. "Perfect," Darla responded. "Sorry, it's getting crazy here, I've really got to go. See you tomorrow."

I hung up the phone and supposed Diamond Lille's would be packed for dinner, too. Besides, I didn't feel like eating alone. I texted Greg to see if he'd eaten.

When the text came back that the gang had been fed a few minutes ago since they were all working overtime on the investigation, I slumped back into the couch. Emma stared at me. "That's it, girl. I've made my only friend mad and my boyfriend is too busy to eat with me."

Emma put her foot on my leg.

"Want to go see if we have frozen fries and clam strips?" I flipped through my movie collection and came up with the first two Percy Jackson movies. You can't go wrong with Greek gods and their half-breed offspring for a good time. A perfect Saturday night. When the devil on my shoulder laughed, I flicked him off with a finger.

I'd just finished the first movie when I gave up, went over to my desk, and grabbed my notebook. Opening it to a clean page, I started writing down everything I knew about Kacey, Austin, and the geo club. It really wasn't investigating, I rationalized to myself. I was just writing down what I knew so I'd remember in case . . . I stopped for a moment to try to think of a good excuse. When I didn't come up with anything, I pushed the thought away. This time, the little devil on my shoulders was rolling around with giggles.

By the time I headed to bed, I knew one thing. I didn't know anything about how Kacey had died, except for the place. I needed to find out whether Darla had gleaned any information from Doc Ames's secretary. I put the notebook in my purse and headed upstairs to sleep.

The sun woke me the next morning. I didn't set an alarm—since I usually got up early, my body would wake me up when I needed to be going. This morning, however, my body clock had missed the wake-up call. I looked at my clock through bleary eyes. Eight thirty. I threw the covers off me and ran to the closet to get clothes. I was going to be late meeting Darla and she didn't like waiting. Besides, I needed gossip to get any further on my non-investigation of Kacey's murder.

Emma whined at the door so I let her out, using the time to sip some coffee. I'd made it out of the bathroom in less than five minutes; now I just needed to set Emma's food and water outside and power-walk to Diamond Lille's. If I was lucky, I might even be early.

The walk did little to ease my nerves. I heard a loud *bang* from behind me and I spun around to see an old car backfiring. Good thing I hadn't thrown myself on the ground, all for a poorly maintained Buick.

When I arrived at the diner, Darla was already seated at a table near the window. I glanced longingly at my regular booth, but this wasn't an Amy and me breakfast. I might have ruined that category for the rest of my life. Darla had a cup of coffee and a muffin already sitting in front of the open chair. Her muffin was already gone, and only the paper lining remained. "Sit down. I ordered you an appetizer."

I didn't realize breakfast had courses like appetizers or desserts. But I couldn't turn one down if I was going to play the game. I slipped into my chair and took a sip of the coffee. "Sorry I'm late. I was up past my bedtime thinking about poor Kacey."

Not quite subtle, but it got the message across. I was interested in her theories.

Darla blinked twice, but then nodded, agreeing with my statement.

I thought she was going to say something, but just then, Carrie arrived to take our order. "Are you still waiting on Amy?"

"Amy's not coming today." I looked at the menu that I'd seen so often I could recite most of the items by heart. "Bring me a Denver omelet with a side of wheat toast. And a glass of orange juice." Carrie had mentioned the wait staff got extra points for more than one drink per customer. I hoped that was still true. I needed some karma credit.

"I'm not very hungry," Darla said. "I'll have a large orange juice, two eggs over easy, an order of bacon, hash browns, and a short stack of cakes. Warm the maple syrup please."

I stared at her after Carrie left. "Not hungry?"

"Don't be all judgmental. I've had a hard week." She stirred some sugar into her coffee. "I saw you at Kacey's memorial yesterday. What did you think of it?"

"Judgment-free zone here." I held my hands up. "I was sad for her. She had all those people who really cared about her and she wasn't around to hear all the good things being said about her."

"Maybe her angel was standing by the coffin. Like in that play the high school does every year." Darla looked at me over her coffee. "Do you think Austin killed her?"

The change of subject threw me a bit. Luckily, I didn't react other than to shake my head. "Who knows? The guy doesn't seem to understand normal things like love and loyalty. Look what he did to Sadie."

"You're still mad? I didn't realize you and Sadie were so close." Darla peered at me, curious now. "Men have their own agendas, I figured you knew that by now."

"What Austin did to Sadie wasn't an agenda, it was just cold and calculating. All the time they were dating, he and Kacey were working on getting back together." I leaned back as a runner from the kitchen delivered our plates.

Carrie followed behind carrying our juice glasses. "Anything else I can get you?"

"We're good." Darla picked up a fork. "Was it as busy here as the winery was yesterday?"

"Lille had to call in all the wait staff. No one got a day off." Carrie patted her tip apron. "But the crowd was feeling generous. I made twice what I typically rake in on a Saturday."

"I thought about coming down for dinner, but after Darla told me about the crowd at the winery, I figured you'd be slammed."

"One woman got all teary-eyed and went over to this Taylor guy and accused him of killing Kacey." Carrie eyed me. "Has Greg told you what killed her? From what I hear, she just fell down dead on the beach. So sad when they're that young."

Now Darla was looking at me as well, waiting for my answer.

"We haven't talked about Kacey's death." I took a sip of my orange juice. My statement was partially true. We'd only talked about Greg interviewing Nick about the food truck incident. And of course, the fact that Sadie's recipes were back in her hands. But we hadn't talked about a cause of death and I was beginning to wonder why a seemingly healthy adult would just die. Or how.

"Whatever. I tell you, though, that chick was fired up. She didn't think Kacey died of natural causes. Her friends had to drag her out of here." Carrie nodded to another table. "Enjoy your meal."

I thought about the memorial and tried to pick out anyone who was upset or seemed angry. Besides Josh. I took a bite of my omelet and realized Darla was watching me. "What?"

"I told you I went to Bakerstown to the funeral home. Doc Ames wasn't in, so Mabel told me what she'd heard." Darla set her fork down on the table and leaned closer. "She said the poor girl's chest was all covered with a rash, and her airway had closed up. Worse case of allergic reaction she'd ever seen."

I kept eating my breakfast. This so didn't replace Sunday breakfast with Amy. We typically talked about the latest star couple breakup or what she'd overheard in the mayor's office. Okay, I'll admit it, we gossiped. This was more of an interrogation.

"Bee sting, I bet," Darla mused. "The news is always talking about those killer bees coming up from South America. I bet she got stung from one of the little buggers who stole away on a cargo ship that docked in the city."

"I thought the killer bee story was an urban legend." I finished my orange juice, hoping to speed up the meal so I could go home and call Amy to patch up our little quarrel. Amy loved debunking urban legends, and the bee thing had been on her list to research.

"I don't know. Any way you look at it, the death doesn't appear to be a murder. So Austin is in the clear to inherit Kacey's estate."

Maybe Darla was right. Kacey could have just died. Then Darla's words hit me. "What estate?"

"Her dad patented the formula for those puffy cookies they sell in stores, you know, the really good ones? When he died, he left her a fortune." Darla started in on her pancakes. "I guess Austin's the beneficiary. Don't tell me Greg didn't know this."

I shrugged. "I don't know. We don't talk about ongoing investigations."

Darla laughed so hard she started to choke on the bite of food in her mouth. Once she got in control of her breathing, she gasped. "You don't have to hold up the party line to me. There's no way the two of you don't exchange any pillow talk around your day."

"I hate to burst your fantasy, but we don't talk about open investigations." I took a ten and two ones out of my purse and laid them on the table. "That's for my meal. I forgot I have another appointment."

Darla smiled. "You just don't want to admit I'm right."

CHAPTER 10

Darla's words still rankled. I wasn't lying when I said Greg and I didn't talk about cases. Well, except for when he was mad at me for getting into his business. I'd turned over a new leaf, and I was actively staying out of investigations. But I had to admit, Kacey's death had me stumped. Darla seemed to think the condition of the body proved she was murdered. I still wondered if the ingestion of the wheat had been an accident. From what the women in my coffee shop had said, Austin was always doing stupid stuff that ended up putting Kacey in danger.

I shook off my unease and decided that instead of worrying about something I couldn't change, I'd call Amy and tell her I was a royal jerk for my attitude yesterday. I had to admit, Kacey's memorial had affected me in ways I didn't expect. However, one fact remained totally clear: Taylor Archer was a jerk. Especially now with the power of the geo club position behind him. As I walked back from Diamond Lille's, the parched look of the wild areas outside of town bothered me. All that water just yards away in the ocean, but the grass was dying of thirst. I didn't really understand how they could send a man to the moon and develop a bomb that could kill off all the living creatures of the world, but they couldn't take salt out of water?

When I reached the house, Greg's truck sat in my driveway. He was on the front step, reading something on his phone. When I opened the gate, he put the phone in his pocket and stood and kissed me on the cheek. "Hey, what are you doing here?"

A confused look passed over his face. "It's Sunday, right? We've got a standing afternoon date. I thought we'd go into the city and get some dinner at one of the restaurants by the bay. I'm craving some seafood. It's been a crazy week."

"I thought since you were on a case, we wouldn't be going out." I put my head on his chest and we unlocked the front door. "I'm so glad you are here, though. I had breakfast with Darla this morning. That girl knows how to wind me up. She tried to get me to spill all the dirty secrets you tell me about your investigations."

"Ha, I bet she was surprised when you told her you didn't have a secret to share. I told you before we went fishing with Jim a few months ago, I'm taking No-Guilt-Sundays, even while I'm on a case. All work and no play makes Greg a boring guy. Not to mention stressed to the gills." He nodded to the kitchen. "You need to handle anything? Or should we take the long way and see if we can find the sea lions this afternoon?"

"You feed and water Emma, I'll run upstairs and get a quick shower and make myself pretty." I kissed him on the cheek. "I really needed to see you today. Amy's mad at me and the breakfast with Darla was painful. Did you know some lady got in Taylor's face after the memorial yesterday?"

Greg sank into a kitchen chair. "Yep. Tim did the report, but I guess the woman was livid. Grief does that to people."

"So you don't think Taylor killed Kacey." I perched on a chair, too, leaning in for the answer.

"I don't think I'm spending my No-Guilt-Sunday talking about work." He stared at me, then sat up. "Look, this is all I'm going to say, then the subject's closed. I know you, and you're not going to be happy until we get the facts out there." I saw him consider his next words carefully. "Kacey's death has been ruled suspicious. She died of anaphylactic shock from an allergic reaction to wheat. We don't know how she ingested it, but it's clear she wouldn't have eaten something with wheat willingly. Everyone said the girl was fanatical about her diet. We have lots of persons of interest, including Taylor and Austin, but nothing concrete at this time."

The breath flowed out of me. "So she *was* murdered. That poor girl."

"I didn't think you liked her all that much." Greg stood to let Emma outside. "And for your information, that last statement is what we're releasing to the press, minus the names, tomorrow. Darla will at least have an official statement to weave into her article."

"I didn't like what Austin did to Sadie. Kacey just got caught up in the mix." I watched him. "You didn't mention Sadie. Is she off the persons-of-interest list?"

Greg filled Emma's water dish. "I don't see how she could have been involved. The day Kacey was killed, Sadie spent the entire day working at the church's outreach program for the homeless in the city. She drove the bus of volunteers, manned the chow line, and was in plain sight for the full time."

I smiled. "Sounds like Sadie. She loves her mission days."

"Well, this time her charity work saved her butt. And before you ask, Nick was in classes all day, then had a debate team practice in the evening. That kid goes from the time he gets up to when he falls into his dorm bed at night. He's going to run the world in a few years." He disappeared into the laundry room and came out with a scoop of food for Emma that he pointed at me. "So, are you getting ready or going like that?"

"Ten minutes." I stood to head upstairs to shower. I paused at the doorway and turned. "Thank you. I know we have a pact not to talk about open investigations."

He held up his hand. "I didn't tell you anything that would get me in trouble or that I wouldn't tell Darla. Well, almost nothing." He grinned and pointed to the stairs. "Go get ready. Our day together is disappearing."

When we finally got to the restaurant, I'd relaxed. We'd talked during the ride about everything and nothing. My camera was filled with pictures from the beach, highlighting the sea lions and the perfect ocean view we'd just kept finding, stop after stop.

As we followed the hostess through the dining room to our table, Greg paused and clapped his hand on a male back. "Great minds must think alike. How you doing, Justin?"

Amy's hand froze as she held her salad fork. She glanced up at me and then Greg but didn't say anything.

"Hey, buddy, good to see you." He looked at Amy, who shook her head. "We're out for a little couple time; you know how hard it is to get time alone."

Greg took the hint. "Us too. In fact, I'm hiding from the investigation right now. Hopefully my phone will stay quiet long enough for me to at least finish my salad." He put his hand on my back and gently pushed me toward our waiting table.

I resisted the movement. "Amy, I'm sorry I was a jerk yesterday."
She didn't look up. "I'm sure you are."

"Wait, that's all you have to say? You think this is all my fault?" I
put my hands on my hips and glared at her.

This time Greg's push wasn't as gentle. "Not here," he whispered
in my ear. Then to Amy and Justin, he waved. "See you around South
Cove."

As the curious hostess set our menus in front of us, I steamed. As
soon as she left, I looked over the menu at Greg. "Did you hear her?
I was trying to be nice and she just blew me off."

"Look, I don't want to talk about your fight with Amy. You two
have too strong of a friendship to lose it over a water conservation
issue." He put his hand on mine. "Think of it this way, she thought
you of all people would be totally in her corner. So when you told her
you wouldn't be part of her 'Nazi patrol,' she was hurt."

"I didn't say 'Nazi patrol,' did I?" Now I wondered if I had gone
too far. I'd stay on the visiting with cookies path tomorrow. Cookies
could smooth over any problem—I hoped.

"Can we get back to our date night?" Greg pointed to the menu.
"I'm thinking about trying these shrimp nachos, are you game?"

I nodded but snuck a glance over toward the table where my best
friend sat. She didn't look too happy that I'd interrupted her date
night, either. This had to blow over. At least, I hoped it would.

I heard Greg clear his throat and turned my attention back to him.
"What are you going to order?"

As I reviewed the menu, I muttered, "First thing I'm getting is a
frozen strawberry margarita."

Greg chuckled and nodded. "I figured. Look, she'll come around.
You two are as close as sisters. Sometimes sisters fight."

And sometimes families broke up over stupid stuff. I didn't say
my thought aloud, just nodded like I believed him. I scanned the menu.
On page five, there was a special category, Gluten-Free. I turned the
menu over and pointed to the listings. "Can you believe the food fads
going around? I mean, I knew there were people with allergies, but it's
becoming such a thing. Austin has the dessert truck, this place has a
listing of gluten-free foods, what's next?"

"Businesses are realizing they can increase profits by catering to
people who want or need a certain menu. Austin thought the food
truck would have paid for itself in less than a year. He'd had inquiries

about doing catering for different events even before he opened. They saw the truck and called the bike shop, wondering who owned it." Greg went back to reading his own menu. "I'm surprised you don't have a mini gluten-free menu for the shop."

"Believe me, I'm looking into it. I've had a lot of people mention how excited they were that the food truck was opening. I didn't want to tell them it might not." I set the menu down, having made my dinner selections. "Do you think Austin will open now?"

Greg shook his head. "This was Kacey's project. Austin doesn't have the drive to work that hard. You know he rarely keeps his shop open except for the weekends. Are you thinking about the truck?"

I hadn't been, but now that Greg had brought it up, I wondered if I could nab the truck this time. Aunt Jackie and I had tried to buy it last summer, thinking that Diamond Lille's was our only competition, before Austin had swooped in with a cash offer Homer Bell couldn't turn down. The good news was that business decision had gotten Homer banned from eating at Lille's for his lifetime or whenever Lille calmed down, which could be longer. I realized the waitress had arrived, and she and Greg were staring at me, waiting for my order.

I ordered the feast plate, which had both lobster and crab along with fried shrimp and as a bonus, mashed potatoes. I added a side salad to give me at least one veggie count for the meal. When she'd left, I looked at Greg. "I guess I'll talk to Aunt Jackie about the truck. We'd have to paint it again, but she was all into the idea that we could take CBM on the road to the local festivals. She's been looking for a truck we could afford since we lost this one."

"You could buy it out of the Miss Emily fund." Greg waited for the server to drop off our drinks and a loaf of hot sourdough bread with whipped butter on the side.

I ripped off a piece of bread and smoothed butter on it. "That's what Aunt Jackie keeps saying. Honestly, I'm a little scared to dump all of that money into the business. What if people stop drinking coffee? I'd be bankrupt."

"I don't think people will stop drinking coffee. Besides, you have the bookstore side as well as the desserts and your touristy things." He took a sip of his iced tea. "Too bad we can't stay over tonight. I'd love one of those margaritas."

"We'll have to make plans for a weekend once the investigation is over." I took a sip of the strawberry delight. "You realize people are buying most of their books online now? That's another reason I don't want to keep all of my eggs in one basket."

"You don't sell to the normal reader. Your book buyers are either tourists who need a book to read right away, or locals who are part of your book clubs or who haven't gone to the e-reader craze. I don't think you need to be worrying about this." He took his own slice of bread. "What does Jackie say? I'm sure she's examined the numbers closely."

"We're up from the last year, and the year before. But you know how things go." I'd read all of the reports my aunt had shoved in front of me in support of her argument to expand, but my gut told me it was too much, and too soon. I watched as the server delivered the shrimp nachos and then I filled my little appetizer plate. Waving a chip at Greg, I continued. "Besides, maybe I want to use that money for something else, like a new house once the wall gets certified. I may need to turn Miss Emily's house into some sort of tourist attraction, and then I'd be homeless."

Greg nodded. "The mission wall project may take over your life, I'll give you that. But for now, you need to worry about today and not all these maybes. You'll be frozen and not wanting to take any action if you don't stop worrying."

I thought about what he said as I consumed the chips and cheese and baby shrimp on my plate. My aunt had made the same argument. Maybe I should be more open to considering buying the truck.

We didn't talk about the issue any more that night. I tried to put my worries on the back burner and enjoy my time with Greg. We'd finished planning our next trip to the city and all the things we wanted to do when his phone beeped. I watched him read the text as I sipped on the coffee we'd ordered with a couple of blueberry shortcakes for dessert. When he sighed, I knew our evening was over. "Work?"

"Sorry. The DA wants me to go over the case with him tonight. He's planning on filing charges in the morning." Greg put his phone away after texting an answer and finished the last couple bites of his dessert. "Looks like I'll have a long night after I drop you off at the house."

"Charges? Against who? I didn't think you had enough evidence against anyone for Kacey's death." I finished my coffee, knowing that we'd be leaving sooner than later.

Greg waved the waitress down and gave her his credit card for our bill before he answered, "We didn't until we got the background report on Austin."

"I don't understand." I slipped on my jacket and snagged my purse.

Greg signed the slip and stood, holding out his hand to help me out of my chair. "Dustin Austin isn't his real name. They found an old report attached to his fingerprints. He's been hiding under an assumed name for the last forty years, and he's wanted for questioning by the FBI."

CHAPTER 11

I was at Amy's desk with a box of cookies at five after eight the next morning. She stared at me when I walked in. "Hey, I thought you might need these when I heard about Austin. How is he? Have you talked to him?"

She watched me set the box on her desk, then shook her head. "Your boyfriend won't let anyone talk to him. Officially, he's not being charged with anything, just held for questioning. I've called his lawyer, Wilson, and he's coming in from the city. I guess he's some big shot who had a case on trial and had to ask for a stay so he could come save Austin."

"I'm glad he has someone good." I didn't sit, not knowing if we were really talking again, or if Amy was too upset about Austin to be mad at me. "So, did you know about this FBI thing?"

"You're kidding, right? I don't even believe it's true. Austin wouldn't hurt a fly. Besides, what could they want to talk to him about? He's been living here for ten years running a bike rental shop. What kind of criminal runs a bike rental shop?" Amy was close to tears now. "The guy has been like a father to me since I moved here. He's always fixing up something in the apartment to make life easier, or just to make me smile. He's a nice guy."

"Look, I'm sure there's nothing wrong. I mean, you don't think he killed Kacey, do you?"

"Of course not." Amy's voice hit a pitch I hadn't ever heard from her. "Austin is the sweetest, kindest man in the world. He loved Kacey, I know it."

"Like he loved Sadie?" The question was out of my mouth before I could stop it. Amy's eyes flared at me, and I knew the cookies weren't going to make up for my second mistake in less than a week. I'd never known Amy to be this sensitive about things.

"You can leave any time." Amy didn't even look at me; instead, she focused on her computer.

Now I sat down. "Look, I didn't mean to suggest that Austin is guilty of murder. He just wasn't very up front and honest with Sadie when they were dating. Even you can't argue that point."

Amy gave me a slight nod, and instead of shutting up, like I should have, I kept going. "So, do you know anything about his past? Did he say where he was born, or where he went to school? Anything?"

This time Amy did look at me. "Are you going to try to help him? Or do you just want to put the last nail in his coffin?"

"If Austin is innocent, I want to know who killed Kacey. I didn't know her very well, but she seemed nice. She deserves for her murderer to be caught." What I didn't add was that if it was Austin, he needed to rot in hell.

She leaned back in her chair. "He told me he grew up in a small town back East. His dad was a minister and his mom stayed at home. They were one of those old religious sects, maybe Quaker? I'm not sure he ever said, but I got that feeling. I know he was against the war, but he never said if he had to serve or if he had been drafted."

"The Vietnam War? He was hiding from being in the service?" I'd remembered seeing the history videos of the anti-war protests, but if Austin was a Quaker, I thought they were pacifists. "What else did he say?"

"I don't know if he really did get drafted, I just know he was very anti-government and had a fear of authority figures. I saw him disappear into the back every time Toby would drive by at night on his regular patrol. I just thought it was Austin being paranoid." Amy leaned forward. "You didn't answer me. Do you think he's innocent?"

I stood and looked at my friend, hoping I wouldn't widen the gap that seemed to be growing between us. "Honestly, I don't know, but at least there's something to check out now."

As I left City Hall, I walked toward Sadie's house. She would be in the garage-turned-bakery today, making treats for my shop as well as Diamond Lille's. I wondered if Austin had ever told her about his past.

I dialed Greg's number. He'd dropped me off last night with a kiss and a wave, and I hadn't heard anything from him this morning. I knew from the gossip grapevine that he and Toby had picked up Austin from his apartment over the bike shop at three that morning. Rumor had it that he was only there for questioning, but my gut told me you didn't bring someone down in the middle of the night to ask them a few more questions. My call went straight to voice mail.

"Hey, I'm thinking of you. Make sure you get some sleep." I clicked off the phone and turned down Sadie's street. The yards here were all as brown as my own, no rain to replace the sprinkler ban that had been announced through a letter from the city council, but signed by the conservation committee.

I knocked on the garage door, and then when I didn't hear a response, I tipped my head inside. Sadie stood with her back to me, using the large, noisy mixer. From the smell of whatever was baking in the oven, it was muffin day. I loved her peanut butter cup muffins, all mixed up with chocolate, peanut butter, and a sweet vanilla batter binding them all together. It was heaven, or as close as I'd come.

The radio played a song I didn't recognize, but I knew she was listening to the Christian music station out of Bakerstown. The song was upbeat and positive, singing about having faith and being rewarded with a dance beat. I stepped toward the radio and turned the sound down a few decibels. Sadie flew around and smiled when she saw me just inside the door.

"Hey, Jill." Sadie turned off the mixer. "Hold on and let me check the oven real quick. Then we can have coffee and you can tell me you love my new muffin creation, Springtime Orange Cream. Or would you rather have a chocolate peanut butter muffin cup?"

"Whatever you're having." I put my purse on the stool next to mine and climbed up, putting my feet on the rungs. The coffee carafe was already on the counter, so I took a cup off the little tree where Sadie kept the clean ones and poured some. I gave Sadie a free pound of coffee once a month. The hazelnut cream filled my mouth without additional calories or creamer. This was the way coffee was meant to be: dark, rich, full of flavor, and without cream or sugar. Greg felt a little different. He liked his coffee with lots of sugar and French vanilla creamer. Of course, you could argue that he liked his sugar and creamer with a little coffee.

I watched as Sadie pulled a rack of muffins out of the oven, turning them out on the wire rack she had on a large metal table nearby. She put two muffins on a plate, pulled a knife out of the drawer, and brought over the butter. She set everything on the counter and refilled her own coffee cup.

She studied me as she sat down, pushing a muffin toward me. "So, what brings you out on a Monday? Typically, you're lost in a book right now."

"You're right, but I wanted to get here before the rumors reached you." I broke off a piece of the muffin and popped it in my mouth, the orange flavoring reminding me of the push-ups we used to buy off the ice cream truck. "These are really good."

"Thanks. So, what's the rumor? I hope your honey's not putting me in the calaboose for killing Kacey." Sadie shook her head. "Say that five times fast, I dare you."

"Not you, Austin." I watched her face, wondering what her reaction would be. Tears, laughter; at this point, it could be either one.

She unwrapped her own muffin, ripped it in half, and then loaded it with butter. "I don't believe he killed Kacey."

Her voice was calm, soothing, and absolutely certain. I hated to break her poise, but she needed to know. "There's something you don't know about Austin. He's been living under an assumed name."

She nodded. "I knew that. He was almost totally honest with me." At this her lips curved into a smile so sad it made my heart ache.

"You knew? Do you know why?" I sipped on my coffee, not wanting to appear too curious.

"Of course. He was accused of a bombing when he was a kid. But he didn't do it, I'm sure he was only protecting his girlfriend. Once they'd left the area, he said she confessed and he didn't know how to fix it, so they ran away to Mexico." Sadie picked at the crumbs on the table. "They can't prove anything, not this long after."

"So you still think he had nothing to do with Kacey's death? Maybe she found out his secret?"

"He told me his secret and I'm still alive. Why would he kill Kacey for finding out something he told me without holding back?"

I thought about her question, and she was right: It didn't make sense. "So what was this girlfriend's name? Did he tell you that?"

"Mary Jane. That's all he said." Sadie sipped on her coffee. "You tell Greg he's not guilty of this. He's just an easy scapegoat."

I took my notebook out of my purse and wrote down *Mary Jane* and *Mexico.* "Did he tell you where he was from?"

"Deary, Vermont. I guess it's a little hole-in-the-wall farm town. His folks had a place outside of town, and I think his dad was a pastor at some church." Sadie had a faraway look in her eyes. "We'd talked about visiting someday, but of course, someday isn't a day of the week."

I kept writing. "What about this Mary Jane? She was from Deary, too?" It couldn't be too hard to find a Mary Jane from Vermont about Austin's age. Of course, I still didn't know his real name.

"No, they met in college. I guess Austin went his first year, and then dropped out. Too many fun things to do rather than studying, at least that was his story." Sadie smiled and sipped her coffee. "I got the impression they were big into the anti-war protests and traveled around the country with a bunch of organizers."

A memory was nagging at me. Something about a group of protesters whose peaceful march had gone totally wrong. "So, that's when he disappeared? While he was working the war protest circuit?"

"You make it sound like the car or horse races. I'm sure he believed in what he was doing." A buzzer went off. "I've got another batch to get ready for the oven or your display case is going to be empty tomorrow. Do you want a couple of those to take to Greg?"

Just like Sadie to worry about feeding the man who'd put Austin in the clink. No matter what, I knew I could always count on her. Even if I said stupid things like I did with Amy. I took the bag with more than a few for the guys at the station, gave my friend a hug, and decided to see what I could find out about Austin's prior life. Facebook and Google had been my research tools before; hopefully they would be as knowledgeable this time.

Esmeralda was at the desk when I walked through the station door.

"Hey, Jill, he's in a meeting with John and I don't think he'll be done soon. They just had me order lunch for the team." She looked at the bag in my hand, sniffing the air. "What do you have in there? Don't tell me you baked?"

I shook my head. "You don't want what I could bake." I set the bag on her desk. "Sadie sent these over for you all. She's trying out a new recipe."

"Well, isn't that sweet of her. She's got a good heart, that's why people tend to take advantage of her." The town's fortune-teller nodded, pointing her finger at me. "You need to protect her from those who want to use her good nature."

"Like Austin?" This message from beyond sounded more like a message from a concerned neighbor.

Esmeralda nodded. "Austin appears to be a wounded soul, but he's got a dark side that Sadie can't see."

"I totally agree with you. Do you know anything about him that I need to know?" I pulled out my notebook and pen, waiting for the gossip I was sure was coming.

Esmeralda leaned closer. "I've already told Greg this, so I don't see the harm. I visit a local nursing home over in Bakerstown and do readings for the residents. They enjoy talking to their friends who have passed on, so I try to go once a month. Last month, I went on a different day and Austin was there talking to a resident. A woman who'd just moved from up north."

"North California?" Now I was intrigued. Maybe this was the mother he'd brought to live closer.

"She was from Oregon, according to Judy. She's the social worker who has me come visit." The phone rang and Esmeralda reached for it, interrupting our conversation. She wrote on a piece of paper and shoved it at me as she listened to the caller. She put her hand over the mouthpiece and whispered, "The name of the nursing home."

As I walked out, I put the piece of paper in my pocket. It was time to make a trip into town. Emma needed treats, I needed to go to the grocery store, and while I was there, I would talk to Judy at Resting Acres Nursing Home. Or at least I'd try.

I pulled my cell out of my pocket and dialed a number as I walked home. When the line was answered, I asked, "Want to go visit a nursing home?"

"Making plans for my retirement?" Aunt Jackie answered. "Do you know something I don't?"

"No, I'm not looking for a place to stick you. Although it might be a good idea to start." I probably shouldn't have said the last bit out loud. "Anyway, I need to talk to someone, and I thought if I brought you, we could pretend we were looking for someone else."

"You mean like an imaginary husband I'm tired of taking care of?"

She chuckled. "I could play that role easily. I'll just pretend it's Josh. I wonder if they do bariatric placements."

"Maybe you could pretend he wasn't that large." I'd hate to have them turn us away without finding out who this mystery woman was. "So, do you want to come or not?"

"You'll owe me lunch. And not some fast-food bag of grease. I want a real, sit-down meal." She paused and I heard the television shut off in the background. "Give me twenty minutes and I'll be ready."

I heard the phone click in my ear. Twenty minutes would be perfect. I'd have time to start researching Austin and his mysterious past. Maybe Aunt Jackie knew something about the era as well. She had been active in political campaigns during that time, she could have knowledge about the anti-war protests. I sped up my walking so I could get busy on the computer.

Thirty minutes later, Aunt Jackie and I were in the Jeep, heading toward Bakerstown. I filled her in on what I'd found. "I think this was the incident that sent Austin and Mary Jane underground." I handed her a page I'd printed off just before I'd shut down my laptop.

"I remember this. The ROTC building was bombed on campus. They never found out who planted the bomb, but they assumed it was an anti-war group." Aunt Jackie looked at me. "You think this was Austin?"

"Look at the next page. There's a picture of the protesters who marched the weekend before. Doesn't that look like him, third one from the left?" I focused on the road as she looked at the grainy black-and-white picture.

"It could be. I've only known him with his gray dreadlocks. This guy must be young, maybe not even eighteen. There's something familiar about his eyes, though." She looked at me. "You think it's him."

"I do. And there's a young woman next to him with her arm in his. I bet that's Mary Jane." I turned off the air. "Sadie said he ran because of what she did. Maybe she set the bomb off. Austin could have just been in the wrong place and felt protective of his girlfriend."

"Not very smart if it was him." She put the papers back into the folder and sighed. "The whole thing seems too cloak-and-dagger for the guy. He'll sit on the beach for hours, working on his tan and ignore the customers who are lining up at his rental booth."

"Maybe he's really good at hiding his true self." But I was beginning to wonder if this was another wild goose chase. It was a good thing I hadn't mentioned my suspicions to Greg, he would have laughed at me. Well, after I got the lecture about staying out of the investigation, I was 90 percent sure he would have laughed. Okay, maybe 75.

I really had to stop testing his level of commitment like this. And I would—right after we visited the nursing home.

CHAPTER 12

"We have an excellent locked ward for our more challenged residents." We were being given the grand tour by the marketing manager, Tess. I kind of felt bad for the woman since there wasn't a real "Uncle Ted" for us to place. She continued with her sales pitch. "The facility is set up for the varying needs of your loved one. Depending on the progression of the disease, they could be in the open ward with little supervision, the medium ward, where we have an increased level of staffing, or finally, the locked ward, where they are limited on their ability to roam the grounds."

Aunt Jackie pointed to the large glass windows looking out onto a hilly area behind the building. "You have such lovely gardens. Are residents allowed outside? Ted loves his walks."

"Of course, as long as they are supervised. We'd hate for someone to fall without us knowing. We use alarms on walkers, chairs, and beds to keep the nursing staff alert to problems such as fall risks." Now Tess looked anxious. "We have an excellent record of fall prevention. You can see that on the government website that ranks homes in the area."

"I didn't realize there was a website." Or really cared for that matter. I guess I should have been more interested in what a good long-term care facility looked like, for Aunt Jackie's sake, but that was one future I couldn't think about today. Or ever, if I was lucky. I scanned the large living room for someone who looked like Mary Jane. Her hair in the black-and-white photo had looked dark, but who knew what color it was in real life. It could be gray now.

Tess nodded. "I'll give you the pamphlet with your visit materials before you leave. I'm sure you'll find our home is top in the area." She opened a door and we walked into what appeared to be the crafts room. "Here's where our more active residents spend their days. We have speakers come in, have quilt clubs, and even craft days. We just had a fifth-grade class visit and lead the group in making Valentines." Tess pointed to the wall. "The residents loved it."

It looked like my elementary hallway with all the lacy hearts covering the wall, some pretty and sparkly with glitter, others with handwriting not much better than a scribble that looked like my primary care physician's script for my prescriptions.

"Isn't this nice, Jill?" Aunt Jackie smiled at me and pointed me toward a woman sitting alone with a journal. Her long gray hair covered her face as she wrote furiously into the notebook. As Tess continued talking about the overwhelming choices of activities a resident had for their week, the woman at the table picked up her travel mug and tried to take a drink. I watched as she tilted her head back and shook the empty cup. Then she slammed the notebook closed and wheeled over to our group.

Tess looked down at her, stroked the woman's hair out of her face, and adjusted her flowing scarf around her shoulders. "Good morning, MJ, how are you feeling?"

"I'm dying of thirst over here. Doesn't anyone check on an old woman anymore? What are we here for? A show for your new victims?" MJ pointed to Aunt Jackie. "You should run as fast as you can before you're warehoused here with the rest of us."

"Now MJ, you know all you have to do is ask and we'll get you more coffee." Tess waved over an aide and handed the cup to the young girl, then whispered to me, "I'm afraid she has a bit of a coffee addiction."

"I'm not deaf, you know." This time, MJ looked at me. "You should be ashamed of yourself, putting your mother into a place like this. I've lived here for years, and it never gets any better."

"Now, MJ, you just moved in less than six months ago. You were in that home in Oregon before, remember?" Tess put a hand on the woman's arm. "We believe in reality theory in the open wards. Once they move into the higher care area, we let them have their fantasy world."

MJ shook her head. "There, or here, it's all the same. Where's that child with my coffee? I need to finish my book. People need to know about the conspiracy, and I'm not getting any younger."

The aide came back into the room with the coffee cup and a bouquet of carnations. "Look what I found at the front desk for you. Do you want them here or in your room?"

MJ took her coffee and waved the flowers away. "Take those to the room. That man needs to stop sending me crap like this. He knows I'll never marry him. I can't be chained to a white picket fence, birth his babies, and raise the stupid sheepdog. I'm a free spirit."

The aide smiled and left the room with the flowers.

Tess waited for MJ to return to her table and take a deep sip of her coffee. Then she opened the notebook and started writing again. "Her boyfriend visits every week and sends flowers. I guess he's been her only family for years. He's such a nice man. A bit eccentric with his clothing and hair choices, but this is California. You expect to see aging hippies, right?"

The rest of the tour I kept thinking about Austin and his real life. How long had he been living under the new name, caring for this woman who had no idea what year it was or how old she'd become? Tess must have sensed my distance because she steered us to her office to get a folder.

"I know it can all be overwhelming. Why don't you come back later this week and have lunch on us? We can talk more then." She handed me the folder. "In the meantime, read up on the industry, and I'm sure you'll agree that Resting Acres is the best placement you could make for your loved one."

We said our good-byes, and when Aunt Jackie and I got back into the car, she opened the folder and stared at the picture. Then she handed it to me. "It's the same woman, right?"

I looked at the younger, smiling Austin and the woman we'd just met. "Almost fifty years later, but yeah, that's MJ."

I let the car sit idling for a while. "I'm not sure what to do next. We may know why Austin was hiding, but all it means is he might not have been involved in the bombing. Of course, MJ is the only one who can verify that, and her testimony would be a little dicey."

"Let's just find out if Austin is the boyfriend first. Don't you know the florist in town?" My aunt stared out at the entrance to the facility. "Seriously, if I get that bad, don't put me in a place like that."

"You want me to hire cute cabana boys to watch over you?" I smiled and put the Jeep into gear, thankful for a direction. I was going to have to confess my investigating sins to Greg, but not quite yet.

"Actually, I'm thinking a cruise ship. I read an article about a woman who is living on one as her retirement home. I could do that easy. Maybe I could get a job running the senior social hours to help pay for my stays." My aunt shrugged. "It's as good a retirement plan as any, I guess."

"I just hope you don't take off too soon." I squeezed her arm. "I don't know what I'd do without you at the shop now. I'd be a mess in a month."

She sniffed. "I'd give you a week before you'd be begging me to come back. Are you still thinking about taking those business classes? I think you need to consider expanding your knowledge about the business world."

I had thought about taking some classes at the local community college, but I'd put it off in favor of spending more time on my deck with Greg. "Honestly, I haven't done anything. I've missed the spring semester, but I'll get registered for fall. As long as they're night classes, my time's free."

"Speaking of nights, can you take my shift on Friday again? I'll work your morning shift on Saturday so you can have the entire day off." My aunt turned her head away from me, but I could see a slight tinge of pink on her cheek.

"You have plans for Friday, again?" I kept my head facing forward, but tried to gauge my aunt's response.

"Fine. Yes, Harrold asked me out again. There's a traveling show in the city and the last night they'll be there is Friday. We tried to get in tonight, but the theater is dark on Mondays." She turned toward me. "Is it a problem for you to work? I could ask Sasha, but I think she's got midterms this week."

"Not a problem at all. Greg will probably still be tied up with this investigation." Especially when I gave him the information that I'd uncovered. He'd have to talk to the nursing home people. I only hoped Tess wouldn't be too disappointed that our imaginary relative wasn't moving in. Did they get commissions like used car salesmen? Five admissions in a month and they earned a trip to Mexico? "And I'll be expecting Josh to show up at closing. What should I tell him?"

"I don't have to explain my life or my choices to that man." She crossed her arms.

"Yeah, but *I* do. So if you don't want me to use the 'she's too sick to work' excuse like I did last week, I need something to tell him." I parked in front of the florist. "You think about what you want me to say, and I'll pop in to the florist shop to see Allison. Then we'll eat over at that new Asian Fusion place near the Pet Palace."

"I suppose you need something for that mutt of yours." Her words were harsher than her tone. "You might want to get her more tennis balls, too. The ones she has are disgusting." She took a book out of her purse. An autobiography of another ex–First Lady; my aunt had a taste for the political life, even if it was just reading about those involved in the national game.

I left the stereo on and my keys in the ignition in case she needed to turn on the air or roll down a window.

Allison Delaine was in the front of the shop, a tiny vase of purple flowers, pansies, and violets partially completed on the counter. She smiled when I opened the door and its chime announced my entrance. "Jill, I haven't seen you in forever. Is this a personal call, or are you here on committee business?"

Allison was my Bakerstown counterpart for the Business-to-Business meeting. Of course, they called it "Bakerstown's Open for Business," which I thought was a little cutesy. Of course, my committee's name could be seen as a little dry. But then, I named my shop Coffee, Books, and More—which demonstrated how I liked names to reflect what was sold in the place. Or the purpose of the committee. Some days, I'd wished I'd thought a little longer and named the shop something cute, like The Human Bean, or A Cup of Stories, but at that point I already had branding stuff done up for CBM.

I made my way through the potted plants, taking in the strong floral smell, which always seemed a little cold to my senses. "Hey, Allison. This is pretty." I touched a petal on a pansy. "Actually, I'm here to ask you a favor, but I don't know if you can tell me or not."

"You want to know who sent a bouquet of flowers, right?" She laughed at my shocked face. "Cards get lost, and it's not like I'm a doctor or lawyer. There's no expectation of privacy." She turned to her computer. "However, I don't remember having a delivery sent to you this week. I sent two batches of flowers to your aunt. Is that what you're asking about?"

"*Two* batches?" Aunt Jackie had told me that Josh had sent flowers, but had Harrold sent the others?

"Yeah, it was weird. One had a Get Well Soon card, and the other was a thanks for the great evening message." Allison raised her eyebrows. "Your aunt is a popular girl."

"Always," I said. "Anyway, it's not about Jackie's flowers, or mine. I wanted to know who's been sending flowers to Resting Acres. It's a recurring order to a woman named MJ?"

"Carnations." Allison nodded, tapping on her keyboard. "I bill monthly, but I've had the standing order for the last six months."

I waited as she pulled up the right record.

"Here it is." She squinted at me. "This is odd. The order's from South Cove, a Dustin Austin? Do you know him?"

I nodded. "Thanks. That's what I thought."

"Is something wrong?" Allison watched me closely. "Don't tell me you're seeing someone else. I thought you were dating that cute detective."

"I am. No, this is for a friend." I tapped on the counter. "Got to go, I'm taking Aunt Jackie to lunch and she gets grumpy when she's hungry."

"Call me and we'll do coffee next week. It's been too long since we've talked." Allison waved and turned back to her floral arrangement. That had been too easy. Now I had to find a way to tell Greg the information I'd discovered without him getting upset.

Or I could just bite the bullet and drop into the station after I dropped off Aunt Jackie.

Driving to the restaurant, I decided that this could wait until morning. After my shift, I'd stop by the station with a cheesecake for the gang and then tell Greg what I knew. After he'd seen the cheesecake.

CHAPTER 13

I hadn't slept well, my mind kicking around the Austin files and what I suspected would be Greg's reaction when he found out that Jackie and I had gone sleuthing. I snorted as I sipped my coffee and read a magazine article on ways to make your kitchen sparkle for under two hundred bucks. The next house project was the exercise room, which would be either upstairs or out in Miss Emily's painting shed. The shed had a lot more room, as Greg kept pointing out, but my fear was I'd never actually make it the twenty steps to work out.

Emma put her nose into my hand and nuzzled. I looked down into my dog's brown eyes and she barked once, then pointedly glanced at the door. I checked the wall clock. We had plenty of time. "Hold on, let me get changed."

I headed upstairs to change into my running clothes. The only way Emma would push me out the door to use a workout room was if she had a bag of bones hidden behind the weight bars. I considered Greg's attachment to it—maybe I could give in there and he wouldn't be as upset about the sleuthing. I shook my head. I was going to get a lecture this morning no matter what and I might as well get it over with.

Right now, though, Emma and I had a date with the seagulls. And maybe, if she was lucky and I wasn't alert, a dead fish.

Sasha was sitting at one of the outside tables when I finally arrived at the shop. I smiled as she tucked her book into her bag; she was hooked on historical romance, although with her schoolwork and the two book clubs she ran for the store, she hardly had any free time. However, the girl still got through a book a week for her own pleasure. I was amazed. Dressed in a patterned dress and tennis shoes, her hair tied up with a headband, she looked more like a college student with a part-time job than a single mom trying to make ends meet.

"If you keep beating me here, I'm going to have to give you your own key." I unlocked and held the door open for her, flipping on the lights as we crossed the threshold.

"And take away my reading time? You'd do that to me?" Sasha tapped her purse. "I carry my book with me everywhere, and if I have ten or even five minutes, that's a few more pages."

"So you're telling me that you like me showing up late because you get to read more?" I laughed as I went to the counter and washed my hands. Then I started the regular pot of coffee as Sasha started the decaf. We'd been working this shift together for over a month now, and we had the chores down to a choreographed dance. Sasha worked a full shift with me on Tuesdays, then on Wednesdays, she worked with Toby and helped Aunt Jackie close. She had Thursdays off, then ran the same schedule for Fridays and Saturdays. We'd carved out full-time hours so we could get her on our health insurance. Toby had benefits with the police department, so Sasha was our only employee with full benefits.

"What can I say, I'm great at time management." She held up the list Aunt Jackie had left by the counter on Saturday night. "You want to handle the extra or the ordinary list?"

"I'll do the setup and any customers who come in. You handle the queen's instructions." I liked to tease my aunt that she tended to over-schedule us with activities, but honestly, most of her ideas were gold, especially in the area of marketing. She'd started the book clubs, sponsored a launch for a well-known mystery author at the store, and even set up the last mystery dinner theater. Of course, finding a real dead body meant that hadn't been in the plan, but the idea was solid.

We worked in relative silence for a half hour before we got our first rush of commuter customers. After the last one, Bob, ambled out of the store and on his way to his job at the bottling plant down the road, Sasha leaned against the counter and folded her bar towel.

"Have you heard from Toby?"

Her question surprised me, and I looked up from cutting a new banana nut coffee cake for the display counter. I set the knife down and ripped a slice in half, giving her the larger piece. My heart sank at the realization. "Crap, something happened with the investigation and he's not coming in today?" I almost inhaled the bread, not wanting to think about what could happen to Austin, especially since I had the information to free him. "What else did they charge Austin with?"

Sasha frowned. "I don't know."

Now it was my turn to be confused. "Then why won't Toby be coming in to work?"

"Who said Toby wasn't coming in?" Sasha paused, then laughed. "Oh no. That's not what I meant. I wondered if you heard how Toby and Elisa's date had gone on Friday."

Relief filled me, and I made a mental promise to go to the station and confess as soon as my shift was over. I went back to checking the prices in the cash register. Aunt Jackie made me do the routine double-check first thing every week, just in case gremlins had come in over the weekend and played with our pricing codes. "I don't know. I guess fine. I mean, I don't really hear from Toby unless it's about work." Or my sleuthing, I added silently.

"Oh." A twinge of disappointment echoing in Sasha's one-word answer caused me to pause from the verification task again.

"What's going on? Anything I need to know about?" This was the second time I'd asked Sasha about her emotional health in less than a week. The girl had me worried.

She waved away my words. "I'm fine. I was just concerned about Toby, that's all. A girl doesn't set up a mandatory dinner for her beau unless she has big news."

My mind started racing. "Oh no. You don't think she's pregnant, do you?"

Sasha's eyes widened. "No. I mean, I don't know. Do *you* think she's pregnant?"

I thought about Toby's complaints about Elisa being moody and hard to deal with. "It could explain a lot, especially her mood swings." I shook my head. "Toby as a daddy, I just can't see it."

Sasha headed toward the back. "I can." Then she disappeared through the swinging doors.

I stepped toward the office, but the bell over the front door stopped me. Harrold strolled through the door and set a leather-strapped briefcase on a table near the window. He waved at me, then came up to the counter. "Hey, Jill, is Jackie down yet?"

"Down? She doesn't work until three." Harrold looked good. Clean jeans, a button-down shirt, and, I sniffed just to make sure, he *was* also wearing cologne. I didn't think I'd ever seen him in anything but T-shirts, mostly ones with different railroad insignias. That was the fun of making a hobby into a profession; you could dress the part. Today, Harrold looked like a successful California real estate broker, or maybe one of those dot-com kings.

"Didn't she tell you? We have our weekly meeting for the water conservation committee today and she's hosting. Let me order up coffee for four and a plate of a variety of the different pastries over there. My treat." He pulled out his wallet and handed me a gold card.

"Let us handle the coffee, but I'll take your card for the desserts. Let me know if the rest of the group wants anything else." I charged him for the order and handed back the plastic. I looked at the clock: ten to nine. "Do you want me to call Aunt Jackie and let her know you're here?"

He shook his head. "Nope, I've got stuff to keep me busy until the meeting starts." He smiled and the crinkles around his blue eyes made him look like Robert Redford. "Besides, a guy doesn't want to look too anxious, right?"

"I'll bring everything over to the table then." As he walked away, my gaze darted to the ceiling. Was Aunt Jackie really into this guy? Could this be my new uncle?

As I filled the coffee carafe, the bell over the door rang again, and Josh lumbered into the shop. I saw his glare toward Harrold, who in turn smiled and waved him over. Instead, Josh headed toward me and the counter.

"Where's Jackie?" Even though the day was just starting, he looked rumpled in his white shirt and black suit.

I pointed to the ceiling. "She hasn't come down yet. I guess you all have a meeting? I'm getting coffee for the table, can I get you something else?"

"Plate up some of those cake things Jackie likes." Josh waved toward the dessert case. "I'll treat everyone to breakfast."

"Harrold's already bought enough for the table." I smiled over at Harrold, who was poring over papers from his briefcase. "Hey, is Amy coming? I need to talk to her."

"I am not in charge of Miss Newman's social calendar. Please let Jackie know I'm here." Josh pulled his jacket straight and spun around, apparently ready to meet the dragon commonly known as Harrold.

"Uh-oh, this might not be good," Sasha whispered as she came to stand beside me. "I'd give the match to Josh, mostly because of the weight-class difference."

I shook my head, not taking my gaze off of the black suit moving closer to the unsuspecting Harrold. "I'm going with Train Guy. He's a few years younger, and a whole lot more in shape."

"Who's in shape?" Aunt Jackie asked from the door leading to the office. My eyes widened, and I stared at Sasha, hoping she'd come up with a convincing lie. Instead, my newest barista curled her lips into a smile worthy of a winning prizefighter and went to clean off the tables in the front dining area, leaving me to face my aunt alone.

"Toby." I shrugged. "For as much as he works, he's really in shape."

Aunt Jackie watched Sasha, who was avoiding making eye contact with anyone. "I've wondered about Sasha and Toby. She's way too interested in him. I think she needs to start dating instead of mooning over a guy who's already involved."

I leaned against the counter and stared at her. "You think Sasha's in love with Toby?"

She laughed and shook her head and I relaxed—until she said, "Not in love, but she's got a major crush on the guy."

"Really? I haven't noticed anything." I put the last of the treats on the tray.

"You're oblivious to most things, dear." My aunt looked at the empty shop and then down at the tray. "I take it those are for my meeting?"

"Harrold thought it would be nice. Then Josh tried to buy some treats for the table, as well." I handed her the coffee carafe and four cups. "Is Amy coming?"

As I asked the question, Amy Newman stepped through the door. She nodded to me, then went to sit in between Josh and Harrold, and handed each a notebook. She put a third in front of the empty chair where my aunt was going to sit.

"Let's get these delivered so I can get the meeting started. Time is money, you know." Aunt Jackie strolled to the table and set cups down in front of each of the members. "Coffee?"

As they nodded in turn, she filled their cups. I set the treats in the middle of the table with an extra set of plates and forks for the group. Then she handed me the empty carafe. "Fill this, will you?"

I'd been dismissed. I went back to the coffee bar, filled the carafe, and walked it back over to the table where they were all talking at once, except for Amy, who was staring down into her notebook, ignoring my presence.

Well, fine. Two could play that game. I returned to the coffee counter, poured myself a cup of hazelnut and took a book over to the couch. Sasha could handle any more random customers. When Sasha finished cleaning the tables, no other customers had arrived, so she joined me with a book on the couch. I thought about my aunt's statement. Was Sasha fascinated with the reformed playboy barista? I knew they liked to tease each other, but I didn't think Sasha was one to poach in someone else's backyard, so to speak.

By the time Toby arrived, the water committee was still in session over at the window table. I stood and stretched, joining him at the counter while he prepped for his shift. "How is everything?"

Toby didn't meet my eyes. "What do you mean?"

"Are you and Elisa talking yet?" I leaned closer, dropping the volume in my voice so Sasha wouldn't hear. I glanced toward the couch and caught her watching us. When she saw me watching her, she returned to her reading.

Toby shrugged. "Not much." He slipped on his apron. "Hey, Greg wanted me to tell you he's heading in to Bakerstown this afternoon and may not be able to stop by tonight."

I jumped off the stool. "Crap, what time is he leaving?"

"He had a few things to finish up, why?" Toby leaned over the counter watching me.

I raced around the counter and snatched my purse out of the back room. "Nothing much, I just need to talk to him."

Halfway to the station, I realized what Toby had done. He'd distracted me from asking about his relationship. Whatever the couple had discussed on Friday, he didn't want to tell me. I'd just have to be sneakier in how I asked the next time. Toby might be tricky, but I could be devious.

The brisk sea air had me chilled by the time I arrived at the station. I'd left my jacket at the shop, thinking it looked warmer than it really was. I rubbed my arms and walked even faster to catch Greg, if he was even planning on leaving town today.

Esmeralda was on the phone at the reception desk when I arrived, and she waved me into his office. Still, I knocked before going through the open door. Greg glanced up at me, his blue eyes crinkling in a welcome surprise. At least he was happy to see me now. Who knew how he'd feel in a few minutes when I unloaded my findings? "Hey, you." His voice softened and made my insides all gooey.

"Hey, yourself. Toby said you were heading to Bakerstown." I looked around his office. It didn't appear Greg was on his way anywhere. I was going to kick Toby the next time I saw him.

Greg looked at the clock on the wall. "I am, just not right now. I don't have time for lunch, but I can spare you a few minutes. What's on your mind?"

"Can't a girl just come in to see her beau?" I drawled as I sank into one of the chairs across from him.

Greg leaned back and put his arms behind his head. "Come on, spill. I know that look. What did you find out? Is the mayor head of the crack cocaine mafia? Or does Amy have a secret boyfriend Justin doesn't know about?"

I frowned. "Neither. Why would you think Amy would cheat on Justin?"

"Just throwing out ideas, since you're not very chatty yet." He looked at the clock again, my clue to get talking or get out.

"Okay, so Aunt Jackie and I went in to Bakerstown yesterday."

He groaned. "I should have known."

"What, can't we go into town?" I knew I was bluffing, but hey, he didn't have to suspect me all the time. Even if he was usually right.

He raised his eyebrows. "Continue."

"Fine. We went to Resting Acres and there's this woman there, MJ, but we think her name is Mary Jane and she's the one Austin is protecting from the Feds and why he changed his name." I stopped for breath, then added, "And he's been sending her flowers for years."

"What?" He put his head in his hands. "You're giving me a headache. Who's been sending flowers for years?"

"Austin. He's been visiting this woman in the nursing home and sending her flowers. Sadie thinks she's the reason he went under-ground in the first place." I paused, watching Greg's face to see if he believed anything I was saying. After I explained Aunt Jackie's and my trip into Bakerstown, Greg took out a pad and wrote down some-thing. "The florist's name is Allison?"

"Yep. So is this important?" I leaned forward, trying to read what he'd written, but he snapped the notebook closed before I could see much more than the name of the nursing home.

He looked at the clock a third time. "Sorry, honey, I've got to run. I'll try to stop by this evening. If you're lucky, I'll bring by pizza from Godfather's."

"And if you're lucky, I'll have a few cold beers in the fridge." I let him pull me from my seat and we walked out into the lobby together. "Are you going to tell me where you're going?"

He kissed me, letting his lips linger a bit on mine, then swatted me on the butt. "Nope."

I watched him disappear through the station's back door, where he typically parked his truck. As I turned toward the other exit, Esmeralda laughed. "You two are so cute together. He's all business and you're always messing with his karma."

I paused at her desk. "I don't mess with his karma, do I?" I wasn't quite sure what messing with karma meant, so I didn't want to totally deny the charge if it was true.

"Girl, you are at the center of all the important stuff going on here in South Cove. I would think the mayor should be paying you big bucks for everything you do instead of that measly salary for running the business committee." She filed her nails, not looking at me.

"You know how much I make?"

She shrugged. "The city budgets may cross my e-mail from time to time." Now she leaned forward and squinted at me. "Have you been on a treasure hunt?"

"No. Why do you ask?"

"Something in your aura." She considered me closely. "You need to be careful when you go out alone to seek the treasure. There's something guarding it and it's not friendly."

"Seriously, I'm not going on any treasure hunts." I smiled at my neighbor. "Hey, your lawn looks terrific. What kind of seed do you use? Is it drought-resistant?"

Esmeralda smiled as the phone rang. "The grass is always greener when it's been watered." She picked up the phone, spun her chair so her back was to me, and answered, "South Cove Police Department, how may I help you?"

CHAPTER 14

When I returned home, a letter was taped on my door. The envelope's printed return address was for South Cove City Hall. Maybe Amy had come by after the meeting and left me a note. I ripped it off the door, and waited to open it until I'd unlocked the door and let Emma out. I dumped my purse on the table and sank into a chair, opening the letter. Instead of a handwritten note from my friend, though, telling me she'd forgiven me for slighting her about Esmeralda, there was a printed letter from the South Cove Water Commission.

I read down to the important part. I was being fined a hundred dollars for watering my lawn. A lawn I hadn't watered in months. Sue me, I wasn't the best landscaper. Greg mowed my lawn more often than I did. I didn't like getting my hands dirty. The way it caked on my hands creeped me out, so I didn't do anything without donning a pair of gardening gloves.

Scanning the letter, I knew they'd made a big mistake. Esmeralda was watering, she'd told me so, and I got fined? Amy must really be mad. But when I saw the signature, I knew the problem.

Josh Thomas had signed the letter. This was retaliation for Aunt Jackie and Harrold. I put the letter on the counter. I'd take it to work tomorrow and have Aunt Jackie take care of it. She caused the issues; she could handle the fallout.

I went upstairs and changed into my running clothes. I needed a taste of the sea air and to run off this bad energy.

When Emma and I returned, there was a message on my answering machine. I punched the button and Greg's voice filled the small kitchen. Emma barked and looked around to see where her friend was hiding.

"Hey, you're in luck. I'll be there just after five with two large pies, so chill the beer." I looked at my dog sitting at attention, waiting for Greg to appear out of the small machine.

"He'll be here soon." I opened the fridge and pulled out lettuce, tomatoes, and what was left of my deli turkey meat to make a salad. Even with the second run, if I didn't make up for the calories I'd be consuming tonight, I'd feel bloated in the morning. Emma sniffed the air and, realizing I wasn't cooking anything on her top-ten list of begging menus, crossed the kitchen to her bed, where she circled three times before lying down with her head on her newest stuffed raccoon.

I finished the salad, dressed it with a raspberry vinaigrette I loved, and poured a glass of sun tea I'd made last weekend. Cleaning up the counter, I moved my lunch to the table and took out my notebook and a pen.

I stared at the list of possible suspects in Kacey's murder, which right now included one person. Dustin Austin. I knew Kacey had died of a severe reaction to a wheat allergy, but the girl was smart. She knew how to keep herself safe, and I'd seen an epi pen in her purse, so why hadn't she used it?

I started writing down the questions that bothered me. Kacey knew about her condition, and as her husband, so had Austin. But it wasn't like she was shy about talking to others about her allergy. I'd had a brief conversation with her at the food truck, and I'd learned more than I'd ever known about gluten allergies. Of course, we had been talking about the new business. I wrote *food truck* in big letters in the middle of the page. If getting her to close or sell the truck had been the motive, I knew of three people who would be suspects: me, Sadie, and Lille. I circled *Lille* a few times, but really, my heart wasn't into suspecting her. The restaurant owner was more into her bad-boy boyfriends and holding a grudge against anyone who'd ever slighted her. Now if Homer Bell, the guy who'd sold the truck out from under me and Lille, had come up dead, Lille would be top of my list. She hated that guy.

I sighed and wrote down Sadie's name under the food truck. Not only had Austin stolen her recipes by sucking face with her and pretending to be her boyfriend, she might have lost business for Pies on the Fly if the food truck had been successful. Although that logic didn't completely ring true, as the customer base for the two businesses were totally different. Thinking about Sadie reminded me of the women who'd asked for gluten-free treats at the shop last weekend. I'd never asked Sadie if she could make up something special.

I dialed Sadie's number and got her voice mail. She got up about three to do her baking, and I'd forgotten this was her nap time, when she turned off her phone. "Hi, Sadie, it's Jill. I wanted to talk to you about some different menu items for the shop. Don't kill me, but I need something gluten-free. Give me a call when you get this message."

One thing off my to-do list. I turned a page in the notebook and looked at the week's schedule. I added *Pizza with Greg* and *beach run* to today's list, crossing off the beach run right after I wrote it. Then I wrote *Gluten-Free Menu Items* on the page for tomorrow. I wanted to talk to Aunt Jackie about her thoughts on the change, too. She could probably estimate how many items we might sell using one of her business school models. I paused, then wrote on today's list *explore back-to-school options.*

If the murder investigation was leading me back around to one of my best friends, then I needed to do something else to occupy my mind. I knew I was missing something, but I kept thinking about that book of recipes now in Sadie's kitchen with Kacey's handwritten changes in the margins. I picked up the phone to call Amy, then realized she was still miffed at me.

Finishing the last of my salad, I rinsed the bowl and fork and put it into the dishwasher. Then I powered up my laptop, turned the notebook to a clean page, and started figuring out what I needed to do to go back to school next fall and get a business degree.

I'd made a plan for my first semester, listed off all the steps I needed to complete before I could apply for admission, and ordered materials to be sent to the house. I had a month before the admissions due date and there were many steps to complete, including an essay on why I wanted an MBA degree. Of course, since my bachelor's had been in political science, I also had several prerequisite classes I had to take just to be provisionally approved.

Worse, there was a placement test. I put a note on my to-do list to order a study guide for the GMAT. I'd ordered several guides for the undergrad test earlier that fall for seniors at the high school, but I didn't have any for graduate school on hand.

Maybe going back to school wasn't such a great idea. After passing the bar, I'd sworn I'd never take another test again. But according to the website, the LSAT test that got me into law school wasn't accepted for the MBA program, so it looked like I'd be sitting at a computer for the next month, getting my student groove back on. Maybe Sasha would help me study.

The knock on the door came at ten minutes after five. I was still in student mode, making choices of what classes I wanted to take which nights. If I went four nights a week, I'd be done in three years, even with the extra classes I needed to boost my business knowledge. How hard could Math for Business Decisions be?

Emma beat me to the door and as I unlocked it, I peeked through the side window to make sure it was Greg. I'd been surprised before by a crazy stalker who thought I held a package from a dead woman. Don't ask, but now I always kept the doors locked and checked before I opened up, even if I was expecting the South Cove police detective. Greg approved of my new habit, which kind of got me off the hook for all the bad ones he didn't like so much.

He was leaning against the doorway, holding the screen open with his foot because in his hands were two boxes from Godfather's. My stomach grumbled as the smell of deep-dish pepperoni and a super garbage supreme pizza hit my nose.

"Come on in. I'm starving." I held open the door, then relocked it after he entered. A little overkill in my view, but it made Greg feel like I was taking my protection seriously. I'd even started carrying pepper spray when I ran, although whoever would mess with me while Emma was around was just plain stupid.

"What, did you only eat one of Sadie's cheesecakes for lunch?" He kissed me on the cheek and moved to the kitchen. "Sorry about pizza again, but we really didn't finish that impromptu dinner and a movie night."

Following him, I answered, "For your information I had salad for lunch. And I don't think I had anything for breakfast." No wonder I was starving, now that I thought about it. I really needed to start eating earlier. Coffee didn't replace real food, although it made a valiant effort in my book.

He set the pizza boxes on the counter and pointed to the table. "You working on the shop's books today? I thought your aunt handled most of that."

I scrambled to close up the notebook and put away the laptop before he went thumbing through the pages and found the *Who Killed Kacey* page. I knew Greg wasn't stupid enough to think I wasn't investigating, but I didn't want the proof to be so obvious. "I'm going back to school for my MBA. Aunt Jackie thinks I need to know more about how businesses run, seeing as I own one."

Greg got plates from the counter and set them near the boxes. Then he took two beers out of the fridge and opened them. "You want a glass for your beer?"

"Waste of a glass. I can drink out of the bottle. Besides, I don't want to run the dishwasher until Friday." I pointed to the letter on the counter. "I'm already in trouble with the committee for watering my lawn. I don't want to waste water on cleaning dishes."

He picked up the letter, read the fine, and laughed. "Seriously? I don't think you've watered the lawn in a year. That's my job since you tend to forget."

"I know, right?" I helped myself to a plate. "I'm turning it over to Aunt Jackie tomorrow and she can rein in her attack dog. Besides, I don't think Josh is upset over the water. I think Harrold's got him worried that Aunt Jackie's going to dump him."

Greg filled his own plate and took it to the table with a couple of paper towels. "I can see why he'd be worried. Harrold would be a perfect match for your aunt. They both like traveling and theater. I don't know why we didn't think of introducing them before now."

"He is more her style." I took a swig from the bottle, letting the cold beer race down my throat. Setting it down on the table, I smoothed my paper towel over my lap. "I don't know, I just feel a little sorry for Josh."

"Don't tell me you want him to marry your aunt?" He picked up his pizza and folded it in half before taking a bite.

"No. I don't want her to marry anyone." I picked off a mushroom and ate it. "That sounded really selfish of me, huh?"

"You're protective. That's a good thing." Greg wiped his mouth. "Of course, dragging her to Bakerstown to follow up on a crazy lead isn't protecting her very well. What were you thinking?"

"I don't think Austin killed Kacey." I held up a hand before he could respond. "I know, not my circus, but just because he was hiding out from the law for over forty years doesn't make him a killer. He sends the woman flowers every week for goodness' sake."

He raised his eyebrows. "Now you sound like Amy. Pro-Austin and not able to see anything but the nice guy he portrays here in town."

"Believe me. I know Austin's a royal jerk. Look what he did to Sadie. I'd like him thrown in jail for breaking her heart, but I don't think you'd get away with it with the DA." I took my first bite of the pizza, wanting to change the subject so I could eat, but not wanting to cut Greg off. He might tell me something about what he discovered the more we talked.

Greg laughed. "I don't know. John's ready to go to court on this guy. If I added reckless endangerment of Miss Sadie's heart, he might just go for the kill. I've never seen him so sold on one person, even if all the evidence seems to prove Austin's innocence."

I thought about that statement. "Any chance John knows what happened to Sadie?"

"Everyone knows what happened to Sadie. I'm surprised Austin wasn't run out of town for the crap he pulled. But it's not illegal to be a jerk." He finished the slices on his plate and looked at my still full one. "I thought you were hungry?"

"I'm worried about Sadie. Amy isn't talking to me. And Aunt Jackie asked me to cover her shift Friday night, which means I'll have to lie to Josh again about where she is instead of at the shop." I took a bite of the pizza, but it didn't taste as good as I'd hoped.

"She shouldn't ask you to lie. Tell her to come clean with Josh." He stood up and took two more pieces of the pepperoni. "Justin called me on the way back from Bakerstown with a plan to get you and Amy talking again."

My stomach tightened. "What's his plan?" I never liked it when the boys interfered in our stuff.

"We're going out to do that geo-whatever stuff again on Sunday. Justin is getting really involved in the group, and he thinks doing an active double date will let the two of you work out your angst while we hike in the woods looking for hidden treasure." He took the crust off his pizza and gave it to Emma, who didn't even seem to chew or taste the buttery bread.

"Wait, what did you say?" I thought about the fortune-teller's earlier comment. "Did you tell Esmeralda we were going out?"

"I haven't seen her since I left the building. I told you that Justin called while I was driving back to South Cove. Callers like him are why I love my truck's Bluetooth. I can't ever get him to shut up." He looked at me. "You look a little green, are you sick?"

"No, I'm not sick." I told him about how Esmeralda had asked if I'd been looking for hidden treasure and told me to be careful. When I finished, Greg shrugged.

"She's messing with you. I'm sure someone has told her that we've been doing this geocaching thing with Amy and Justin. Probably Amy told her." He took a last bite of the slice on his plate and gave the rest to Emma. "You have to stop letting her play you."

As I ate my pizza, I thought about his words. The explanation sounded logical, and even Esmeralda had admitted she could piece together bits of information she heard from different sources to figure out what people needed to hear. But for some reason, the hair at the back of my neck was standing up and I had goose pimples on my arms.

"So, are we on for Sunday? Justin wants us to meet at the parking lot at the trailhead. That way if you two are still snippy, we can separate you for the ride home." Greg finished off his beer.

"I'll be good if she is." I picked up the plates and took them to the sink, putting the leftover pizza in one box, keeping two pieces out for my lunch tomorrow. Greg would take the rest to the station, and Toby and Tim would scarf down the leftovers. It was like having kids to feed. Big, hungry kids with size-ten feet.

He put his arms around me and gave me a tight squeeze. "I know you'll be good. So, do you want to watch a movie? I can't promise when or if you'll see me again between now and Sunday."

"Let me finish cleaning up and I'll be right in. I'll even let you choose the movie." I leaned into his body for a second, enjoying the warmth of his embrace.

"You will probably regret those words," he whispered into my ear.

I nodded. "I already do."

We stayed like that for a long minute, then he kissed me on the neck and left the room, Emma on his heels. During an investigation, we rarely got couple time except for the No-Guilt-Sunday time he'd implemented last year. And even then, if there was an emergency, all bets were off. Tonight, I wasn't going to worry about anything but spending time together. I could pry him for information tomorrow when I stopped by the station with a slice of cheesecake or two.

When I entered the living room, he sat in the middle of the couch, Emma on one side and a small portion of the seat cushion for me on the other. I slipped into the space and hit Play on the DVD remote. "So, you never told me why you're able to have date night in the middle of the week. Is John out of town for some reason?"

"He's trying to deal with the information you brought to my attention this morning. He says thanks, by the way. He didn't mean it when he said it, but I know his heart is in the right place." Greg leaned back into the couch and put his arm around me, pulling me closer.

"What's he deciding?" I put my ear over his heart and listened to the strong, comforting beat.

He put his hand on my head, stroking my face very gently as if I were a china doll to be protected from crashing and breaking. "Whether to drop the charges on Austin. Apparently John was convinced that Austin did in Mary Jane as well, and now that we found her, he's in the clear, so the 'kill one, kill them all' motive doesn't really apply."

We both left the other question hang in the air without an answer. *If Austin didn't kill Kacey, who did?*

CHAPTER 15

I hadn't slept well, my dreams filled with wandering kittens that kept getting into harm's way. When I woke early, I dressed in my running clothes and took Emma out for a quick run hoping to clear my head of the stress dreams. I still opened the shop early.

After the morning commuter customers left, I dialed Aunt Jackie's number. Three rings and she answered. "What? Is there a problem in the shop?"

"No, there's a problem with Josh." I could hear her favorite morning show in the background.

The sigh was long and loud. "What's he done now?"

"Come down to the shop and I'll show you. You really have got to get a handle on him." I clicked off and waited for her to make her way downstairs.

I read another chapter in the mystery I'd been nursing along not wanting the story to end, when I heard the door close in the office. She pushed through the doors, still dressed in her lounging clothes, a silk robe, silk pajama top and long pants, and her fuzzy slippers. With her hair wrapped up with a matching turban, she looked like a gently aged Lucille Ball, but with more makeup. She might not have gotten dressed to talk to me, but she had put on the full face treatment. Foundation, eye shadow, liner, mascara, and lipstick. She poured a cup of coffee and leaned against the counter sipping it. "So, what's so important?"

I pushed the letter toward her. "I got this on my door last night. Did you guys talk about me during your meeting?"

She pulled her reading glasses up off the chain where they hung around her neck and read the citation. "He didn't have the authority of the commission for this. I mean, we talked about someone who appeared to be watering his or her lawn, but I never got the impression it was you. You hate gardening."

"I know. And it wasn't me. My lawn is as dry as everyone else's. I think your committee needs to get their facts straight before they go off issuing citations." I grabbed the paper back from her and started waving it. "This is America. I have rights. What about innocent until proven guilty? Let Josh prove I water my lawn. Does he have pictures?"

She gently took the citation from my hand. "Calm down, dear. I told you it wasn't the committee. I'll handle this and Josh. You just relax."

"Okay, so that was over the top. I just hate being accused of things I didn't do. Especially since we both know this is about your date on Friday." I studied her. "You will tell him about you and Harrold, right?"

"Now, don't go all crazy on me. Telling him to back off you is one thing, but hurting his feelings by telling him about Harrold and me is quite different." My aunt tucked the letter into her robe jacket and took off her glasses. She sipped on her coffee.

"You know he did this because he suspects something is going on. He's vindictive." I almost said a "little vindictive," but nothing about Josh was little, unless you counted his emotional stability.

"You're probably right. I'm just not ready to talk about Harrold with Josh yet. I've been fair both ways, I don't talk about Josh to Harrold, either. I'm sure Harrold doesn't even care that I ever dated Josh." She pushed a wayward curl off her face and back behind her ear. "If Josh comes over Friday night, tell him I've gone out. That's all. No details, no with whom, not even a guess about what movie or theater. The man needs to learn to respect my privacy." And with that declaration, my aunt spun around on her fuzzy slipper and left. I'm sure it would have been a more satisfying exit if she'd had on shoes that actually allowed me to hear her stomp away.

With that problem solved—sort of—I returned to the *Kacey* page of my notebook. I knew I was missing something. I put a line through Austin and Sadie's names, but Austin's cross-out was much lighter than my friend's. As soon as I finished, the bell rang over the door and Sadie walked in the shop. If I'd believed in signs, this was a clear one that I was on the right track. Maybe Sadie's memories hid a clue even she didn't realize she knew.

Or maybe she was just responding to the voice mail I'd left her yesterday. I'd like to believe it was the former.

She slipped onto one of the stools and looked at me, putting her purse on the counter next to her. "Let me get this straight. You want me to develop a gluten-free dessert for your customers since the jerk and his now-deceased wife aren't opening up a dessert truck that could have run both of us out of business."

"You have to admit, it's a good business decision. Besides, we just need one or two choices, besides the fresh fruit cup we offer now." I smiled what I hoped was a winning smile when in fact it was probably serial killer creepy.

Sadie's shoulders sagged. "I'm being emotional about a business decision, aren't I?"

"You have a right to be emotional. Austin was a total butt to you. He led you on and stole your recipes. He should go to jail for being a bad man." I poured her a cup of her favorite chocolate-flavored coffee and filled my own cup before I walked around and sat next to her. "If you don't want to help me with this, you don't have to do it. I'll figure out something else."

She wiped away tears that had begun to fall. "I'll start playing around with some things. I have Kacey's notes, but I think instead of changing one of my recipes, I'll create something new and name it after her."

"I think that would be lovely." I put my arm around her and gave her a quick hug. "You are such a kind person."

"A kind person who wants to murder Austin? I think that's the definition of unkind, although Pastor Bill seems to think my rage is perfectly human." She pulled away from my hug and took a sip of her coffee. "I'd always thought I was above hate. I chair the South Cove Methodist Women Against Violence Committee, for gosh sake."

I pressed my lips together to keep from laughing. "You were hurt. Hurt people, like hurt animals, lash out at times." I was glad Toby or Greg wasn't here listening to Sadie's rambling. They might take her anger out of context and instead of Austin sitting over at the station, she'd be sitting there. Sadie was likely to admit to being guilty for not being more understanding than actually committing a real crime.

"I appreciate you looking at all sides of the issue." I returned to my coffee. "If you can't figure out something to make that we can serve, it's not a big issue. I don't get a lot of requests for gluten-free products." Well, that was a big fat fib, but I didn't want to make her feel bad.

"I'll figure out something. It will help me take my mind off poor Austin. I can't believe Greg is still holding him in that cell. Doesn't he have to charge him or let him go?"

"I think the DA is the one actually holding off on releasing him. It's not like he hasn't disappeared before."

Sadie waved her hand, pushing away the thought. "That was when he was a kid. She lured him into helping her escape. And you know some people will do anything for love."

I turned toward the door, where the bell had announced Toby's arrival. He looked like he'd been rode hard and put away wet, or in layman's terms, like crap. His usual crisp white shirt was replaced with a rumpled T-shirt I was pretty sure I'd seen in the corner of the police station's locker room when Greg had asked me to get him his coat out of a locker last week. I felt Sadie turn to see what I was staring at and heard her audible gasp.

"I look that bad, do I?" Toby shook his head and went behind the counter. "I'm kind of in between places right now and didn't feel like going to Elisa's for a clean shirt this morning."

"Well, I'd better be going." Sadie air-kissed me and skittered to the doorway. "Lots of baking to do, you know."

As she left, I turned back toward Toby, who now had a clean apron over the logo of the classic acid rock band. He looked better, but still drawn and pale. "What do you mean, you're in between places? I thought you were living with Elisa."

"She kicked me out. Or we broke up. I can't remember the exact order, but as of ten o'clock Friday night, I've been homeless. I sublet my apartment to a buddy when I moved in with Elisa, and now I can't find a place that's close and in my price range. I'm pretty sure I'll have to look in Bakerstown or even Collinsville."

"Oh Toby, I'm so sorry. How are you dealing with the breakup?" I wanted to ask about what he'd said a few days ago, that he thought she might be seeing someone else, but I didn't want to scare him off. It had taken him days to tell me this much.

"I miss that little girl like crazy." Toby arranged the cups. "But it's over, so I guess I'd better deal with it. Hey, you don't know of any apartments going up soon, do you?"

"Did Josh rent out the second apartment next door?" My eyes drifted to the Antiques by Thomas building. Josh lived in one of the top floor apartments, but he had an extra.

"Kyle's living there now that he's moved out from his mother's house. I'd see if I could bunk with him, but he has a girlfriend who stays most nights." Toby shrugged. "I'm sure I'll find somewhere to stay. For the last couple nights I've been at the station. Greg's been awesome about letting me crash there, but I need someplace I can sleep past six, since I get off patrol at two."

"You could stay with me." The words were out before I really thought about it, but I did have a guest room and a second bedroom up-stairs that had a bed in it. The guest room was probably too frilly for Toby's taste, but he could get used to it until he had a place of his own.

"Not an option. I don't want to intrude on both of my bosses during our time off. I'd be out of one job or maybe both within the month. And I like working for you." He grinned one of his special Toby Lady Killer smiles, but I could tell his heart wasn't in it.

"I was talking about the shed behind the garage. Miss Emily put a bathroom in with a shower. I guess she would get dirty painting and didn't want to come into the house that way." I was turning over the idea. I had initially meant the main house, but this was a much better idea. "You would have a private entrance from the driveway. It's insu-lated, so you wouldn't be cold, and it has a window air-conditioning unit when it gets hot. The only downside is that it doesn't have a full kitchen, just a fridge."

Toby seemed to be considering it. "I have a microwave in storage and I could move my bed, couch, and dresser in, and leave most of the other stuff in storage. Except my television. That would definitely have to come along." He watched one of his regulars climb out of her car, her stacked high heels making it hard for her to walk on the brick sidewalk. "Can I move in tonight?"

"Of course. Just come by after you get off and I'll give you a key. I don't have much in there except some boxes of Miss Emily's that I haven't gone through yet. And we can put those in the loft."

"You're sure it won't be a problem?" Toby ran a hand through his hair. "I mean, we already spend a lot of time together, maybe this is a little too close."

I picked up my purse. "You'll be doing me a favor. Greg wants to turn the place into a home gym. Now I have an excuse to put it off." I nodded my head toward the woman applying lipstick in the window reflection before she entered the shop. "Although, if you'd rather ask one of your friends . . ." I let the implication hang for a second.

"No way. I'm done with the dating life for a while. Elisa did a number on me, and I'm still not sure why we broke up. I really thought she was the one." Toby let his smile drop, and I saw the pain in his face. "I'll never again date someone with a kid. I'm going to miss that cupcake."

As the bell rang announcing his first customer, Toby put back on his fake smile and then nodded to me. "I'll see you after my shift. Thanks for doing this. I really appreciate it."

"Just no wild parties. Emma will have a cow if there are too many people running back and forth." I squeezed Toby's arm and exited out the back into the office. Now I had another reason to stop by Greg's office. I needed to tell him about Toby moving in before the gossip got there first. And maybe I could find out more about what was going on with Kacey's murder investigation.

I exited out into the back parking lot that held Aunt Jackie's car and nothing else. Even when we were slammed by tourists in the summer, our back lot stayed open, mostly due to the fact the alley entrances were several blocks up and down the street. The town had blocked off several of the intersecting streets to build places for street vendors. Sometimes that made it hard to get out of the lot since tourists used the alleys for pedestrian walkways, but I rarely drove into town anyway.

I touched the large cement planters surrounding the building, empty except for the dirt. Typically these would be planted with spring flowers by now, pansies and primrose, with a few bulbs in the middle. This year, because of the lack of rain, we were holding off planting. Hopefully the delay wouldn't last all summer. I would hate to see South Cove without the flowers overrunning the planters that ran the length of Main Street.

Thinking of the drought made me think about Josh and his water citation. I narrowed my eyes and stared at the building next door. If I hadn't told Jackie to handle it, I would march right into his store and give him a piece of my mind. I turned and made my way through the narrow walkway that separated our two buildings. Glancing at the doorway of Antiques by Thomas, I realized the store was closed. Josh had cut his hours down for winter even more drastically than I had. Of course, maybe I got more coffee addicts and he was catering toward a more select clientele. And there was the thing about being less available making you more desirable. If anyone besides me worked the dead hours my shift typically held, I would be cutting my store's open hours, as well, but I didn't pay myself a salary. My monthly income was based on the profit margin. So the more hours I worked, the better for the bottom line.

Well, Josh just avoided a butt chewing from me. Hopefully Jackie would take care of it before I had to say something. I knew I wouldn't be as tactful as my aunt would be. I crossed the street and headed to the police station. The morning was warm and I could feel the sun kissing my upper arms that had gone pasty white over the winter. I wasn't a big tanner. Sure, I'd sit out in the yard, but I didn't have the patience to be totally committed to the cause. Besides, the swing on the shaded back porch was a perfect place to spend the sunny summer days reading.

Maybe that would be my afternoon activity today. I had a new thriller in my bag that I'd scarfed off the advance reader copy pile that Jesse, my book salesman, had left last week when he'd come to visit. He came more often now that we were having a higher sales volume. And the happier he was with our sales, the more free books he left. The book in my purse was one of those big-name authors who had people writing his books for him. I'd been hooked on the first book in the series, so now I read everything this coauthor wrote. Readers are like that. You get attached to an author's world building and you just want to stay in their reality.

I was thinking about the love interest in the last book and wondering if the same character would be in this release when I ran into Greg coming out of the station. He dropped his file, and we both bent to pick up the papers before a gust of wind took off with them. I looked at the first page, and it was a warrant to arrest Austin. "What on earth are you arresting Austin for?" I shook the paper in front of him.

"You weren't supposed to read that." He took the page out of my hand. "Seriously, Jill, how are you always in the wrong place at the wrong time?"

"Maybe I'm at the right place at the wrong time?" I paused, rethinking my words. "Or the wrong place at the right time." No, that wasn't right, either. Now Greg was grinning at me. "Oh, you know what I mean. And you didn't answer my question."

"I'm not arresting Austin. I'm going in to Bakerstown to try to talk John out of this. There is no way that guy killed Kacey, you and I both know it. But John is out for bear. He has something stuck in his craw about this case, and I'm going to find out what it's all about." Greg kissed me on the cheek. "Now, can I go, or do you need to confess something else about sticking your nose in my investigation?"

"No. I was coming over to work my magic and get you to tell me something about the case." I eyed the folder with the loose papers sticking out at all angles. "And I guess it worked."

"Your sleuthing methods are unscientific and yet, sometimes, successful." He shook the file at me. "You know if I convince John that Austin isn't the murderer, I'm going to have to figure out who really did kill Kacey."

"I have faith in you." Besides, I was starting to think I could help somehow on the problem. I nodded to the other end of the street. "I guess I'll head home then."

"I could drive you." Greg tossed his keys in the air and caught them with his free hand.

"I'll walk. I might stop at Lille's and get lunch before I head home." I held my hands up. "Besides, it's a beautiful day."

"Let's just hope Sunday is as nice." Greg turned toward the parking lot, where he'd parked his truck.

"Sunday?" My question stopped him, and he turned around and pointed at me.

"Do not tell me you've already forgotten. We're going out with Justin and Amy to that geocaching club event. You are not stranding me with the treasure hunters." He narrowed his eyes.

"I forgot. Sorry." I waved, then turned back. "One more thing?"

Greg hadn't moved from his spot. "Yes?"

"Toby is going to move into the shed for a while. He needs a place to stay until the sublet on his lease is up." I shrugged. "I guess we'll have to put off that home gym remodel for a while."

"You did that on purpose," Greg grumbled.

I put my hand to my chest and widened my eyes. "I assure you, I have no idea what you're talking about."

"Evil woman," Greg muttered, then strode to his truck. "I'll get back at you for this."

As I walked down the sidewalk, I decided I would stop at Diamond Lille's for lunch. Looking in the storefront windows, I noticed the smile on my face. Yep, today was a good day.

CHAPTER 16

By the time I went to bed that Wednesday night, Toby was all moved into the shed. I had to admit, the building made an excellent bachelor's pad. He put his bed in the loft, along with Miss Emily's boxes. With Tim's help, he had even moved a small dresser to the makeshift bedroom. Downstairs he had set up a television game room with a couch and a recliner, and even a small kitchen area, using a microwave stand next to the fridge and a table under the back window that looked out onto what might someday be the mission wall.

I was impressed with his ability to quickly move in after rescuing most of his belongings from storage. He even had a coffeemaker for his morning java. Ten minutes after he unloaded the last box, I gave him the keys to the shed, and he disappeared for his shift at the police station. Emma and I returned to the big house, and I made a quick dinner of a frozen potpie and a bowl of ice cream. I took the ice cream upstairs after I'd eaten along with the book and started reading.

The next morning I woke with the sun and stretched, enjoying the peace. Since this week, like last, I was working Aunt Jackie's late shift and Aunt Jackie had agreed to take Saturday's early shift, I had four mornings of no alarm bliss to look forward to. I stretched and dressed in my running clothes, giddy about my ability to sleep in late tomorrow. I'd pushed bedtime back last night, wanting to read one more chapter. Tonight I'd finish the book, no matter what time it was when it ended. I could get used to this schedule. Maybe I should make it a permanent change?

Emma and I took off for the beach. The run was glorious. The waves pounded the shoreline, keeping time with the slap of my running shoes. Emma ran ahead, then back to me, then ahead again. When I realized the shape in front of us was actually a man walking toward us, though, I put her back on the leash.

"Good morning, Miss Gardner." Taylor Archer stopped in front of me, dressed in jeans and a sweat jacket. "I understand you and your friends will be joining in our fun on Sunday."

"That's what I hear." I scanned the far parking lot and saw a white van. "I didn't realize you lived around here. It's a great place to run in the morning before the beach gets busy."

He put his hands in his jeans pocket. "I'm not much of a runner, bad knees. But I do enjoy getting out and walking. It clears my head."

He stepped closer, and Emma growled low, back in her throat.

Taylor stepped back. "I can see it's going to take some time for us to make friends." He looked up at me. "And you're skeptical of me, as well."

"I wouldn't say that." Of course, I really would, but not to the guy's face. I do have some manners.

He looked past me. "I can be a really good friend." His words dropped, like he really wanted to add, "*or a bad enemy,*" but maybe that was just a feeling I got.

"I'm sure you can be . . ." I paused, looking for a word besides *nice*, which really didn't describe the guy. Instead of responding, he put a hand up to wave me off and walked away. As I turned to watch him go, I saw what he'd been looking at: Bill and Mary Sullivan were walking toward us, holding hands.

They nodded to Taylor and waved to me. As they approached, Emma lay down in the sand, wiggling her pleasure at seeing the two.

"Hey, Jill." Bill crouched down and petted Emma on the head. "Who's the good girl?"

Mary gave me a quick hug. "I haven't seen you in weeks. How have you been? How's Jackie? With this new committee, her job, and now Harrold, I barely get to talk to her."

"I've been good. Busy." I watched as Taylor disappeared into the woods where the greenbelt started. It was only then that my shoulders sank, and I realized I had been holding my breath.

"Do you know that guy?" Still crouching, Bill turned to see what I was looking at.

"Kind of. He's part of that geocaching club that Kacey was into. I've talked to him a few times. Emma really doesn't like him."

"She's a good judge of character." Bill gave Emma a kiss on the nose, then stood. "You should take her warnings to heart."

"Bill, you shouldn't scare the girl. No one's going to mess with her when she's got Emma in tow." Mary leaned in to her husband, her arm going around the crook of his elbow. "So, you tell your aunt to call me. Just because she has a new man in her life doesn't mean she can ignore her friends. Men come and go, but girlfriends are forever."

"I'll tell her that." I checked the time on my watch. "I've got to open the shop in less than an hour. I guess I'd better head home."

"Do you want us to walk with you?" Bill scanned the beach in the direction Taylor had disappeared.

"I'm fine, but thanks." I grinned. "I've got one of South Cove's finest living in my shed."

Mary frowned. "Greg moved in with you? Are you sure that's a smart idea? You know what they say about free milk and cows."

I tried not to giggle at her analogy. "No one's living with me. Toby needed a place to stay, so we set up the back shed for him. It makes a nice little apartment."

"Well, isn't that nice. I'm sure the extra money comes in handy." Bill gave Emma one last pat. "Being a good landlord is all about setting boundaries. Just remember that piece of advice from the professional here."

As Emma and I ran home, I thought about what Bill had said. Was I really a landlord? Bill and Mary ran the South Cove Bed-and-Breakfast, so they knew what it took to rent out a place. I hadn't even talked to Toby about charging him rent. And would people think he was living with me? Like in a boyfriend-girlfriend kind of way? I hadn't thought this idea through enough. Of course, most of my decisions were made that way, spur of the moment and by the seat of my pants. Why should this be any different?

Toby was just pulling in the driveway when we got back. He looked tired from his night patrol. I waved as he unlocked the shed door and disappeared inside. Emma and I went in through the backyard gate and I entered the house through the kitchen door. My dog went right to her water bowl. I, on the other hand, went to the coffeepot and poured me a large mug. I took the black liquid upstairs with me to shower and change into my work uniform: a T-shirt and capris. In the summer, the uniform became a tank top and city shorts or on rare occasions, a sundress. Really rare occasions.

No one waited for me at the shop. Sasha had a class this morning, so I wouldn't see her until tomorrow. I opened the doors and started my morning setup routine. Ten minutes after opening, my first commuter coffee drinker came in and I was kept busy until eight. I took the time to scan through the bookshelves, looking for a book or two to take home since I'd have a long weekend.

As I checked out a couple of possibilities, the bell over the door rang, and Bill Sullivan walked in. Relief filled his face when he saw me. I raised my eyebrows in a silent question and he shrugged. "Sue me, I was worried about you. Mary told me I was being stupid, but something about that guy really bothered me. I'm glad you made it home all right, and I guess I'll be going."

"Do you want a cup of coffee? I actually need to talk to you about the water committee, they're getting out of hand." I walked to the counter. "Or are you on board with this crazy idea of Mayor Baylor's?"

Bill met me at the counter and sat on one of the stools. "No, I think you're right. There's something wrong about separating out the power like this. The decisions about the town's water conservation should come from the city council. I have an agenda item for our meeting next week. I want to make sure the committee knows they are only advisory."

"Josh is issuing fines for watering." I watched Bill's face to see if he'd known this, but the shock on his features told me it was news to him. "Without even checking with the committee, it seems. I got a letter about my nonexistent watering taped to my door."

"He shouldn't be doing that. He could put the city in jeopardy of being sued for false citations." Bill shook his head. "I knew this would be an issue when the mayor insisted on the committee. Josh is too much of a hothead to be put into a power position. The man drives me crazy sometimes."

"You and me both." I poured Bill a cup of coffee and warmed my own up before I walked around the bar to sit with him. "So you'll talk to the mayor and council about this? I told Aunt Jackie, but I think she has a vested interest in the committee's stature. And besides, I think he cited me because of his relationship with her. What's to say he won't go off the deep end when she does talk to him?"

"The Harrold issue, right?" Bill nodded. "I can see Josh being upset. I mean, he thought he and Jackie were an item. I always knew there would be a day when she found someone who made her pause."

"I'm happy for her. I just don't want to be drawn into the fight." I ran a finger around the edge of my coffee cup.

Bill tapped my arm. "Don't worry about it. As of today, the committee has no standing to issue citations to anyone. And if I play this right, by the end of the month, there won't even be a committee to have to deal with." He finished his coffee and stood. "I need to get back to the B&B. Mary's been complaining about the oven not working right, so we have a repair guy showing up this morning. I sure hope he doesn't just recommend we purchase a new range. I'd need to be in tourist season to finance a purchase like that. Especially since I've seen the ones that Mary's been looking at online."

I said good-bye to my friend and went back to pulling a few books for the weekend. By the time Toby arrived, I had my tote filled and was ready to head home.

"Busy shift?" He smiled as he entered the empty shop.

I pulled the tote over my shoulder and waved. "Yours will be. It's always a good shift when you're working."

"See you at home," he called out as two of his regular customers came in. The women looked at me, narrowing their eyes. Apparently the rumor mill would be buzzing again that Toby had left Elise to move in with me. One woman's eyes filled with tears, and her friend put an arm around her.

"He's probably kidding," I heard the woman whisper. "Look at her hair, and no makeup? He's not living with that."

My hand started to raise to my head to tamp down the unruly curls, but I stopped myself before it was noticeable. I wasn't going to play the I-can-snag-Toby game, even if he'd put me in play with these women. I pushed the front door open and ran smack into Josh Thomas.

"Oomph," he uttered as the wind was knocked out of him and he went backward onto the sidewalk.

"Oh no! Josh, are you okay?" I knelt beside him, making sure he hadn't hit his head or something. I stuck two fingers up near his eyes. "How many fingers am I holding up?"

He swatted my hand away. "Two, and if you don't leave me alone, you'll lose both of them." He struggled to a sitting position. "Seriously, Miss Gardner, do you have to attack me every time we meet?"

"I didn't attack you," I muttered, knowing my words weren't going to change Josh's opinion of me any more than saying something to Toby's girls would have helped.

Toby hurried through the doorway and bent down to Josh's level. "Do you need an ambulance? Should I call the paramedics?"

Josh glared at Toby. "No, you *should* mind your own business." He waved Toby away, then sighed. "You could help me to my feet, though."

Toby put his hand under Josh's arm and with me on the other side, we lifted Josh to his feet. Once he was stable, he shrugged off our assistance and peered into the storefront. "Jackie's not in there, is she?"

"She wasn't when I left," I muttered. I kind of hoped Aunt Jackie had seen Josh on his butt, especially now that he was being a jerk about our help. "Do you want me to call her?"

"I know how to use a phone, Miss Gardner. Your aunt asked me to meet her here for coffee at noon." He glanced at the digital display on his watch, which I could see read eleven thirty-four. Josh was early.

"I'm sure she'll be down soon." I adjusted the strap on my tote. "Well, if you don't need me, I've got some reading to do."

I could feel the glare from Josh on my back as I power-walked away toward the house. I thought I knew why Aunt Jackie had asked to meet with Josh. I wanted to be locked safely in my house before he realized he was being dumped.

The rest of the day was uneventful. I didn't hear from Aunt Jackie or Greg. I saw Toby come back to the shed to change as I was reading out on the porch. A few minutes later, he was dressed in his South Cove Police Department uniform and waved as he backed his truck out of the driveway.

I ate dinner alone in front of the television watching one of the crime dramas I had recorded. I was too far behind on most of them to ever catch up, but I enjoyed checking in with my imaginary friends every once in a while.

I let Emma out and watched her through the back screen door. Toby had left a light burning in his new apartment. Some things were going to be hard to get used to, including having people around me at all times of the day. Of course, Toby worked longer hours than I did, so I probably wouldn't see him much, except on days when the shop was closed or on weekends.

Emma had done her business and was whining at the door. We climbed the stairs and I fell into a fitful rest, with too many unknowns flying around in my head to sleep well.

* * *

Even without the alarm, I was up by six the next morning. My eyes felt gritty and my body ached. My body's internal clock had me trained to get up early. I tried to fall back to sleep, but sensing my movement, Emma licked my hand, indicating her need to go outside. I pulled myself to a sitting position. "Fine, but we're coming right back to bed."

I opened the back door to let her out and was about to close the screen, when I heard a step on the porch. I whirled toward the noise, my hands up in a defensive position. Ten years of martial arts classes had taught me one thing: the stance.

"Hold on, slugger. It's just me." Toby put his hands up to protect his face. "Seriously, you've got to lay off the caffeine. You're getting a little jumpy."

I leaned against the doorway, taking in a few deep breaths to calm myself before I did kill him for scaring me. "What on earth are you doing out here?"

Toby shrugged. "I thought if you were up, we could have coffee together." He held out a box. "I stopped at Lille's and got some donuts."

I could smell the grease and fat, and I made a decision. "Come on in. The coffee's made but I'm running upstairs to change." I narrowed my eyes at him. "Don't think this is going to be an every-morning occurrence."

He held the door open so I could walk through. "Of course not." His words were promising, but for some reason I didn't believe my new neighbor.

I climbed upstairs and went into my bathroom. My hair looked like I'd teased it using a blender. I brushed it into submission, then washed my face, brushed my teeth, and changed into cutoff shorts and a long tunic. I put my hand over my mouth to stifle a yawn. I wasn't ready to start the day, but I guess I didn't have much of a choice. Tomorrow morning, I'd definitely sleep in, I promised myself as I made my way downstairs.

I poured myself a cup of coffee, then grabbed one of the donuts and sat at the table across from Toby. I pointed the donut at him. "So, why are you here?"

"I got to thinking last night that you typically have an idea on who the murder suspects in a case are, sometimes before we can narrow it down. This Kacey Austin investigation is totally stalled and unless

Greg can come up with a viable suspect, I think Austin is going to go down for a murder he might not have committed." Toby opened his cop notebook. "So spill. What do you have on the murders so far?"

"Nothing." I kept my eyes on the coffee I was sipping like it was ambrosia from the gods.

He pushed. "You can't lie to me. It's not very polite, and you are my boss. You're supposed to set a good example."

I glared at him. "Fine, you want to know what I have?" I pulled out my notebook where I'd started writing out clues. "Nothing. I have nothing, and it's driving me crazy."

He held out his hand. "Let's see. Maybe two heads are better than one."

I paused, wondering what his game was today. "You're going to be in trouble with Greg."

Toby shrugged. "Actually, I won't. He's told me I won't be working the case. Something about the mayor and overtime issues so he's not allowed to devote any hourly manpower to the investigation, unless the DA approves another suspect. I guess the mayor isn't in the Save Austin camp."

"So you thought you'd work the case in your spare time?" I grinned. "Seriously Toby, when do you sleep?"

"Right now, after this thing with Elisa, I don't sleep very much." He ran his hand through his hair. "Can you just give me a break here? Working helps keep me sane, and I need the distraction."

I didn't want to pry about why Elisa had called it quits. Okay, I really wanted to know, but I didn't want to ask. I kept hoping Toby would just tell me. I looked at my notebook. "I'll share on one condition. You can't even think that Sadie or Nick are suspects."

"You're kidding me, right? The pie lady and her soon-to-be-president son? You think I might consider them falling off the path of good to the dark side?" He tapped the notebook. "Just what have you got in there?"

"I need your promise." I thought about Sadie's tearful confession about how she'd harbored bad feelings in her heart for Kacey. The woman would take the fall for her guilt alone even though I knew she couldn't kill anyone.

Toby sat back in his chair and looked at me. "You're really serious here, aren't you?"

I watched his face for a tell or reaction to my condition.

Finally he put his hands up in the air. "Fine, I'll take them off the possible suspects list no matter what I see in the notebook or what we find out later. You just better be right."

I opened the notebook and started walking Toby through what I'd considered so far—especially my notes on Taylor. Of course, he hadn't done anything wrong, really. As I listed off the evidence, I could see the dismissal of Taylor as a real suspect in Toby's eyes. As I shared my facts and theories with my new sleuthing partner, I prayed that Sadie didn't look half as guilty to him as she did on the surface to me.

When we finished, Toby stood and refilled both our coffee cups without saying anything. Finally, he sat down and pushed the untouched cup away. He tapped the book. "You're right. The circumstantial evidence all points to our pie lady."

CHAPTER 17

Toby and I made a plan of attack for the day. He'd go and research what was happening with Austin, but we both knew that hoping Austin was the killer was far-fetched even for South Cove. The guy just didn't have it in his DNA. I needed to tie up Sadie's alibi for the night the food truck was vandalized. We agreed to meet again over breakfast Saturday morning with what we'd found out.

After Toby left to get a few hours of sleep before his next shift at the shop, I took Emma for a run, my mind filled with what-ifs. I kind of liked having someone besides Aunt Jackie to bounce ideas off of. I knew that he couldn't be totally impartial since he was an actual police officer, but Toby was classified more as the brawn of the force than the brain. That was Greg's job, and apparently Toby had been restricted to his normal traffic cop, bar bouncer duties.

But one thing was clear in my mind: No matter who was helping me think through this puzzle, I needed another suspect. If Austin was too granola to kill, and Sadie was too nice, there had to be a third suspect and probably a different reason. Taylor and the club presidency seemed a little far-fetched, even for me. I started thinking about the food truck. I'd already considered and discarded Lille, but what if the food truck break-in was just a distraction? And what better way to set someone up by giving Sadie her recipes back?

I plopped down on the warm sand and watched Emma play in the surf. The seagulls were swarming around her and playing with the waves as she chased after them. What if Kacey was involved with the mob? Okay, a totally crazy idea, but I needed to separate out the real from the possible. If she was killed as part of a mob hit, she'd have a bullet hole rather than being killed with an overdose of wheat germ.

Which told me what?

My eyes widened. The method of death told me it wasn't a random or professional murder. Someone she knew killed her because only someone she knew would know that she was that allergic to wheat products. There was a big difference between following a gluten-free diet for your health and doing it because of a deadly allergy.

Kacey knew her killer.

I called Emma to come back from the shoreline and stood up from my thinking place. I dusted the sand off my hands and clicked Emma's leash back on her collar. I needed to talk to Austin.

By the time I needed to leave for work, I hadn't had any luck reaching him by phone. I packed my notebook in my tote and took off for town. If Austin was at his store, I'd stop in there and see if I could get a list of people who knew Kacey that well.

The bike rental shop was closed when I arrived. It looked like it hadn't been open for a week, and it had a handwritten sign on the door apologizing for the closure due to a death in the family. Well, that and an almost arrest of the shop owner. I went around back to the door where I could walk up the three flights of stairs to Austin's apartment.

I was a little winded when I reached the top floor, but that was probably due to the fact I'd run earlier, certainly not the donuts I'd had for breakfast and an early lunch. I knocked on the door. No answer. I knocked again. Nothing. Tempted, I tried to twist the doorknob. Locked. Defeated, I wrote a quick note and slipped it under his door. Hopefully he'd call me soon.

I started down the stairs and heard the door to the stairwell open. My luck was changing. I sped down the stairs to the second floor and stopped in my tracks. Amy was walking toward me.

"What are you doing in Austin's apartment?" Her cold stare made me a little angry.

I leaned against the stair rail. "I wasn't in his apartment, I was looking for him."

"Sure, like you didn't know your boyfriend carted him off to the station a few days ago." Amy shook her head. "For the sake of our friendship, at least you could do me the favor of not lying to me."

"I wasn't lying." My voice rose a little, and the words echoed in the stairwell. "Look, I thought he'd be home by now and I wanted to ask him some questions about people Kacey knew. There's nothing wrong with that."

"So you're snooping again. Does Greg know?" Amy's eyes narrowed as she waited for my answer.

"No, he doesn't. And he doesn't need to know. I'm not doing anything wrong." I felt my cheeks burn a little at that statement.

"Well, maybe we'll just see what he thinks about that." Amy put her key into the lock and disappeared into her apartment, slamming the door on me.

I stood at the door, shocked about what had just happened. I leaned closer to the door. "You just keep your nose out of things, Miss Amy. If you don't, I'm sure there are a few things I can mention to Justin. Like how you turned on the GPS on his phone so you could find out where he went on his boys' nights."

The door flew open. "You said you wouldn't tell him about that." Amy's eyes were wide and crazed. "You promised."

"Then don't be a tattletale to Greg." I started down the stairs, then turned back, leaning against the stair rail. "We've known each other too long, and we both have a lot of ammunition in our arsenal. Can't we just stop?"

"Whatever." Amy closed the door again, this time a little quieter, but it still echoed in the empty stairwell.

I stood stock-still, suddenly realizing I might not ever get my friend back. Tears filled my eyes, but I wiped the back of my hand over them to keep the tears from falling. I wouldn't cry. By the time I'd reached the shop, I'd kept that promise and now my emotional center bubbled like lava. Amy Newman was a self-centered egomaniac who could just disappear. I pushed through the front door and the bell clanged and the door slammed against a chair someone had left in the wrong place.

I picked up the chair and pushed it next to a table a few feet away. The table rocked with the force, and I had to steady it to keep it from falling over, too.

"Uh-oh. You're steamed. Who got you riled up?" Toby waved me over to the counter. "Come over and tell Uncle Toby all about it."

"Does that line work on anyone?" I went to the counter and put my purse on one stool and climbed up on another. "Pour me a double-shot mocha with whipped cream and chocolate drizzle."

Toby glanced at the clock. "It's already five, you sure you want a double-shot?"

I narrowed my eyes at him, trying to summon a superpower I didn't possess. The one that kept people from saying stupid things. "Just do it."

Toby held up his hands. "Fine, just don't be blaming me when you can't sleep tonight. I'll be out on patrol and not even available to play rummy with you."

A smile played on my lips, but I forced it away. "I don't play rummy at night."

"That's not what Greg says. He's always complaining about your card habit. I hear you have a tendency to cheat." Toby set my coffee in front of me, and I took a big sip before answering.

"He's a downright dirty liar." I took a napkin out of one of the dispensers I'd found at a used restaurant supply store. I was sure they came from some 1950s cafeteria complete with bobby socks on the waitresses' feet and beehives in their hair. Wiping the whipped cream off my lips, I took another big draught. Coffee and chocolate mixed, that was an elixir of the gods. I sighed my approval.

"Better?" Toby leaned against the counter, watching me. I looked around. The place was empty except for a couple of teenagers who were over in the book side, reading on the couch and nursing frozen lattes.

"Much." I pointed to the empty shop. "It been like this all day?"

He threw a bar towel over his shoulder and poured himself a glass of ice water. "Nope. I always have a good steady run of customers from about noon to three. Then it starts to slow down. The kids go home about now to get ready for their dates, or to eat dinner with their folks. And most of our walk-in customers have already returned to the bed-and-breakfast to get ready for their evening out."

"You really have a handle on this shift, don't you?" I took another sip of my coffee.

Toby eyed me. "You really want to talk shop, or are you just keeping me from asking what's going on? Who were you so mad at? I hope it wasn't Greg. I like working for both of you."

"Not Greg, Amy." I told him about my brainstorm on the beach and then explained how we needed to cast a bigger net for Kacey's murder. "It has to be someone she knows, right?"

Toby nodded. "Good thought. I'll talk to Greg tonight and see if he's interviewed any of Kacey's friends. The real ones who didn't like the fact she was going back to Austin."

"Like the women who visited the coffee shop before the memorial? Both of them seemed to hate Austin. Hey, I thought you were banned from working the case?" The mocha was making my body all warm and squishy. Some people used alcohol to get a buzz. I'd take my coffee fix any day.

Toby took off his apron. "I can't work the case. Nothing wrong with me talking to my overworked boss about what he's done." He paused in front of me. "You going to be okay here alone? According to Jackie, this is kind of a dead night lately. Everyone heads out of town for their Friday night entertainment."

"Then I'll get a lot of reading done." I patted my tote. "Besides, I brought my notebook. Maybe I can figure out some more avenues of investigation we haven't come up with yet."

"I love it when you talk sleuthing to me." Toby grinned. "You know if Greg finds out we're doing this, we're both dead."

I found myself defending my perceived slights against my boyfriend for the second time that day. When I paused to take a breath, Toby started laughing. "You are just trying to wind me up tonight."

"I want you to be on your feet. I'll drive by a few times once I start patrol." He held up a hand. "Hey, I could shuttle you home if you'd like?"

"I don't want a ride in the police car." Toby had a habit of putting me in the back like a recently caught criminal. Not as sexy as it sounds in the movies: The backseat reeked of sweat, alcohol, and a faint odor of vomit. And that was when it was recently cleaned. "I can walk home all by myself. I've done it for years."

"Call me if you change your mind." Toby disappeared into the back office.

I walked around the counter and stashed my tote bag, pulling out the notebook and starting to doodle. The teenagers left a few minutes after Toby, and I was alone in the shop. After an hour of no customers, I tucked the notebook back into the tote, frustrated with the lack of progress I'd made. I really needed to talk to Austin. I picked up the contemporary romance I'd started yesterday and went over to the couch to put my feet up on the coffee table and read.

The jangle of the bell drug me out of the story, and I looked up and saw Dustin Austin standing in the middle of the shop. Surprised,

I looked around the store and realized it was just the two of us. Had I somehow called him telepathically since I'd been just thinking about him? I shook off the unease and stood. "I thought you were still in custody?" The look on his face told me I'd overstepped. "I mean, what can I get for you?"

"For your information, I am only a person of interest. Your boyfriend sure isn't keeping you in the gossip loop." Austin walked toward the counter and sat on a stool. "I thought your aunt worked the evening shift."

"She does, but she had plans tonight." I felt like a jerk so I repeated my question. "What can I get for you?"

"Coffee to go, black, three sugars." He leaned on the counter. "Can you give your aunt a message?"

"Sure." Now I was curious. What would Austin have to say to my aunt?

He pointed outside and toward his shop. "Tell her that I'm interested in selling the food truck, for the right price that is. Just because you'll have to repaint it doesn't mean I'm going to take any lowball offer."

"Why do you want to tell Aunt Jackie this?" I pointed to my chest. "You know I'm the owner of the store, right?"

Austin smirked as I gave him his coffee. "Give me a break. Everyone knows that your aunt runs things around here. You may hold the purse strings, but she's the decision maker."

"Nice to know what people think, but it's not true." I rang up his coffee. "Two fifty."

He gave me the exact change and then stood. "Just tell her I'm willing to talk about a fair price. I know you and Diamond Lille's were both interested in the truck when I bought it off of Homer. I'm coming to you first, as I promised him I wouldn't sell it to Lille, no matter what. I guess they aren't on the best speaking terms."

I thought about Lille kicking Homer Bell out of her restaurant when he'd told her he'd sold the truck without even allowing her to make a better offer. If she'd had a gun, Homer would have been dead that day. "I'd say that was an understatement."

Austin tapped a finger on the counter. "Just say I'm motivated for you guys to be the buyer." He turned toward the door.

"Hey, Austin? Who was Kacey friends with?" The pain that shot through his eyes told me I hadn't been as delicate as I could have been. "I mean, who did she pal around with? Go out on girls' nights with?" *Cry on their shoulder when you left her* was one friendship task I didn't list out for the grieving widower. Who said I couldn't be sensitive if I tried?

"Kacey had a lot of friends. Everyone loved her." He paused and I could tell he was thinking about the past. "After we separated, she started with that stupid GPS club. I don't think she'd hung with anyone who wasn't part of the club in years."

"She was the president." I thought about the people we'd met on our first outing. Maybe someone there hated Kacey enough to kill her? Over what? Finding too many geocaches? I wondered if this would be another wild goose chase.

"She loved that stupid club. I kept telling her just to quit, that we had enough going on without spending time tramping around the woods." He walked toward the door. "Call Ginny over at the bathroom place. She and Kacey were close."

Ginny, the woman who worked for Jen. Well, maybe she still worked for Jen. The last time I'd visited, Ginny had been late, again. I'd heard the sigh in my friend's voice when she talked to her about her hours. Too committed to the geo club to make sure she got to work on time or sometimes at all. I made a mental note to visit Linens and Loots tomorrow. Austin was almost to the door, so I called out, "Anyone else you can think of?"

He turned and stared at me. "I may not know a lot of my wife's friends, but I do know she didn't like that man who kept trying to get her to step down as president." He smiled a little sadly. "She said he would be president of the club over her dead body. I guess she got her wish."

I watched Austin leave the shop and shuffle down the street. I knew he was only in his fifties, but right now, he looked older than Aunt Jackie, Harrold, or even Josh. I took out my notebook and put a note in to talk to Taylor on Sunday. With Greg and Justin around, maybe he wouldn't seem as creepy and they could help me decipher his cryptic answers. Of course, I'd have to be a little cryptic myself or I'd show my hand to Greg and get a lecture about staying out of his investigations. I also put visiting Linens and Loots on my to-do list for tomorrow.

That done, I put the notebook away and glanced at the clock. Seven thirty. Technically, I had an hour and a half before I could close the doors, but I might just fudge the closing hours since my traffic had been little to none all night. I went over to the sideboard in the dining room where Toby had set up a water station. I'd have to mention that it wasn't our policy to have a water station again. Sometimes being a boss was like being a kindergarten teacher. You had to keep saying the same things, over and over, until the kids got it and stopped running in the halls. Or setting up water stations for the customers.

I took the half-full pitcher, and after filling a glass for myself, poured it out into the sink, setting the empty container way back in the cabinet where maybe Toby wouldn't see it tomorrow. My mind turned to my aunt and her night out.

She and Harrold were going to a play that Aunt Jackie had wanted to see for months. The production was getting ready to close up shop here and move on to Salt Lake, I believed. I'd done some research a few weeks ago, planning on giving her tickets for her birthday, but Harrold had beat me to the punch.

He was good for her. She was getting out more, having more fun with him than she had since she moved to South Cove. Or at least she talked about it more. I knew she and Josh had done some antiquing trips, but he was more interested in his own hobbies and activities than what my aunt wanted to do.

I sipped my water and when I turned around a face was peeking around the side of the building, trying to see into the shop. The street lamps were on, but the corner of the building was too dark to see clearly. When I looked that way, the shadowed figure jerked back. With shaking hands, I set down my glass and picked up my cell.

"Hey, Toby." I was glad he answered. I would have felt embarrassed calling this in to the 911 number. "Are you patrolling?"

"I'm sitting out here by your house waiting for speeders, actually. What's up?" He turned the music down in the car.

"Can you drive by the shop? There's someone lurking around the west side of the building, and they're looking into the shop trying to see who's here." I kept my eyes on the window, wondering if the man was still there.

"Go lock the front door. Don't hesitate, just walk over like you're cleaning off a table, then throw the dead bolt. I'll come down the alley without lights and see if I can catch him." Toby paused. "Are you walking?"

I groaned inside. "Yes, I've got the phone in one hand and a wash towel in the other." I paused at the door and turned the locks, not looking over at the side of the building as I did it.

"Fine. I'll be right there." I heard a *click*, then my phone rang back.

"This is Jill." I kept my back turned to the window so no one could see how white my face must be. I'd caught a bit of my reflections in the window and I looked scared to death.

"You do have the back door locked, right?" Toby asked. He knew it was a rule that when only one person was working, the back door stayed locked. A rule I'd made and one I forgot to implement on most days I worked.

I headed to the back office. "I'm checking. I think I do."

"Stay on the line with me. I'm coming up on the alley entrance now. I'll be there in two minutes tops." Toby sounded concerned.

I got to the back and jiggled the door, locked. Then I went to the door that led to the inside hallway between my aunt's apartment and the shop and locked it, too. "There, I'm locked in. Now what?"

"Wait for me to knock on your door. Stay in the back, there's more cover there."

What Toby hadn't said was if the guy had a gun, he couldn't see me to shoot me if I was hiding in the back. I could read subtext, even when I was shaking like a leaf. "No problem here."

I heard the tires crunch on the gravel, then heard, "Seriously?" The line went dead. I peeked out the back window, but all I could see was Toby's squad car with the driver's door still open. The car was still running. I opened the swinging door to the shop and tried to see Toby through the front, but apparently he was still on the side where I couldn't put eyes on him. Well, I could, but I'd have to unlock the stairwell and run up to the second floor landing where the windows looked out over the parking lot and Josh's building.

I figured Toby would consider that not staying put, so I kept pacing between the two doors, wondering which one he'd knock on when it was safe. I was peeking out the back door into the gathering darkness when I heard the knock on the front of the shop.

"Jill, come open up. It's safe," Toby called out and I skittered toward the front. When I saw who was standing next to Toby, I stopped in my tracks.

Shaking my head, I walked the rest of the way and unlocked the door. Josh came inside first with Toby following. "What in the world is going on?"

Josh didn't look at me until Toby nudged him. "Tell her."

He glared at Toby, then looked at me. "I'm sorry I scared you. I was just trying to see if Jackie was working tonight."

"I thought she told you she wasn't going to be here." I met eyes with Toby, who had a wide smile on his face. "*Not funny*," I mouthed to him.

He held up a hand with his thumb and forefinger separated a bit, signaling he thought it was a little funny.

Josh didn't see our exchange as his gaze was still on where his feet might be if he could see over his gut. "I know what she said, but I thought maybe she was just trying to make me jealous."

And right then, for just a second, my heart ached for Josh. He adored my aunt, and now that Harrold was in the picture, even he knew his days were numbered. Then he opened his mouth again. "Or maybe you were trying to break us up and sent Jackie off on some wild goose chase to make me think she wanted to end it."

Delusional. That was all I had to say. Of course, I didn't say it aloud. "Well, the next time you want to see if Jackie's working, just come in the shop."

This time he did lift his head. "I am sorry I scared you. It was never my intention to be seen."

"Now that I believe." I glanced at the clock. "It's time for me to close up for the night—for real this time."

Josh turned to the front door. "Have a good evening." And then he disappeared into the night.

Well, really he walked to his building and climbed the stairs to his apartment. I was reading way too many mysteries. My brain saw danger even when it was just Josh and his stalker persona.

"You okay?" Toby looked around the shop. "Need me to help with anything?"

I waved him toward the door. "Just leave so I can lock up. And no, before you ask, I don't want a ride home."

Toby chuckled. "But I cleaned out the backseat just in case you needed an escort."

"For the first time since when?"

He started walking toward the door and I followed so I could lock it again. "Last month, but I've only had three DUIs since then, and most of those haven't been pukers."

"Charming." I motioned him outside, but he paused before I could close the door.

"Do me a favor and text me when you get to the house. That way I won't worry." Toby looked at his cell. "And I'm off to the winery to break up a fight. The fun never ends around here."

"Be safe, and yes, I'll text." I closed and locked the door behind him and turned off the main shop lights. As I moved to the back, I thought about my aunt and hoped her date was worth all the trouble it was causing around here.

The thought might have been totally unfair, but the way I felt tonight, I didn't even try to take it back.

CHAPTER 18

I woke to a rapping downstairs and Emma barking at the side of my bed. I leaned over and looked at the alarm clock next to my bed. Six thirty. I was going to kill someone. I dragged myself out of bed, threw a robe over my pajamas, and headed downstairs, Emma in front of me. Instead of heading to the front door, she swerved into the kitchen. Either she wanted to go out, or Toby was our morning visitor.

It turned out to be both. Emma quickly greeted him, sniffing at the Diamond Lille's bag in his hand, and then raced to the yard to check for any stray bunnies or groundhogs in her yard. Once, she'd brought a dead snake up to the porch. I'd about had a heart attack before I realized it was already deceased.

Toby pushed past me and headed to the coffeepot. He took two cups out of the cabinet and poured the coffee I'd set to brew last night before going to bed. Handing me a cup, he raised his eyebrows. "You miss out on sleep last night? Don't tell me that Josh's little stunt had you worried."

I ran my hand over my hair. "I slept fine, thank you." Of course, I'd read long past my bedtime thinking I'd sleep in this morning as Jackie was handling my opening shift. I took a sip of my coffee and motioned to the table. "Sit and I'll be back in a few minutes after I get dressed."

"Works for me. You look a little too comfortable in those shortie pj's. I'd hate to have Greg walk in on our breakfast strategy meeting." He grinned and held up the bag. "I brought muffins from Lille's."

"Another reason to run this morning," I grumbled, but my stomach gave me away with a large growl in response to the sweet smell. "There better be a blueberry crumble in there when I get back."

I climbed back up the stairs and dressed. The shower could wait until after I took Emma for our run. I smoothed hair that looked like I'd put my finger in a light socket sometime during the night and twisted it into a ponytail. After brushing my teeth, I called it good and headed back downstairs for my muffin. Before I sat down, I took my notebook out of my tote along with a pen.

"Eat before we start. You'll be in a better mood." He nodded to the plate with the blueberry crumble muffin set in the middle. He stood to refill my coffee cup.

"Thanks." I unwrapped the muffin and took a big bite, savoring the sweet, moist cakelike texture. I opened my notebook. "I talked to Austin last night."

Toby sat across from me. "He find your note?"

Shaking my head, I sipped the dark coffee. "I don't think so. He was there to talk to Aunt Jackie about Coffee, Books, and More purchasing the food truck from him. I guess the gluten-free dessert business is done."

"I got the feeling that was more Kacey's dream than Austin's." Toby took another muffin out of the bag and broke it in half, spreading butter on both sides. "But doesn't it seem a little quick to be selling off the parts?"

"Maybe seeing it parked in front of his rental shop brings back bad memories. I didn't ask." I stood and let Emma into the kitchen. "I was too annoyed about him thinking he needed to talk to Jackie instead of me. Sometimes I think everyone believes it's her shop."

His eyebrows raised. "It's not? She hired me, not you. She runs most of the staff meetings, and she's always making changes in what we're doing."

"That reminds me, I saw you set up the water station yesterday." I waited to hear his response before bringing down the hammer. I could be the bad cop in the business relationship, not just Aunt Jackie.

Toby shrugged. "I had a lot of kids in yesterday doing homework before the weekend started. They kept asking for water, so I set up a station. I was too busy to wait on them all the time."

"I get it, I do. But until this drought is over, we've committed to doing our part to conserve, and I dumped a half of a pitcher down the drain last night." I smiled. "I'll let Aunt Jackie give you the next warning."

"I'm so scared." Toby polished off the last of his muffin. "Enough of the small talk. I want to know what you found out from Austin, or was it just about the food truck?"

I told him about asking about Kacey's friends and getting Ginny's name. "I'm heading in to Bakerstown to Linens and Loots to try to talk to the woman. At least, I should be able to get her address or phone number out of Jen."

"Sounds like a good lead." Toby sipped his coffee as he considered my information. "Greg told me they went to the nursing home and interviewed MJ."

"How did that go?"

"Apparently not well. The woman has early onset Alzheimer's, so most of what she talked about was how her Quaker family had disowned her due to her radical views against the war. She really railed about their hypocrisy. She told Greg that change doesn't come from speaking out against an immoral war, change comes from destruction and blood." Toby let that statement hang in the air.

"So the story Austin told Sadie was probably true. Mary Jane was the driving force behind the bombings on campus and he was just trying to keep her safe." I scribbled some notes on a new page in my notebook.

"She told Greg that she duped some guy who was in love with her into driving the getaway car. She seemed pretty proud of the way she used him." He shook his head. "I even felt for the guy. Here he's gone into hiding for the woman, dedicating his future to her, and she's just not that into him."

"No wonder women like Kacey and Sadie were attractive to him. They're both kind and attentive." I focused on Toby. "Do you think he killed Kacey?"

"Austin?" He shook his head. "The guy's a lover, not a killer. I don't even think he knew about the bombings until after they happened."

"That's what I think, too." I darkened the line through Austin's name. "But now, the only other suspect we have is Sadie. And I know she couldn't kill anyone."

"No, Sadie's just the only one we know about right now. Nothing's ever done until someone is in jail." He pointed to my notebook. "Anyway, you have a great lead. Women tell their best friends everything. Maybe someone was bothering Kacey."

"Austin said something about Taylor being upset when she kept getting elected to run that geo club." I stared at Toby. "You don't think he was really that upset, do you?"

Toby stood, refilled his coffee cup, and put the last muffin on the table in front of me. He threw away the bag and the muffin wrappers. "I've heard of people killed for stupid reasons. This could be the reason."

"Seems petty." I didn't like Taylor, but I didn't think anyone would kill to get control over a group of hobbyists. That was like killing the winner of the blue ribbon in quilting so your creation would stop taking second place every year.

"See what Ginny has to say. Maybe she's got some insight we haven't thought of." Toby opened the back door. "And Greg hasn't gotten any information about Kacey's friends, so we're ahead of the investigation with this lead."

Somehow that didn't make me feel any better.

After Toby left, I made my shopping list. The cupboard was bare, and Greg had already made our plans for Sunday. Besides, I needed a good excuse to go to Bakerstown besides talking to Ginny. After the list was complete, I started a load of laundry, changed into my running clothes and took a long run, trying not to think about anything but the way the salt air tasted in my mouth and the sound of the seagulls as they flew over the waves.

Driving in to town later that morning, I planned my day. First I'd hit the Pet Palace for chew toys for Emma, then Linens and Loots to talk to Ginny. Jen had complained about needing all her employees to work on the weekends, and since I knew the club had an event tomorrow, I was betting Ginny would be on-site today. Finally, I'd hit the grocery store and top the trip off with a quick stop at a locally owned drive-in that served the best fish tacos in the area. The place was a dive, but clean, and the food, amazing.

First stop done, and I found myself in the parking lot for Linens and Loots. I decided to splurge on the grill pans Greg and I'd been talking about so we could cook fresh veggies over the grill easier. And a grill brush cleaner tool.

My cover purchase decided, I locked the Jeep and strolled into the store. Jen hadn't been kidding, the place was packed. Women pushed undersized plastic carts through the narrow aisles, filled with bedsheets, towels, and kitchen equipment. I saw Jen at one of the registers and waved. I didn't see Ginny on a register, so I wandered back through the store. I found her folding towels in the bath section. I ran my hand along one of the towels and pretended to consider it, but then was shocked at how plush and soft it felt.

Ginny must have seen the reaction on my face because she laughed. "They are the best we carry. If I could afford to, I'd replace every towel I owned with these. I buy one a month. That's all I can do on my salary."

I looked at the price tag. She wasn't kidding. But then I felt the fabric again and sighed. "I might just have to eat peanut butter sandwiches for a month to afford these."

She continued to fold and stack the new shipment. When she saw me still standing by the towels, she paused. "Can I help you with something?"

"You're part of that geocache club, right?" I kept my hand on the top of one stack of towels, pretending to consider a purchase.

"How did you know?" Now I had her attention and she stopped folding.

"My boyfriend and I went to an event last month. I thought I saw you over by the food booth." I shook my head. "I heard about that poor girl who died on the beach. It was so nice of the club to give her a memorial."

Ginny snorted. "Well, the members owed her at least that. Kacey was the heart and soul of the Coastal Geocache Club. She built that group from just a few people who liked to get together on weekends to geocache." She smiled at a memory. "That's how we met. I was her best friend, especially during her breakup with her jerk of a husband. She and I went everywhere together."

"I'm sure you're going to miss her. So sad for a young woman to just die like that." I knew I was pushing buttons, but that's what I was there for, right?

Her hands tightened on a towel, squeezing the softness out of the plush. "She didn't just die. She was murdered. And I know who did it."

The overhead speaker buzzed, then Jen's voice came over. "Will all available associates come to the front to open more registers? Customer service alert."

Ginny shook her head. "I've got to go up front. You should get the towels, you won't be disappointed."

I watched her disappear, disappointed I hadn't heard her theory on who had killed Kacey. Of course, she could be in the "hang Austin" camp since she didn't seem to care for him at all. I decided I'd have another chance with her on Sunday. No way would she miss the monthly club activity. I picked up two of the bath towels in a powder blue that would match my current bathroom décor and decided against the grill accessories. I'd come back later.

By the time I got to the checkout line, I was three people back. Ginny's line was packed with people who had several carts filled to the brim and seemed to be redeeming gift cards. I looked at my watch and decided to stay in the line I was in. Jen paused by the cashier's station as I was checking out. She bagged my towels.

"I see you found the good stuff." She squeezed each towel as she put it into the bag. "I adore this brand. If I had my way, it would be the only towel I sold."

"Your associate, Ginny, told me how wonderful they were, so I decided to take a chance." I handed the cashier a credit card.

Jen looked toward Ginny's line. "That's interesting. I didn't think she recommended anything we sold." She flushed and glanced at the cashier, who was soaking in all the gossip. "Anyway, I'm serious about coming in to South Cove for a coffee date. Text me next week and we'll set up formal plans." Jen nodded to Ginny and me, then walked toward a cashier who had been waving her over.

The cashier handed me my slip and credit card. "Here you go, thanks for visiting." Then she leaned forward. "I didn't realize the boss had any friends. Glad to know she's human."

I nodded and tried to act very friendly so maybe my own persona would make Jen seem more in tune with her employees. As I walked out of the store, I thought about the pressure to perform that corporate bosses put on managers like Jen. And for not the first time, I blessed my luck in owning my own business and being my own boss. Well, after Aunt Jackie.

As I headed to the grocery store, I rolled down the window to let the warm air into the car. It was a beautiful day. As I walked into the store, my phone rang. I answered without looking at the display. "Hello?"

"Hey, yourself. Are you home?" Greg's voice always contained a bit of honey, especially over the phone.

"Nope, I'm walking into the grocery store. What's up?" I took a cart and headed toward the produce section.

"Good, pick up something for dinner. The case has stalled and I'm declaring a night off." Greg chuckled. "Unless you're going to grill me for information."

"No grilling here except for meat on the porch. You want steak and corn on the cob?" I spied some out-of-season corn that some local farmer probably had delivered this week.

"Sounds like heaven. I'll stop at the shop and pick up one of Sadie's cheesecakes. You have much stock this week?"

I glanced at my watch. "Tell Toby to pull one out of the freezer. It will be thawed by the time we're ready. And we can invite Amy and Justin over for coffee tomorrow. Maybe it will sweeten things a bit between us."

"You two still fighting?"

I wheeled the cart toward the soup aisle. "I guess. I wish I'd just ignored her request to spy on Esmeralda. Or I could have agreed and then ignored it."

"You tend to say exactly what's on your mind. That's why I love you so much." He must have covered the phone because I heard mumbled conversation. "Look, I need to go. Don't forget a six-pack."

"Do I ever?" I clicked off my phone and slipped it into my purse. I started checking things off my shopping list. The good thing about living alone: You got to eat whatever you felt like for dinner. The bad thing: You got to eat whatever you felt like. I'd decided to try to eat at least a little healthier on nights when Greg didn't come by, and I thought stocking my shelves with a variety of soups might convince me to heat up something rather than finishing off a bag of chips in my cabinet.

It was a theory at least. I finished my shopping and went to get some tacos.

I'd missed the lunch crowd at Jose's Hangout, so it took me just a few minutes to be back on the road to South Cove. I had just un-wrapped a taco when my phone rang. "Yep?" Or at least that's what I tried to say with a mouth full of amazing fish taco.

"Hey, boss. You okay? You sound weird." Toby's voice echoed through my Bluetooth.

I chewed fast, then swallowed. "I'm trying to eat."

The line went silent for a minute. Then he came back on. "Aren't you driving? You know it's not safe to be distracted while you're driving."

"I wasn't distracted until you called." I slowed for a turning car. "So, what's up?"

"Josh just dropped off an envelope with a citation for the water station yesterday. Man, if I'd known what was in the stupid thing, I probably would have wrung his neck. If my hands would fit around it."

"Put it on the office table and forget about it. I've already talked to Bill, and the committee has no power to be citing people. It's an advisory committee, and he's had plenty of complaints about Josh's heavy-handedness. Give it to Jackie when she comes in to work." I looked at the taco and my stomach growled. "Oh, Greg's coming by to pick up a cheesecake. Take one out of the freezer for him."

"Yes, ma'am. You're kind of calm about this whole water citation thing."

"Not my first envelope." I said my good-byes and clicked off the phone. Then I picked up the taco and scarfed it before anything else could happen to stop me. By the time I'd made it home, I'd eaten both tacos, a serving of seasoned fries, and drank most of my frozen lime soda. Just call me the queen of emotional eaters.

I had a few hours before Greg would show up, so I made good use of the time. I put away the groceries, made a quick pasta salad and put it in the fridge to cool, then I set a new jar of sun tea out. Filling my glass with the last of the tea from the previous pitcher, I took a book out of my tote and Emma and I went to the porch to read.

Six on the dot, I heard Greg's truck pull into the driveway. Toby had arrived earlier and had his truck parked by the garage. I assumed he was asleep since he started his Saturday shift at nine. Tim was technically on all day Saturday with Greg filling in when needed, but in the off season, nothing much happened on the weekends, so the guys played a lot of *Halo* in the station's break room.

Greg came up on the porch, the cheesecake box in his hand, and kissed me. "Let me put this in the kitchen. You got a cold beer in there?"

"Of course. Bring me out one, too." I hurried to finish the few pages I had left in the chapter and then slipped a bookmark to keep my place and set the book on my side table.

When Greg returned, he nodded to Toby's truck. "Did the Jeep break down?"

Confused at the question, I took the beer. "No, the Jeep's fine, why?"

"So why is Toby's truck parked in your driveway? Shouldn't he be getting some shut-eye before his shift tonight?" Greg leaned back on the swing, his arms hung over the edge.

"I told you before." I pointed to the shed. "I have a new neighbor."
"That's right, Toby's living here. I hope he's out before we start on
the exercise gym this summer." He grinned, staring at the shed that now
held his number two, who was postponing his hope for a home gym.

"Maybe. Anyway, he won't be there forever. When he moved out
of Elisa's, he needed a place to stay until the sublease on his apartment
is up." I shook my head. "What do you guys talk about at work?"

"Work." He grinned. "And basketball. What do you talk about at
work?"

"Mostly we gossip about what's going on in town. Now we talk
about Jackie and Harrold and when Josh is going to get a clue. As
long as Aunt Jackie's not in earshot, that is." I avoided the subject of
who killed Kacey. Greg didn't need to be upset at Toby for keeping
me involved in the investigation. Or worse, order him to stop telling
me things.

"Well, you can bet that we'll be talking about the rules. Like not
intruding on our time together." He reached down and tickled my
foot. "You are charging him rent, right?"

"We haven't talked about that yet." I shrugged. "It's not like I need
the money. The place is paid off and the shop's doing good."

"You need to charge him something. You can put the money toward the gym once he moves out. Do you want me to talk to him?"

I slapped his hand away from my feet and sat up straighter. "No.
I'll handle my own business, thank you very much."

"Doesn't sound like you're handling it." He shrugged and put his
hands up when I opened my mouth to let him have it. "Let's get off
the subject. The information just surprised me, that's all."

"Why don't you start up the grill? I'll get the steaks and the rest of
the stuff ready." I headed quickly for the kitchen door.

Greg followed me and took me into his arms. "I'm sorry if I'm
grumpy. This case has been crazy, and I'm still no closer to locking it
up than I was the night we found Kacey's body. I don't mean to take
it out on you."

I relaxed into his arms. "Let's only talk about fun things tonight.
Like where we're going on the next trip."

"Or how we're going to set up the home gym once Toby moves out?"
I furrowed my brow at him.

Laughing, he held up his hands. "Fine, I surrender. Hearts and
flowers conversations only. Can we at least talk about tomorrow's

outing? I can't believe Justin conned me into another day of hide-and-seek, techy-style."

"He's trying to fix things between me and Amy. So what if his technique is a little off? He has good intentions." I paused at the kitchen door. "You going to start that grill or what?"

He threw me a mock salute. "Yes, ma'am."

Laughing, I went into the house to get the rest of dinner ready to go. I loved our times together. Fighting or not, I felt comfortable with Greg, more than any man I'd dated or even the one I'd been married to. It was like all my relationships had had something missing: a solid friendship. Greg and I truly liked each other, which made the love part easy. I shivered at the word. Love. It felt like such a big commitment. I pulled out the steaks and started tenderizing them with my meat mallet, hammering in the seasoning and thinking about our relationship with each swing of the mallet.

CHAPTER 19

The parking lot was crowded on Sunday with vehicles owned by the Coastal Geocache Club and a few hikers who'd chosen the wrong venue for their quiet Sunday stroll. Greg parked the truck near the edge of the lot, and as I climbed out, I scanned the area for Amy and Justin. "Maybe they didn't come."

Greg locked the truck and came to stand by me. "I think you're avoiding fixing this with Amy. The two of you have been friends too long to let a misunderstanding ruin your friendship."

"I know." I thought about the exchange we'd had on the stairs to her apartment. "I'm just not sure she's ready to talk to me yet."

"It would help if she didn't think you were trying to get Austin arrested for Kacey's murder." Greg took my arm, and we walked toward the booths the club had set up for registrations.

"I wasn't trying to get Austin arrested." I sighed. "I guess you've heard that I wanted to talk to him about Kacey's friends."

"I did." He held me back as a compact car whizzed by us, going way too fast for the speed limit in the lot. "Idiots."

"Maybe you should have Toby come and hand out speeding tickets. I bet you'd make enough money here to pay for his overtime this month."

"Not our jurisdiction." He hugged me. "But you're trying to change the subject. What did you want to know from Austin?"

I told him about Austin coming into the coffee shop that night to offer the food truck for sale to Aunt Jackie. Then I told him about what he said about Kacey's friends. "I met Ginny Dean at Linens and Loots a few days ago. She's convinced Kacey was murdered."

"I know. She's been in the station a few times, demanding to know when I'm going to arrest someone. The woman is a pain in my behind." He pointed to a grassy hill where Amy and Justin stood. "There they are."

Justin waved at us and Amy turned away, looking in the other direction.

I sighed. "This is not going to be a fun day, I can tell already."

"Just be your cheerful, bubbly self. She'll come around." He kissed me on the head. "Let's go into the lions' den, dear."

When we reached them, Justin gave me a hug and slapped Greg on the back. "Welcome. Thanks for coming out, guys. This means a lot to the club. They are donating the profits today for Kacey's funeral costs."

"Now, if someone could just find her murderer," Amy muttered. Justin had his arm around her and he squeezed her tightly, in what appeared to be a warning. She rolled her eyes, then sighed. "I mean, I'm sure you're working hard to solve the case, Greg."

"We're not here to talk shop, right? I've been looking forward to today all week." Greg nodded to Justin. "You ready to get started?"

Justin's head bobbed like a two-year-old who had just been offered ice cream. "I sure am. But first, I got us all a present." He dug into the bag and handed each one of us a device with a *South Cove Rocks* lanyard.

I stared at the item that looked like a cross between a cell phone and the old pager I'd found in Miss Emily's desk drawer. "Thanks, but what is it?"

"It's a handheld GPS locator. I know, we can all get an app on our phones, but this way, you can keep your phone free, like for Greg, and still be on the hunt. Cool, right?"

"This is great. I'm sure it will come in handy when we come out to these events. But you didn't have to buy us each one, I'm sure we could have just followed your directions." Greg hung the cord around his neck.

"What if one of us gets separated? Or you want to come up and do your own search without me? No, each of us needed our own, it's only logical." Justin grinned like he'd just given us the keys to the bank vault.

"Thanks again." I put the item around my neck, hoping that this would be the last time our double date would lead us out to the forest to find caches. I'd rather be sitting on the beach getting a tan and reading a book than doing this. Once I ran, I was done with my work-out for the day.

Justin beamed. "I knew you all would love them. Taylor helped me pick out just the right model, but I don't think he realized I'd be buying us all one. The guy should get a commission from the company on this sale alone."

A woman ran up to me. "I'm so glad you're here." Ginny Dean stood by my side. "I wanted to talk to you about Kacey's murder."

I glanced at Greg, but he and Justin had headed over to the registration table. Amy stood off to the side, ignoring me. I took Ginny by the arm and led her a few feet away from the group so we wouldn't be overheard. "Do you know who killed Kacey?"

Ginny nodded solemnly.

"Can you tell me?" This chick was getting on my nerves. She needed to be telling this to Greg, but apparently she'd been causing so much trouble at the station, who knew if he would even listen to her at this point.

"I've left all the clues." She handed me a slip of paper. "I'm trying to save my own skin here, you've got to understand. If he knew what I really knew, I'd be dead just like Kacey."

"If who knew?"

She started to walk away and pointed to my hand. "Follow the clues. I've left a clear path."

This was stupid. "Look, you need to just tell me what you know." As I watched, Ginny's eyes widened and she skirted away through the crowd. I muttered, "Total nutcase."

"You got that right," a male voice said from behind me. I twirled around and found Taylor Archer standing behind me. Way too close for my comfort. I wanted to take a step backward but decided not to give him the satisfaction.

"That's not a nice thing to say about one of your members." I hated that he'd heard the "nutcase" comment.

"You said it first. The girl was always hanging out with Kacey. I warned Kacey that she was mentally unhinged and to be careful, but she never listened." He widened his eyes. "You don't think Ginny killed her, do you? I hate to say negative things, but the girl is certifi-able."

"Who's certifiable?" Greg stepped between us, and Taylor took a step back. Intimidating women must be more his style. I wrapped my arm around Greg's, thankful for the comfort and the interruption.

"He thinks Ginny killed Kacey." I knew it sounded blunt, but I wanted to see if Taylor would stand behind his statement or if he was only blowing smoke.

Greg cocked his head and considered Taylor. "How did you come up with this theory? Are you a member of the Bakerstown police force?"

"I'm not with the police," Taylor said. "And I'm sure I didn't say anything like that. She must have misunderstood me."

Taylor was apparently one of those men who didn't like talking to women at all if he could help it. I bet to him, women were second-class citizens and should be seen but not heard. I tucked Ginny's slip of paper into my pocket and looked at Greg. "Are we ready to go?"

"Yep." He nodded to Taylor. "We'll talk soon."

Greg's words sounded more like a threat than a salutation. As we walked toward where Amy and Justin were waiting, I relaxed. "Thanks for saving me. The guy gives me the creeps."

"Why do the crazies always find you to play with? I swear, Jill, you must have a beacon built into your system that only the insane can hear."

"You tell me and we'll both know." I stopped for a minute before we reached the other couple. "Ginny says she knows who killed Kacey."

"Yeah, did she tell you?" Greg looked through the crowd, trying to find the woman.

I pulled out the paper and looked at it. It was just a string of numbers. I showed it to Greg. "She gave me this."

He took the paper, looked at it, then gave it back. "Give it up, Jill. The woman is crazy. Taylor might be a jerk, but he's spot-on in his description of Ginny."

I stuffed the paper back in my jeans pocket and walked with Greg to meet up with Amy and Justin.

The boys were chatty as we hiked up the trail toward our first cache. Amy and I were behind them, but she kept three steps ahead and anytime I tried to catch up, she'd go faster. As a team-building event, today was failing. When we reached the first cache site, she paused next to Justin.

"You could talk to me, you know." I put my hands on my knees, trying to take a deep breath.

Amy shrugged. "You were the one who decided we didn't need to talk."

"No, I was the one who said I wouldn't be a rat for the water conservation committee. Since when are you so gung ho about one of the mayor's programs?" I stood, finally able to breathe from the climb. "Who's paying him to sponsor this committee in the first place? You know he doesn't do anything without knowing what's in it for him."

"This time he is." Amy rolled her eyes. "I was the one who convinced him to participate in the regional water conservation committee. Some of my friends from college are involved, and they reached out to me a few months ago. All I wanted was some support. I knew it would be hard to get people on board, but I never questioned your commitment. I guess I didn't know you quite as well as I thought."

"Amy, I didn't know this was your project. Why didn't you tell me?" I felt like a heel now. Not only did I tell my best friend her idea was stupid, but I'd compared her group's goals to those of Nazi Germany.

She pressed her lips together. "I would have thought you would have guessed. No one else in City Hall gives a darn about clean drinking water. You shouldn't have to beg people to do the right thing."

"I really am sorry. You're right, we should have supported it based on the fact it was a good idea, not who brought it to the table." I saw Greg and Justin giving each other a nonverbal high five behind our backs. Or they were, until Amy spoke again.

"I just don't know you anymore." She turned to Justin, who ran a hand through his hair, trying to keep Amy from seeing his celebratory dance with Greg. "Take me home. I'm not having fun."

I watched her walk alone down the path toward the parking lot. Justin hurried after her, stopping for a second. "She'll get over this. She can't stay mad at you forever. I guess this just wasn't such a great idea right now."

I kissed him on the cheek, wondering if I'd ever see him again. I'd loved our double date nights, or at least the ones that didn't involve geocache searching. "Go take care of her. We'll work this out later."

Greg stood by my side and we watched Justin disappear. He hugged me quickly. "Well, there is a bright side to all of this."

I wiped my eyes with the back of my hand. "There is?"

He nodded. "We can go home now and we don't have to search for hours for one of these trinkets."

As we walked down the hill, following the path that Amy and Justin had just taken, we talked about other ways to fill our Sunday afternoon and decided to go sit on the beach outside South Cove with a basket of Diamond Lille's fried chicken and a six-pack of beer. We'd even bring Emma along to play in the surf. The day sounded wonderful. Or it would have, if I didn't have to think about losing the best friend I'd ever had.

As I got undressed that night, I pulled Ginny's note out of my pocket. Looking at the numbers, I realized that I'd seen them before, or something like them. I ran to my purse and found Justin's handheld GPS coordinator. I keyed in the numbers and got a location. Twelve miles north and five miles east would put me right back into Los Padres National Forest. It made sense in a twisted way. Ginny had hidden her clue in a geocache, and I was supposed to use her clues to find the stash. I picked up my phone and called Greg.

"Hey, thinking about me?" His voice felt warm and inviting in my ear. I shook off the tingles he was giving me.

"Nope." I cleared my throat and pushed away the mental image of him lying in his bed. "I was looking at the note Ginny gave me, and I think these are GPS coordinates."

"Seriously? That's what you called at ten thirty to talk about? I've got a meeting at eight in the morning to evaluate other possible murder suspects, and you want to talk about geocache stuff?" The warm tenor in his voice had disappeared. Now he just sounded mad.

"Hear me out." I repeated my words. "So I just keyed them into the GPS thing Justin gave me, and it's coming up as a place in the forest where we were today."

"Jill, listen to me carefully. Ginny's been hospitalized in the past for issues with mental illness. That's even how Kacey met her, she was volunteering over at the state psych ward a few years ago and Ginny was in the facility because she was a danger to herself. The note is just her way of keeping herself involved in Kacey's murder investigation. I'm pretty sure she's going off the deep end again." Greg's words floored me.

"So Taylor was right, Ginny's crazy?" My voice fell to almost a whisper.

Greg yawned. "Well, she was crazy. I don't know what her mental stability is these days, but I'm sure losing Kacey had to have an effect."

"So you think the note is just a wild goose chase." My heart sank as I considered the entire scenario.

"Exactly. She isn't playing with a full deck on the best days." He chuckled. "I need to get some sleep if I'm going to have to listen to John try to drown out the rest of us as he makes a case to arrest Austin again."

"I'll let you." I hung up, not feeling great about waking Greg for no good reason, according to him. But I also felt like if I didn't at least try to figure out Ginny's note, I'd be wondering forever. Just because someone had been in a mental institution didn't mean they were totally bananas. There had to be some truth in there somewhere.

My phone rang at three that morning. "Hello?" I stared at the ceiling, trying to will my eyes to stay open.

"I've got to run to Bakerstown Critical Care." Greg paused.

"Why are you calling?" I sat upright. "Aunt Jackie? Did something happen?"

"Calm down, Jill. It's not Jackie." He turned down the music in his car. "It's Ginny. She was found out on the trails about nine last night. She took a nasty fall and has some head trauma. She asked to talk to you, but then they put her under to try to keep her brain from swelling."

"Ginny? Why would she ask to talk to me?" I thought about the piece of paper. Maybe it did mean she knew something.

"My guess is she didn't mean you, but your friend Jen McKarn was at the hospital, and she mentioned you were the only Jill she knew. Maybe Ginny has a sister or a friend named Jill."

"Maybe." I wasn't as convinced as Greg.

I heard the beep come over his line. "I've got another call that I have to take. I'll call when we know more about Ginny."

"Let me know when I can visit. I didn't know her well, but I don't think she has a lot of friends."

"Will do." And then he clicked off to his next call.

I lay in bed for an hour, wondering if Ginny really had cracked

Kacey's investigation but the murderer had tried to stop her from talking. It happened.

I threw off the covers and got dressed in jeans and a light sweatshirt. Time to update my notebook.

When Toby showed up at five, I didn't even question his being in my kitchen with donuts. "Did you hear about Ginny?"

He nodded as he poured a cup of coffee. "Tough luck she's been having lately."

"Could someone have pushed her?"

Toby frowned, thinking about the question. "I haven't been on those trails in years, but I used to jog there. Sure, someone could have pushed her off a cliff, but that's a long way to go off the trail. Maybe she was looking for a place to relieve herself and got disoriented."

I shuddered, thinking about the lack of restrooms in the park. "Greg says she asked for me. Well, she asked for a Jill. We're thinking it's me."

"Were you friends? I've never heard you talk about her." Toby polished off an apple-cinnamon bear claw.

"She gave me this yesterday when she told me she knew who killed Kacey." I handed him the piece of paper.

"And this is?" Toby's confusion filled his face.

I handed over my GPS handheld device. "The directions to the clue that proves who killed Kacey."

He handed me back the paper and the device. "Sorry Jill, it just seems a little cloak-and-dagger for me. Who would do that kind of thing?"

From what I knew about Ginny, she would. "I don't know. I guess I'm just grasping at straws. I'm beat. I'm going to go upstairs and take a shower."

Toby nodded. "Can I look at this again? I'll be long gone by the time you're out of the shower."

I nodded. "Knock yourself out." I left my cell on the table, figuring if anyone called it would be Greg and he could just wait a few minutes before I called him back.

The hot water in the shower was glorious, and I took my time shaving my legs and just standing in the warm spray. When I got out, I listened for footsteps downstairs, but apparently Toby had let himself out. I knew he'd be off doing his own laundry while I played lady of leisure.

I waited for Toby's truck to pull out of the driveway, then I picked up my phone. There was only one person I knew who would be up for this.

When the call was answered, I jumped into my story. Finally, I asked the important question: "So, do you want to go see if she really planted a clue at this spot?"

CHAPTER 20

Sadie set a basket filled with treats on the backseat before she climbed into my Jeep. "This is so exciting. I never get to go sleuthing with you."

"You may not think that if we come up short. Greg's going to be a little testy about me taking off today." I pulled up one corner of the plaid fabric that covered the basket and dug out a blueberry muffin. "Thanks for bringing these, but we shouldn't be out that long. And I was planning on buying you lunch at that Mexican spot in Bakerstown."

"You can still do that. It's a great excuse for Greg, right?" Sadie grinned. "I'm not an idiot. I know how to cover my tracks."

I thought that was probably as close to Sadie got to lying, but it wasn't her fault since she didn't realize she didn't have a clue. "I'm sure he's right and we're on a wild goose chase, but it just feels like we need to try to find this before someone else finds it and the evidence disappears."

"You are pretty certain that Ginny knew who the killer was, aren't you?" Sadie set her travel mug into the cup holder and strapped on her seat belt. "Well, let's go find this cache. I've got Bible study tonight, and I want to bake some cookies before I go."

I took a bite of the muffin and pulled the Jeep out onto the road. If things went right, Sadie would be home about one and have plenty of time to bake before her group met. At worst, someone would know we were missing at seven when Sadie and the cookies didn't show. If I've learned anything from my sleuthing adventures it's that having a backup plan wasn't a bad idea.

I glanced up at the gathering clouds as we drove to the hiking trailhead. "Looks like rain. Of course, it's probably wishful thinking."

"I got a letter from the water conservation committee with a refrigerator magnet on how to save water. It seemed very in-depth. Make sure you tell your aunt what a great job the committee's doing." Sadie pulled out a notebook along with a bunch of thank-you cards. "The church just had a fasting day of prayer, and I need to get these ready for Pastor Bill to send out this week. You wouldn't believe the amount of money we raised for the child care center just by the members skipping meals for a day and donating that money."

"I could not not eat for a day. I'd pass out." I slowed, looking for the turnoff that would take us north to the forest.

"You'd be surprised at how long your body can really go without food. Water, now, that's another subject. You have to stay hydrated." She pulled two oversized water containers with straps on the edges. "I brought these for us to take on our adventure. We should be good."

"You think of everything." We settled in for the ride, me listening to the country music station and Sadie writing Pastor Bill's thank-you cards. Sadie did a lot for the man, probably because he was a widower. If he'd had a wife, she would probably take care of many of these tasks.

The thought of Pastor Bill being single and needing someone like Sadie in his life started turning over in my head. The man wasn't half bad-looking. He was a little nice for my tastes, but for Sadie, he'd be perfect. I wonder if Greg would object to a small dinner party at the house. We could invite Sadie and Pastor Bill, Harrold and Jackie, Justin and Amy—my party planning stopped short. Amy wasn't even talking to me. No way she would come to a dinner party if I was hosting.

I sighed and turned down the stereo.

"What's wrong? You've been out of sorts for weeks." Sadie had finished all the thank-you notes and already slipped them back into her tote.

"I don't like it when people are mad at me." This statement was the truest way to explain. I didn't like having anyone upset at me, and I tended to put up with way too much for way too long to avoid this scenario. However, the thing with Amy was killing me.

Sadie patted my hand. "I wasn't really mad at you. Now, Greg got called a few choice words by me before Pastor Bill got me calmed down. But that's just about me protecting my baby."

"I wasn't really—"

She didn't let me finish. "I know, he's not much of a baby anymore, but you'll understand when you and Greg get married and start having kids. You just want their lives to be smooth, you know?"

"You think Greg and I are going to get married?" I hadn't even got that far. I was having trouble saying the three little words, and Sadie had us married off and popping out young ones.

"Of course, everyone can see how great you are together." Sadie's eyebrows furrowed. "Greg's not mad at you for this little trip, is he?"

Not yet. I shook my head. "I wasn't talking about Greg, or you. I am glad to know you aren't mad at me anymore, but I was talking about Amy. She's still hot about me not supporting her when she really wasn't right in what she wanted."

"That's what friends do. We might not totally agree, or do what the other person wants, but we always support them." Sadie pointed to the upcoming road sign. "Looks like it's the next turnoff. What did you say to Amy that has her this upset?"

"All I said was no." I turned on my blinker and angled the Jeep up the ramp to the parking lot. It was the same place we'd been yesterday when Amy and I had gotten into it, again.

"Well, maybe it's the way you said no." She pointed to an empty row of parking spots near the front of the trailhead. "Park there, it's close to the entrance."

I followed her directions and thought about my abrupt answer to Amy's request. I could have been nicer, but honestly, I didn't think at the time that Amy was taking this so personally. Now that I knew it was her project, I understood her reaction a lot better. I just didn't know how to fix our problems, and I was pretty sure cookies and cheesecake weren't going to do it this time.

We climbed out of the Jeep. Sadie carried our water bottles, and I brought another muffin. I took two waterproof jackets out of the back of the truck. "I might be being hopeful, but it still looks like rain."

Sadie looked up at the clouds and shrugged. "Maybe, but it doesn't smell like rain. You know how it smells like metal just before it downpours?"

I thought about her description and it was spot-on. "Humor me about the jackets then. I'll carry yours back if it's seventy by the time we get this cache found." I locked the Jeep and studied the handheld locator. I had my phone in my pocket, just in case. Sadie's water bottle was hanging around my neck and I was munching on my second muffin of the morning. I'd say I was prepared for a hike.

I pointed to the trail in front of us. "Looks like we follow this for a while."

An hour later, we were at the location Ginny had mapped and were looking for some sort of cache site. The place was pretty isolated, so I was sure there wasn't another cache set up by one of the club members nearby. Soon I found a metal box wedged into an opening in the rock side of the mountain. "Here we go."

Sadie hurried over to watch me open the box, but inside was another sheet of paper. "Read it and tell me who killed Kacey."

My heart sank as I read the note. Instead of a name, or the name I'd expected, another set of coordinates were written on the paper, along with another notation, 'one of two'. I began to think that Ginny was just pranking us and she didn't know squat.

"Key it in, we didn't come this far only to go halfway." Sadie watched as I keyed the new coordinates into the locator. This time we were to head east, toward the mountain range. Twenty minutes later, we'd found the new site. A cave opened up in front of us on the side of the mountain. I looked at Sadie.

"You don't have rope and a couple of flashlights in your tote, do you?" The cave was big enough to walk into, if we bent down a bit. But who knew how far back it went or where Ginny had hidden the box?

"Sorry. Should we go back?" Sadie leaned her head into the cool cave. "It looks like we could walk forward for a bit."

I fumbled with my cell. "I've got a flashlight app. Hold on."

The light blazed as I turned it on and I held it out toward the cave. We inched our way in, then a *bang* sounded behind us. A grate had slipped over the entrance, locking us in. We ran toward the opening, only to stop when Taylor Archer appeared, a gun in his hand.

"Well, look what I just caught. Two big ol' snoopy people." He grinned. "Get it? Snoopy, like the dog?"

"Let us out." I knew it was fruitless to ask, but I had to try.

"Let me think. Um, no. I'm not letting you out. In fact, I'm pretty sure no one is looking for you, so I'm just going to leave you here. Lucky for me, Ginny chose an old abandoned mining shaft for her final cache. Don't bother to look, I've already found and removed it." He leaned closer to the grate. "But since you did such a good job tracking the clues, I'll give you the answer. I killed Kacey. The witch wouldn't give up her presidency, and the club needs new blood."

"You killed her because you couldn't beat her in an election? For a hobby club?" I couldn't believe what I was hearing.

"Well, that and a few other issues." He pointed to Sadie. "Like Austin stealing your recipes. That was just cold, man. He bragged about it one night when we all went out for drinks after a club event. Too bad you couldn't just stay away from this one, although it still does put that doofus in the spotlight for your disappearance, as well."

"I don't understand, why kill Kacey then?" Sadie's entire body shook next to me, and I put my hand on her arm for support.

"You are dense, aren't you?" Taylor squatted down at the entrance, looking at the edges where the steel screen hit the dirt. "Kacey had to go, and I needed a scapegoat. And since Austin had a history of killing his girlfriends, your death will just go down as another one on his list."

"You knew about MJ." The pieces were all coming together now. "You're the source that called the DA."

"Getting Austin's fingerprints attached to a really old disappearance case wasn't as easy as it makes it seem on television. John just needed a little push in the right direction. So he got a packet in the mail about the bombings." He grinned. "It's not like it was a lie. The guy was knee-deep in that bombing, or at least helping the person who did it. You didn't know I was a CNA, did you?"

"You work at Resting Acres." The connection was becoming clear.

Sadie whispered to me, "I don't understand, what's a CNA?"

"It means," Taylor responded, proving that he'd heard Sadie's question, "that I work with old people who only remember the past. MJ was a treasure trove of information as long as I kept her coffee cup full of the real thing. Not that decaf crap they usually give the residents."

Rain started hitting the trees. Taylor held his hand up and a drop fell on it. "I guess I'd better get down the mountain. These places are known for their flash floods."

I couldn't help it, I swung my flashlight app to the back of the cave. Solid rock. If we did get much rain, Sadie and I wouldn't die of starvation, we'd drown.

"You could let us go. We wouldn't tell anyone," Sadie called after the retreating Taylor. We heard his laughter echo through the cave.

I sat on the dirt, all the energy drained out of me. "Toby was right, this was stupid."

"You told Toby? Doesn't he report to Greg?" Sadie sat next to me. "If you were trying to keep Greg unaware of your actions, talking to his deputy doesn't seem like the smartest plan."

"Toby said Greg wouldn't let him be part of the investigation due to money issues with the city. I felt bad for him since he broke up with Elisa. He needed something to think about besides her." Something about what Sadie had said was tinging in the back of my mind, but before I could formalize it, I heard dogs barking in the background.

Sadie and I both stood, making our way carefully to the opening. "Are those search dogs?" She looked at her watch. "We've only been gone a total of three hours. No one should be looking for us yet."

Another bay from a hound sounded closer. "But they are." I pulled out my cell to try to get a signal, but between the cave and the steel grate, no bars appeared. I returned the cell to my pocket and pushed on the barrier. It didn't move an inch.

"Help me push." I motioned Sadie to move up next to me and counted down, "One, two, three."

The grate moved less than an inch. No way would we be able to get it open enough for us to crawl out. We'd have to take a chance that those really were search dogs—and that it was us they were looking for.

"Help! We're over here!" I yelled at the top of my lungs. A hound's bay answered my words. Sadie grinned at me.

"I think the dog heard you." She stood on tiptoe and called out, too. "Help, we're in a cave!"

I heard rustling down the path, and then two Bluetick hounds appeared, sniffing at the grate. One sat down and howled, the other came up and licked my hand where it was sticking out of the grate. When he saw the other dog doing his job, he, too, sat and howled.

"I think we're saved." Tears filled my eyes as I watched the dogs announce their finding us. Two men burst through the brush and went directly to the dogs, clipping leashes on their collars. One of the guys smiled at us.

"I take it you two are Jill and Sadie?" He examined the grate.

"Unless there's two other women lost on the trails this morning, I think you're right."

"You okay in there? Are you hurt? We have an ambulance down at the trail site. I can call someone up." The other man peered into the cave toward us.

"Just get us out of here." I hugged Sadie. "My friend has a Bible study to get to tonight."

A few minutes later, Toby and Greg burst through the bush and stopped short when they saw the grate locking us into the cave. Greg came close and studied me. "You're something else, you know that?"

"Can you get us out of here?" So far, the men had just been studying the situation. "Sadie and I tried to get it to move, but we didn't have much luck." I was beginning to feel a bit like the lions at the zoo, closed in with time to pace.

"I don't know." He looked back at Toby. "At least with you in there, I know you're safe."

Looking at the rain puddling around us, I shrugged. "Until the cave fills up with water. What a day for the drought to end."

"One rainstorm doesn't end a drought, but it's a good beginning." Greg squeezed my fingers. "Hold on, slugger, we'll get you out of there."

The men gathered around the mouth of the cave, and after a few test runs, lifted the grate up far enough for Sadie and me to squeeze through. Greg handed me a bottle of water, but I shook it off.

"Sadie had us well-stocked." I held up the water jug that I'd strapped over my shoulder that morning. "So, if you found us, you probably found Taylor, as well?"

Greg and Toby exchanged a glance.

"Don't tell me you let him go. The guy is crazy. He locked us in here."

"And he killed Kacey and vandalized the food truck to make it look like Austin had done it." Sadie paused. "But I guess I should thank him for returning my recipes. The man's not all bad."

"The only reason he returned them was to make Austin look guilty." I couldn't believe my friend. She was always seeing the best of people, even the ones who left her for dead in a cave.

"Hold on, he's not gone. Tim has him in the back of the patrol car cooling his jets. I can hold him for your kidnapping and attempted murder, but I got nothing tying him to Kacey's murder except your word." Greg held up a hand before I could speak. "I didn't say it wouldn't sway a judge, but he might be able to play a jury."

"Believe me, he killed Kacey." I started shaking in the rain, and Greg put his arm around me.

"Let's not worry about that right now. Let's get you down the mountain and into a warm vehicle." Greg took my arm and motioned to Toby to help Sadie down the trail.

"How did you find us so fast? I figured we wouldn't be missed until Sadie didn't show up at the church tonight." I leaned my body into Greg's to try to feel some of his warmth. The guy was like a furnace.

"I don't know if I want to tell you."

That made me stop dead in my tracks. "You were following me?"

Greg laughed and, with his hand, gently pushed at the small of my back to get me walking again. "Not exactly."

"How is it, 'exactly'?" Now I was on the edge of mad. If he was following me around or worse, having Tim or Toby follow me, I was going to give him a royal piece of my mind. *Even though he found you before the cave filled up with water?* Sometimes I hated my logical side.

"Well, Toby set the tracker app on your phone after you told him about the GPS coordinates that Ginny gave you. So when he saw you leave in the Jeep, we just tracked your phone. Once we knew you were heading here, we figured we wouldn't be the only ones here." Greg looked at me. "Don't tell me you didn't see Taylor watching Ginny give you the paper. Come on, even I saw that."

I hadn't. I'd been too involved in trying to figure out what Taylor knew, he'd played me like a little violin. I shrugged, not wanting to admit my mistake.

"Then when Ginny was found, she'd said more than just your name. She told us that Taylor was going to get you, too." Greg stopped near my Jeep. He threw Toby his truck keys. "Take Sadie home. I'm going to drive Jill back."

When we got into the car and turned up the heat, Greg passed the basket of muffins that was in the backseat. "You want one of these?"

I took a couple. Greg chuckled, took one, and then pulled up next to the patrol car. "Hand out the rest of these to the volunteers and make sure the basket gets back to Sadie." He handed the basket to

Tim, who grinned. "Oh, and take Mr. Archer to the station. I've got some questions for him before I decide what charges I'm going to ask John to file."

We drove in silence as I consumed the first muffin. Then I leaned back in the seat and thought about all that had happened.

"You really don't have anything linking Taylor to the murder except our testimony?" I aimed the heater vents to blow the warm air toward me. The rain was still falling, making it hard to see out the window to the road. Thankful Greg was driving, I put my leg up under me and turned toward him.

"Nada. At least not yet. I wish I could put him in South Cove the evening of Kacey's death." He put his hand on my knee.

"Did you check Kacey's planner? Maybe she made a note about meeting him." I leaned my head against the seat. I felt so tired, I was going to sleep for days after this.

"What planner? How do you know she had a planner?"

I yawned. "She told me when Austin was trying to get her away from me before I told her about him and Sadie. She said she'd bought it in Bakerstown when they started working on the food truck."

"Interesting." Greg's voice seemed very far away. When I woke up, we were in my driveway.

"I guess I was tired." I turned toward the door, but paused. "So Toby turned on the GPS on my phone, that little tattletale. I'm going to have to give him a piece of my mind when I see him."

Greg smoothed down my hair. "I guess I should tell you all of it. I was having Toby spy on you."

"That's why he moved into the shed?" I looked out to the back of the driveway. Toby's truck wasn't there yet.

"No, that was all the two of you." Greg chuckled. "I asked him to keep an eye on your investigating since I knew you were up to something and I couldn't figure it out. He gave me reports daily, then we decided what information to feed you to hopefully keep you safe and out of harm's way. The friend thing was supposed to keep you researching on Facebook, not locked in an abandoned mine shaft."

"Now I'm really going to have words with the boy. He tricked me." Actually, he'd tricked me several times, but I wasn't going to admit that to Greg. I was just happy to be home, where I could listen to the raindrops hitting the roof without worrying about anything.

CHAPTER 21

I got a text from Aunt Jackie Monday night. Actually, two.

Are you all right?

When I sent back a yes with a smiley face, I got a quick response:

Stay home tomorrow, I'll cover your shift.

Okay.

And that was how I came to sleep in this morning. But as usual, my body had other plans, and I was up and wandering the house by seven. I called Aunt Jackie at the shop to see how things were going.

"You need to be resting. I swear, you get in more trouble than anyone I know." She called out to Heidi, one of my regulars who only came in the morning, mostly to avoid talking to my aunt. "I've got to go. Customers to serve. I suppose you'll want to work tomorrow?"

"I suppose so." When I chuckled, she hung up on me. I knew she was just worried about me, and that gave me a warm feeling. Emma whined at my feet. "Your aunt says hello."

I got a bark from that, and she headed to the door. After letting her out, I called Greg.

"Hey, sunshine. I figured you'd sleep in today," Greg said.

I slumped into a chair. "I tried. No luck. Anything in Kacey's planner about meeting with Taylor?"

"Yep. And she was going to cut him from the club. There was a whole discussion written out on a sheet of paper about how she caught him skimming from the treasury. We asked him, and the guy confessed to everything." Greg chuckled. "I guess he thought your testimony was going to send him up the river anyway."

"What did his lawyer say?"

"He talked before his court-appointed lawyer got there. We tried to get him to shut up, but he waived counsel. Man, that woman was hot when she got to the station. But it was all on tape, and we didn't do anything wrong. John is over the moon since he only has to do the sentencing part of the trial." I could hear Greg tapping on his computer.

"Sounds like you're busy tying up loose ends. I'll let you go."

He stopped typing. "Just want you to know I love you. And stay out of trouble."

"Trouble seems to follow me." I tried to remember what the line was from the movie, but it wasn't coming to me.

"Honey, you dive in feet first. It doesn't follow you, you find trouble." When I started to object, he laughed. "Go read and take care of yourself. I've got a delivery coming from Lille's for your lunch."

A knock on the front door had me distracted. "Is it here already?"

"Shouldn't be. I told them to deliver about noon. Don't hang up until you check to see who's there." Greg didn't like me having unscheduled visitors, especially living so close to the highway.

I peeked out the side window; a woman stood there with a large flower arrangement. "Crap, I forgot that Allison was coming over for coffee this week." I started unlocking the door. "Sorry, hon, I've got to go." I hung up the phone and set it on the table in the foyer.

When I swung the door open, I greeted her. "I didn't expect you to show up today. At least not with flowers."

The woman thrust the flowers into my hands. Then she spoke. "I figured as horrible as I've been, I'd better arrive bearing gifts."

It wasn't Allison on my doorstep, it was Amy. She looked me over. "Are you okay?" She paused. "Can you forgive me?"

"I'm fine, and of course." I set the spring arrangement on the table and pulled my friend over the threshold and into my arms for a hug. "I missed you so much. Have you ever had a meal with Darla? She's impossible."

"Justin says I've been a total brat about this. When we heard the news last night, I wanted to come then, but Greg said you were worn out." She walked over to the couch. "Come sit down and tell me everything. I'm tired of getting my gossip from secondhand sources."

Leave it to Amy to put it all in perspective. I sat down and the two of us talked until the second knock on the door brought a basket of fried chicken along with mashed potatoes and gravy. It was enough to feed ten adults.

"I wonder who else is showing up." I carried the boxes into the kitchen and started unloading. Amy got out the good paper plates and silverware.

"Greg told Justin to be here just after noon. I guess Greg will be arriving anytime." Amy looked in the refrigerator. "Good, you have sun tea."

As she set the jar on the counter, Toby knocked on the kitchen door. "Am I too early for lunch? Sasha's bringing your aunt from the shop. They closed down for the afternoon."

"Seems like everyone but me knew there was going to be a party here today." I hugged him. "Thanks for watching out for me, even when I don't think I need it."

He held his hands up in surrender. "Not my fault at all. This was all Greg's plan. He knew you were investigating, but he couldn't figure out what you were doing. So I was his mole."

"Just remember to take the GPS locator off my phone. I don't need Greg knowing everything I do." I shot Amy a knowing look, and she blushed.

Toby's phone rang and he glanced at the display. "Sorry, I've got to take this." He walked into the living room.

"So Greg found you by using your phone app?" Amy handed me a glass of iced tea. "That's kind of awesome."

"It's kind of invasive, but I'm glad they took that step. Sadie and I didn't even have time to finish the water we'd brought for the hike." I sipped my tea.

"You shouldn't joke. That guy was crazy, he could have killed you." Amy leaned against the cabinet. "Do you know how he killed Kacey?"

I shook my head. "He didn't say. He was just so excited about having done it."

"I heard that he mixed a wheat germ into water, let it steep, then strained it. While they talked, he switched out her water bottle." Amy shrugged. "Another reason why water's bad for you."

"I guess so." I thought about Kacey and her love of people. "I feel bad she didn't get a chance to really be a resident of South Cove. I think once the Austin and Sadie thing blew over, she would have been fun to have around."

Amy walked over and put her arm around me. "That's why I adore you. You're always thinking about the underdog."

"Well, maybe not always." I held my hand up, stopping Amy from disagreeing. "Look, I was wrong to say I wouldn't support you in the water conservation plan. I should have been more understanding whether or not I knew it was your project."

Amy shrugged. "Thank you. I kind of went overboard crazy with my reaction, too. I guess I was trying so hard to not tell people it was my project, I forgot to get buy-in before I went all psycho water saver on you."

I looked out at the gently falling rain. "I guess two days of rain doesn't stop a drought?"

"Two days might not, but the forecast is rain for a week. We'll be disbanding the water conservation committee next week when the council meets. Bill's already talked to me about it." Amy dug through the chicken and pulled out a wing.

"Are you okay?"

She nodded. "I've learned a lot the last couple of weeks. I know I'll do the next project totally different."

Toby came back into the room, and Greg followed him along with Sasha and Aunt Jackie. The kitchen was full of people. Emma sat out on the porch, looking in through the screen door. She whined when she saw Aunt Jackie.

"That was the hospital," Toby said. "Ginny's awake and talking. They are predicting that she's going to make a full recovery."

I sighed. Ginny needed some good news. I just hoped she could find her way in the world now that she was going to be all right.

Greg came over and put his arm around me. "I just wanted to bring together Jill's favorite people and celebrate the fact that we have another day with the most beautiful woman in South Cove. Thank you for being who you are, even when it drives me crazy."

"And risks your life," Aunt Jackie added.

"Here's to Jill." Amy held up a glass of iced tea, and the rest of the group held up their empty hands. "We love you."

After we ate, Greg and Toby had to get to the station to start the paperwork. Amy had to get back to work. She squeezed me tight before she left. "Girls' night Thursday. We'll go to Bakerstown and do that painting and wine thing."

"Greg and Justin can take us and pick us up. Then we can come back to the house for a movie." I adjusted our plan so we wouldn't be drinking then driving back.

"Sounds perfect." She waved and headed out the door.

Sasha looked at my aunt. "You ready to get back?"

Aunt Jackie slouched into my recliner and kicked off her shoes. "Why don't we stay and talk a bit."

I sank down on the couch and Sasha sat on the other end. "Hey, I'm getting ready to go back to school, and I have to take a test. You want to help me study?"

"I can do that. I've gotten really good at testing lately. In high school, I'd freeze up, but now, if I don't know the answer, I just guess. And usually, I'm right." Sasha twisted her hair between her fingers.

"What's going on between you and Toby?" Aunt Jackie asked.

Sasha didn't miss a beat. "I'll tell you right after you tell us what's going on with you and Harrold."

"Touché." I grinned. The girl was learning. "What other gossip have you heard?"

"There's a new store opening across the street next to The Glass Slipper. Some kind of china shop, from what I hear. The name is really cute, Teattee." Aunt Jackie closed her eyes and leaned back her head. "I'm so glad we closed the shop for the day. I'm beat."

"Cheesecake and movie afternoon?" I thought about my movie collection. "Romance, mystery, or comedy?"

"Comedy. Let's watch *Ghostbusters*. Or anything with Bill Murray." Aunt Jackie sat up. "Soda in the fridge?"

"Yep. Bring me one." I stood and grabbed the movie off my shelf. I also grabbed *Groundhog Day*. We might as well make an afternoon of it. I put the DVD into the player and messed with the remote.

Sasha was looking at the movie case.

"Excited?" I pressed Pause on the DVD as we waited for Aunt Jackie.

Sasha looked at me and shrugged. "I guess so. I mean, I love hanging out with you guys."

My aunt handed her a soda and then gave another to me. "But what? You think you need to study or something? Relax, the books will be there tomorrow."

Sasha shook her head. "It's not that. I just have a question." She paused, looking at the movie cover again. "Who's Bill Murray?"

Don't miss any of

The Tourist Trap Mysteries!

Available now from

Lyrical Press

In the gentle coastal town of South Cove, California, all Jill Gardner wants is to keep her store—Coffee, Books, and More—open and running. So why is she caught up in the business of murder?

Guidebook to Murder

When Jill's elderly friend, Miss Emily, calls in a fit of pique, she already knows the city council is trying to force Emily to sell her dilapidated old house. But Emily's gumption goes for naught when she dies unexpectedly and leaves the house to Jill—along with all of her problems . . . *and* her enemies. Convinced her friend was murdered, Jill is finding the list of suspects longer than the list of repairs needed on the house. But Jill is determined to uncover the culprit—especially if it gets her closer to South Cove's finest, Detective Greg King. Problem is, the killer knows she's on the case—and is determined to close the book on Jill *permanently* . . .

Mission to Murder

Jill has discovered that the old stone wall on her property might be a centuries-old mission worthy of being declared a landmark. But Craig Morgan, the obnoxious owner of South Cove's most popular tourist spot, The Castle, makes it his business to contest her claim. When Morgan is found murdered at The Castle shortly after a heated argument with Jill, even her detective boyfriend has to ask

her for an alibi. Jill decides she must find the real murderer to clear
her name. But when the killer comes for her, she'll need to jump
from historic preservation to self-preservation . . .

If the Shoe Kills

As owner of Coffee, Books, and More, Jill Gardner looks forward to
the hustle and bustle of holiday shoppers. But when the mayor ropes
her into being liaison for a new work program, 'tis the season to be
wary. Local businesses are afraid the interns will be delinquents,
punks, or worse. For Jill, nothing's worse than Ted Hendricks—the
jerk who runs the program. After a few run-ins, Jill's ready to kill
the guy. That, however, turns out to be unnecessary when she finds
Ted in his car—dead as a doornail. Detective Greg King assumes it's
a suicide. Jill thinks it's murder. And if the holidays weren't stressful
enough, a spoiled blonde wants to sue the city for breaking her heel.
Jill has to act fast to solve this mess—before the other shoe drops . . .

Dressed to Kill

Of course everyone is expecting a "dead" body at the dress rehearsal
. . . but this one isn't acting! It turns out the main suspect is the
late actor's conniving girlfriend, Sherry . . . who also happens to be
the ex-wife of Jill's main squeeze. Sherry is definitely a master
manipulator . . . but is she a killer? Jill may discover the truth only
when the curtain comes up on the final act . . . and by then, it may
be far too late.

Killer Run

Jill has somehow been talked into sponsoring a 5k race along the
beautiful California coast. The race is a fund-raiser for the local
preservation society—but not everyone is feeling so charitable . . .
The day of the race, everyone hits the ground running . . . until a

local business owner stumbles over a very stationary body. The deceased is the vicious wife of the husband-and-wife team hired to promote the event—and the husband turns to Jill for help in clearing his name. But did he do it? Jill will have to be *very* careful, because this killer is ready to put her out of the running . . . forever!

GUIDEBOOK TO
MURDER

A TOURIST TRAP MYSTERY

Dying for a visit…

LYNN CAHOON

MISSION TO MURDER

A TOURIST TRAP MYSTERY

Don't miss the deadly landmark...

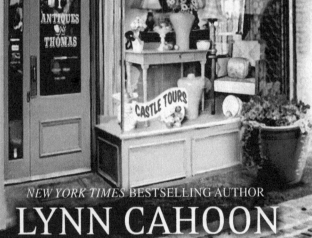

NEW YORK TIMES BESTSELLING AUTHOR

LYNN CAHOON

IF THE SHOE
KILLS

A TOURIST TRAP MYSTERY

The Glass Slipper

NEW YORK TIMES BESTSELLING AUTHOR
LYNN CAHOON

DRESSED TO KILL

A TOURIST TRAP MYSTERY

What you see is not what you get...

NEW YORK TIMES BESTSELLING AUTHOR

LYNN CAHOON

KILLER
RUN

A TOURIST TRAP MYSTERY

She's
running
on empty...

THE
MISSION
WALK

NEW YORK TIMES BESTSELLING AUTHOR
LYNN CAHOON

Angela Brewer Armstrong at Todd Studios

New York Times and *USA Today* bestselling author Lynn Cahoon is an Idaho expat. She grew up living the small-town life she now loves to write about. Currently, she's living with her husband and two fur babies in a small historic town on the banks of the Mississippi River, where her imagination tends to wander. *Guidebook to Murder*, Book One of the Tourist Trap series, won the 2015 Reader's Crown Award for Mystery Fiction.

Sign up for her newsletter at her website (www.lynncahoon.com) and never miss a new release announcement.

Printed in the United States
by Baker & Taylor Publisher Services